CHRONICLES

OF

SWORD

AND

FANG

ELIZABETH R. JENSEN

CHRONICLES

OF

SWORD

AND

FANG

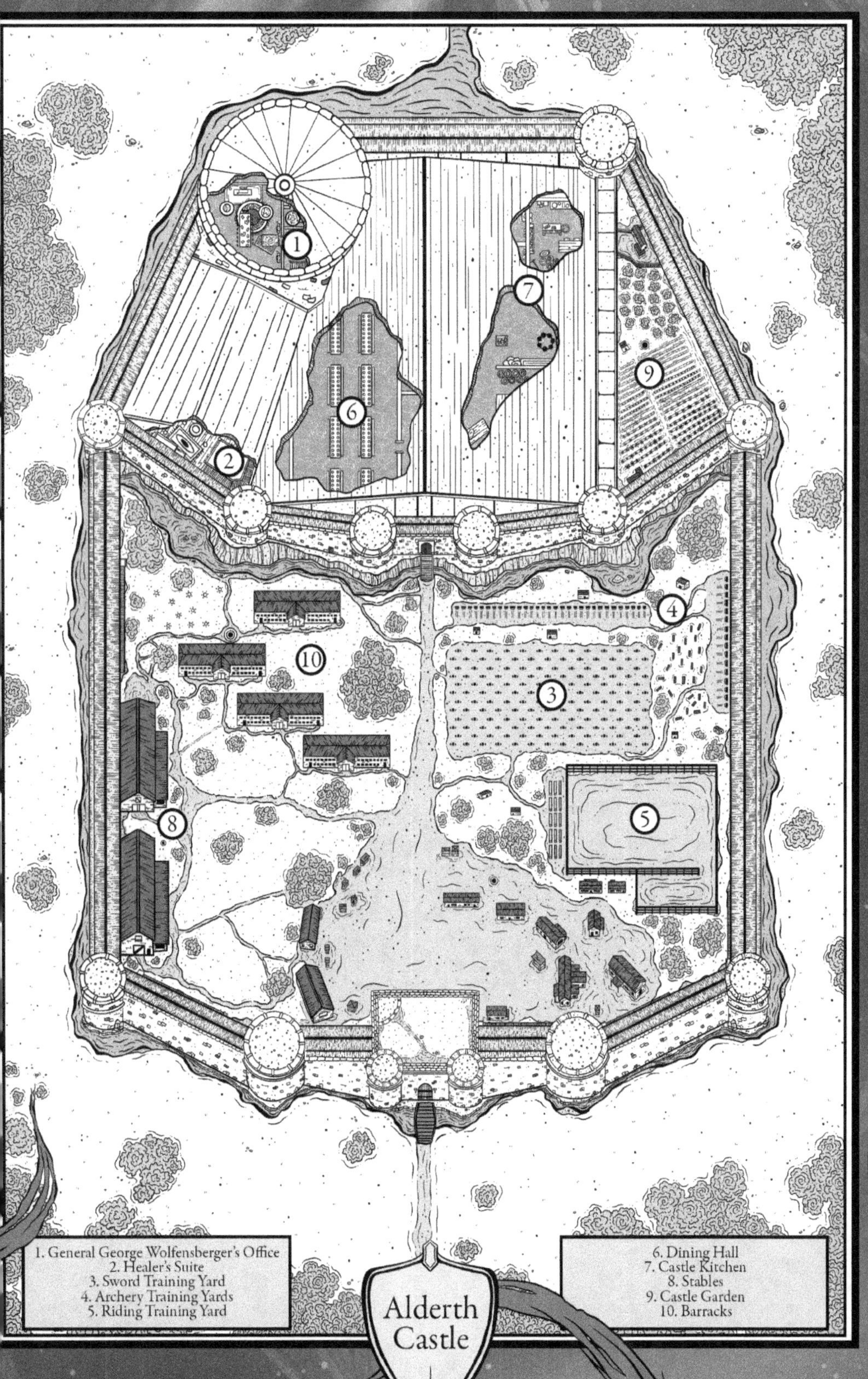

1. General George Wolfensberger's Office	6. Dining Hall
2. Healer's Suite	7. Castle Kitchen
3. Sword Training Yard	8. Stables
4. Archery Training Yards	9. Castle Garden
5. Riding Training Yard	10. Barracks

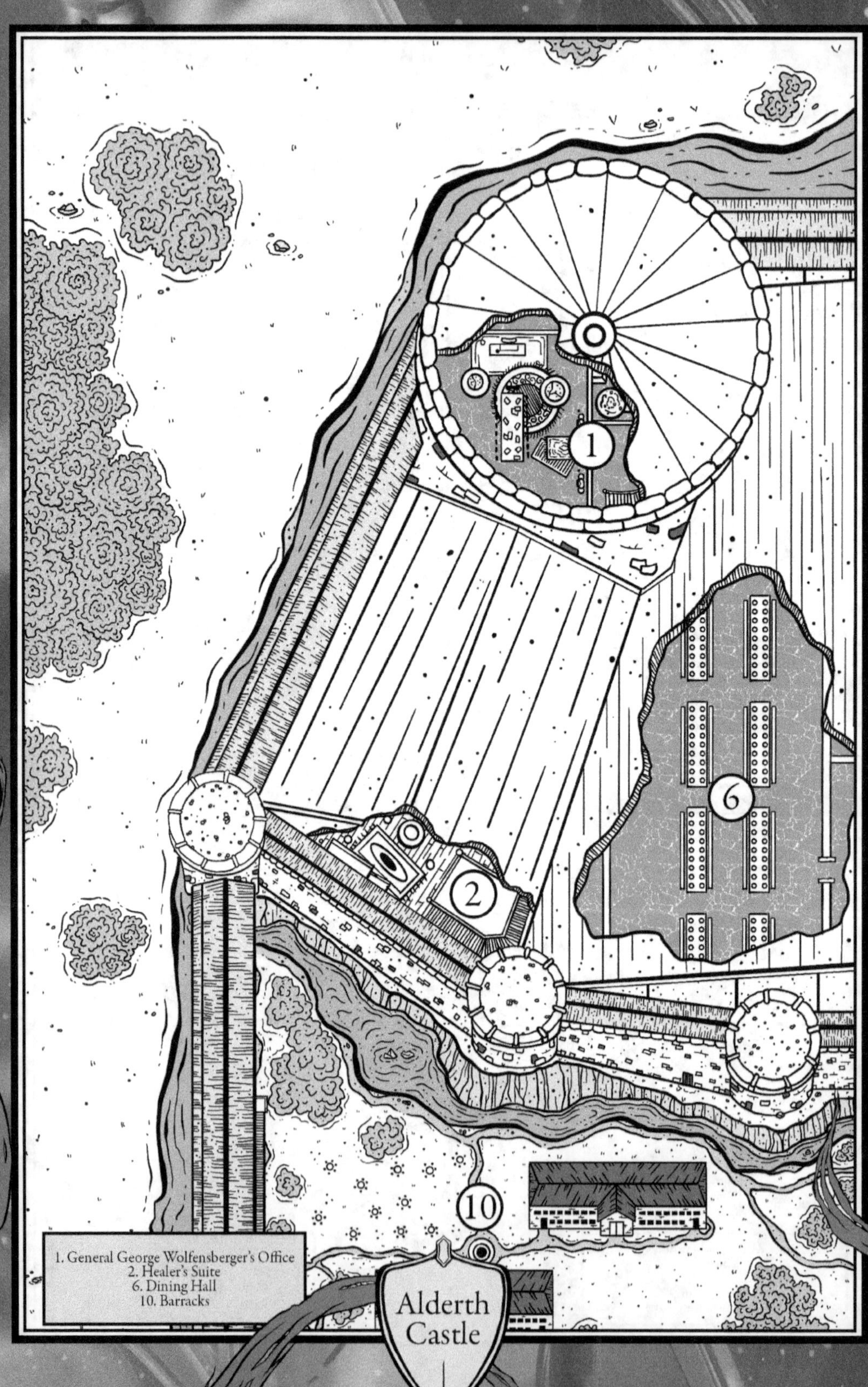

1
2
6
10
1. General George Wolfensberger's Office
2. Healer's Suite
6. Dining Hall
10. Barracks
Alderth Castle

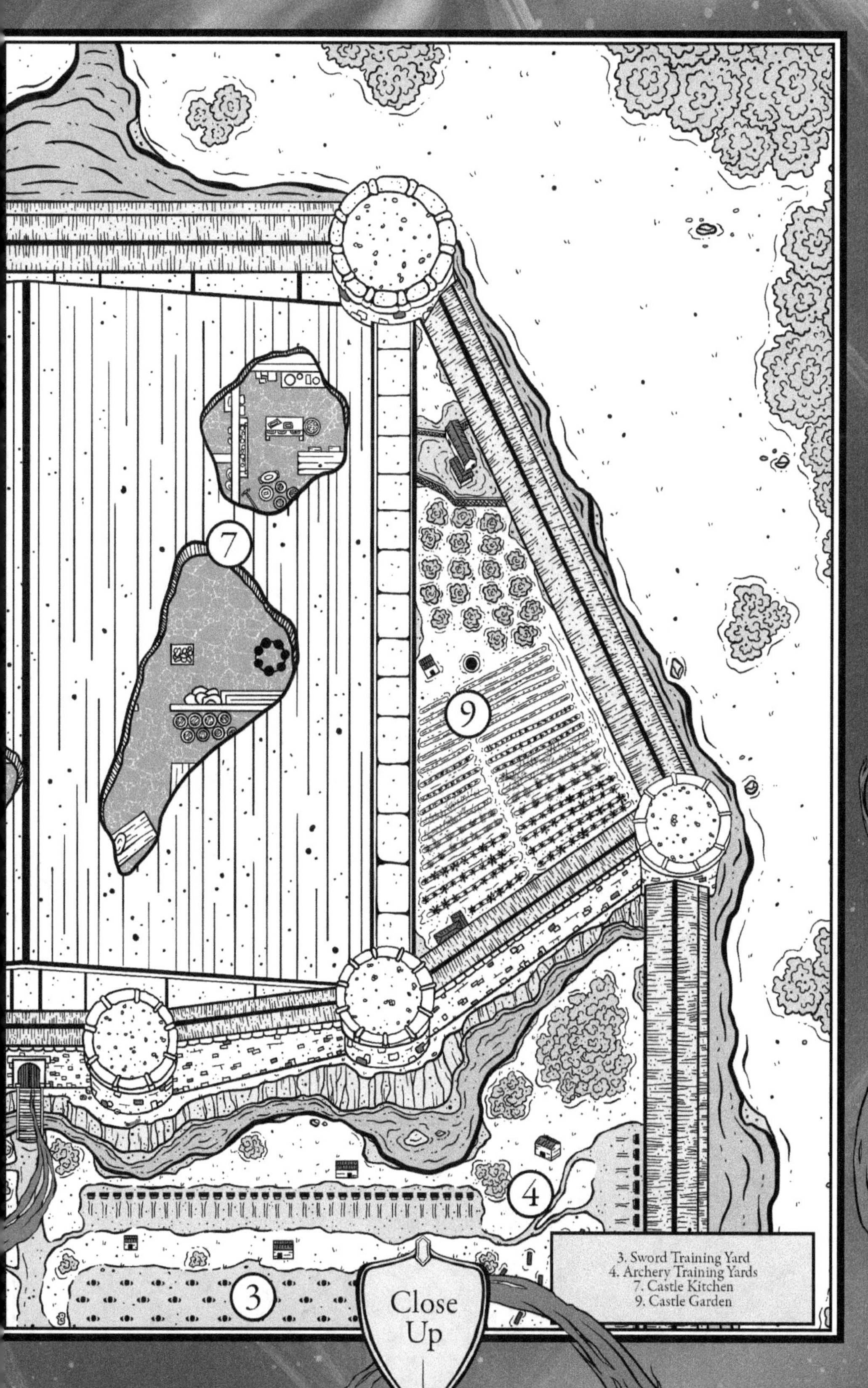

7
9
3
4
Close
Up
3. Sword Training Yard
4. Archery Training Yards
7. Castle Kitchen
9. Castle Garden

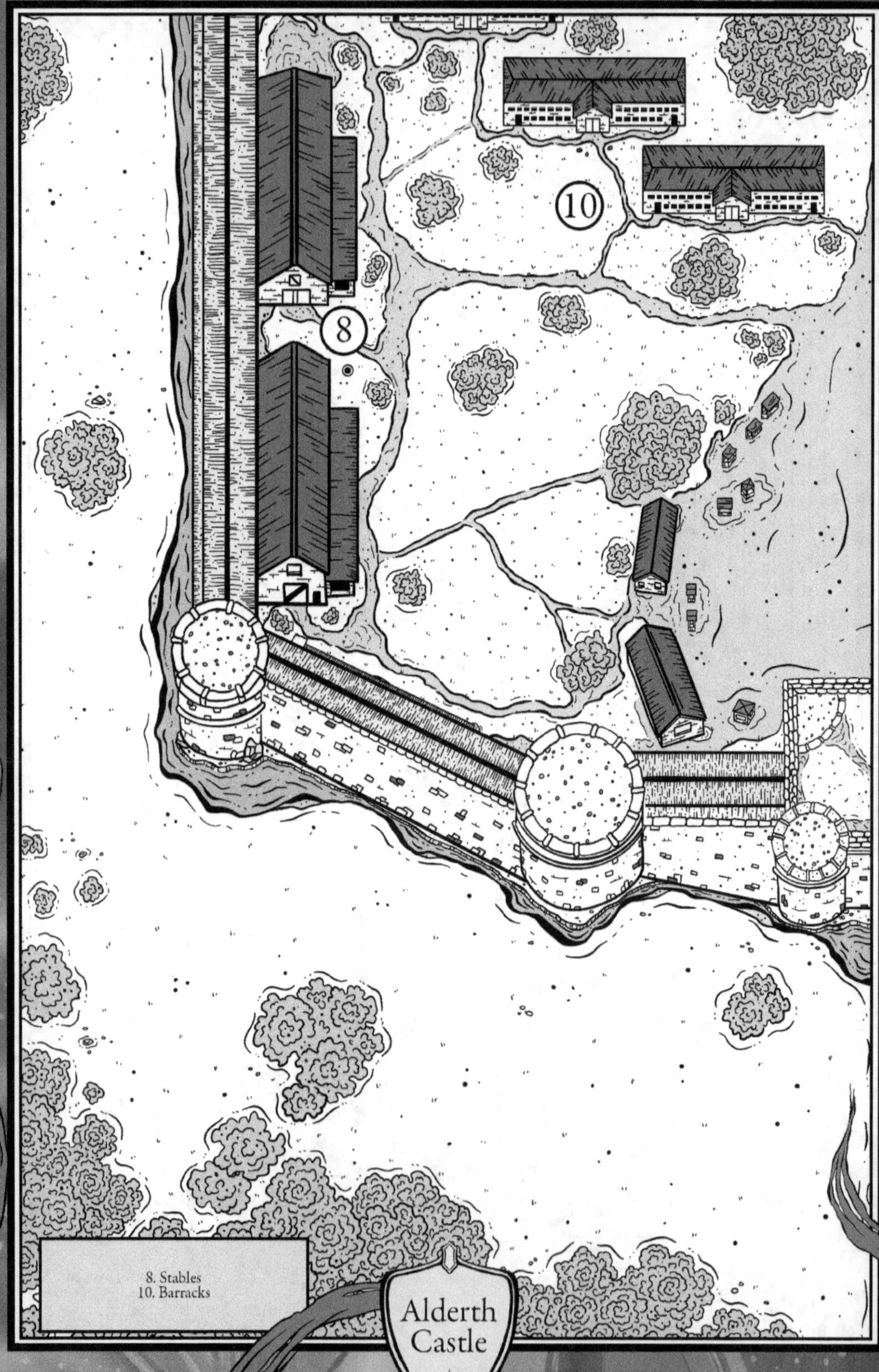

10
8
8. Stables
10. Barracks
Alderth
Castle

3
4
5
Close
Up
3. Sword Training Yard
4. Archery Training Yards
5. Riding Training Yard

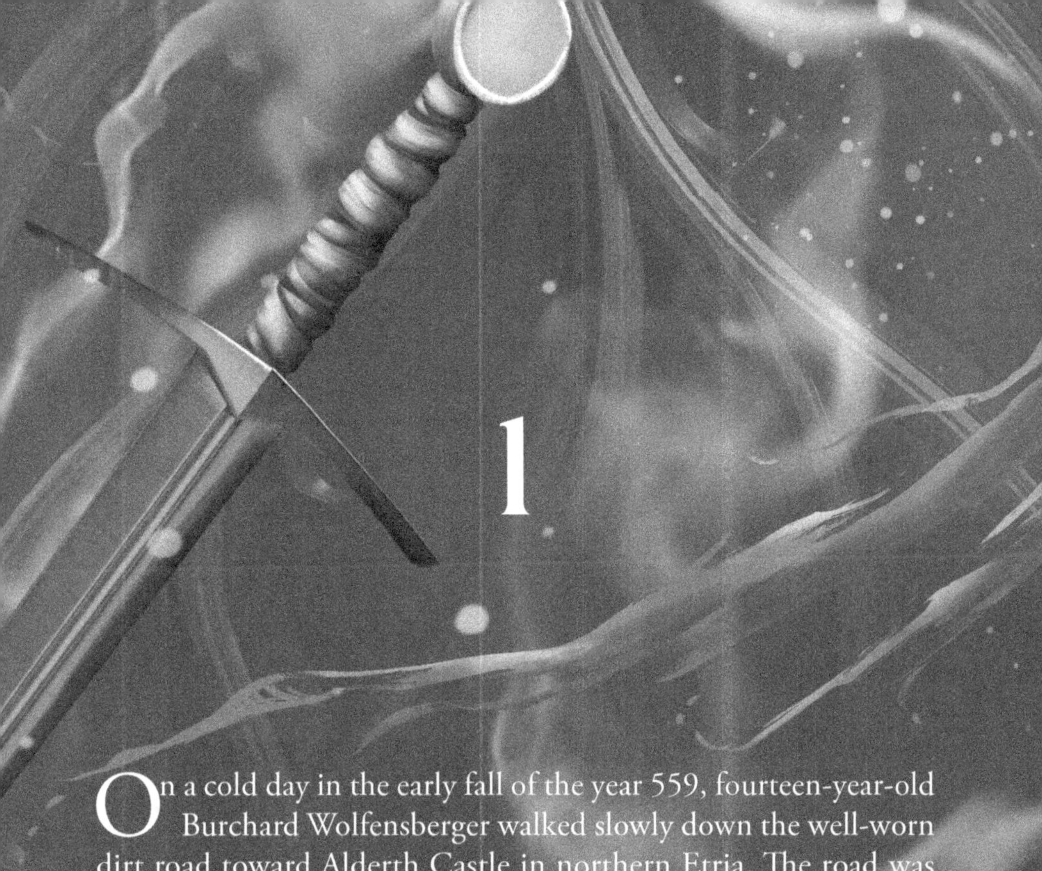

1

On a cold day in the early fall of the year 559, fourteen-year-old Burchard Wolfensberger walked slowly down the well-worn dirt road toward Alderth Castle in northern Etria. The road was lined with a mix of oaks and large pines. The oak leaves had already begun their annual change to the deep reds and oranges of autumn. His horse ambled next to him with a prominent limp, reins draped loosely over its neck. Burchard glanced at his horse and gave him a quick pat before returning to keeping an eye out for any more bandits.

"I think we scared them off," he said quietly, more to himself than the horse. The horse tossed his head as though in agreement.

Why did I comply with this? Burchard thought. *Oh yes, because the assignment was going to be simple. I just had to go to the farm a few miles down the road, give the farmer a letter, and then come back. Except then there were bandits.*

Burchard got lost in his thoughts and stopped watching the road. Suddenly, the ground began to vibrate.

"Uh-oh," Burchard whispered to the horse and scooted them to the side of the road. The vibrations turned into a rhythmic clanking of chain mail and plate armor of at least a full squad of knights, if not more. Keeping his eyes trained on where the knights would become visible, Burchard gave an involuntary shudder. *Please don't be Father. Pease don't be Father,* he fervently prayed.

The knights came into view. He could clearly see a dark-blue standard with a howling white wolf. With a deep sigh, Burchard threw his shoulders back to stand at attention, waiting for his father, General George Wolfensberger, to reach him. Now that Burchard had been under his father's command for several weeks, he knew what was expected of him when they were around other knights. The first day at Alderth Castle, his father had put him in the stocks in the yard for over an hour for speaking out of turn. He had clearly been mistaken in assuming his father would at the very least treat him like any other squire. Instead, it was obvious that whatever had come between them five years ago was still at the forefront of the General's thoughts when it came to his middle son.

At the General's signal, the squad halted a few paces from Burchard. Burchard held his breath, crossing his fingers behind his back, hoping his father was in a good mood. To Burchard's surprise, the General dismounted from his horse and walked over on foot.

"General Wolfensberger," Burchard said formally, with a bow.

"Squire Burchard," the General replied, before he stepped closer to the injured horse. Burchard watched as his father expertly ran his hands over the horse's legs. The inspection stopped when he reached the deep cut on the left hind leg. "Explain yourself," the General said quietly.

Burchard straightened his shoulders and responded, "General, I took the letter to the farmer as ordered. When I was far enough away from the farm that I could not call for help, three bandits attacked me. I was able to scare them off. My horse was brilliant…" He gulped, realizing his slip—his father didn't care about horses or what they did or didn't do. Burchard fell silent, waiting for his father to reprimand him. Once again, his father surprised him by ignoring the comment about the horse.

"The wound is clean, or as clean as you can get it in the field. Would you like to ride back? I can have one of the other knights walk your horse," the General offered.

Burchard narrowed his eyes, trying to keep his face as blank as possible. *This is a test. It has to be. He would never let me trade places with a full knight for an injured horse.*

Doing his best to not roll his eyes at his father in front of the squad of knights, Burchard cleared his throat. "Thank you, General, for the kind offer. I would prefer to walk the horse back myself and make sure he is under the care of the medic." Burchard stood quietly, waiting for his father's response.

The General reached out and squeezed Burchard's hand—recognition that he had said the right words. "I will see you tonight at dinner. Don't be late."

With that, the General turned on his heel and mounted his horse. With an unspoken command, the knights resumed their march toward Alderth Castle.

Burchard let out a shaky breath he didn't realize he was holding as the squad disappeared. "C'mon. We'd better get going so you can get to the medic, and I can get cleaned up before dinner."

The horse grabbed ahold of Burchard's shirt and mashed it around his mouth before spitting it out.

"Ewwww," Burchard said, looking at his shirt, now covered in green slime and drool.

A couple of hours later, an exhausted Burchard trudged into the stable at Alderth Castle.

"Burchard!" a familiar voice called to him from one of the stalls.

Burchard laughed and shook his head. "Captain Thomas?"

The captain stepped out of the stall with his medical bag in hand. "The General said you would need my services," the captain said, and then whistled as he laid his eyes on the horse's wound. "What happened?"

Burchard watched as the captain ran his hands over the horse's back leg, fingers gently probing around the wound. "Bandits. When we got clear of them, I cleaned the wound as you taught me, but I didn't have any supplies with me to dress it."

The captain shook his head. "You did well. I just can't believe your horse was willing to walk back for you."

Burchard shrugged nonchalantly. "It's not like he was going to just lie down and refuse to walk." The captain gave him an odd look. "What?"

"Most horses would have done just that if all you did was clean this wound. You have an uncanny way with horses…although I suspect it's not just horses," the captain said as he rummaged through his bag for a packet of herbs to make a poultice. "Are you sure you're not a mage?"

Burchard gasped, his eyes narrowing in anger. "Me, a mage?" His temper flared. "How can you say that?"

The captain held up his hands in surrender. "Sorry…it's just some mages can, you know…talk to animals. Some can even become animals. I just thought…"

Burchard growled before forcing words out. "I am *not* a mage. Just because I like animals and they like me doesn't mean there is magic involved." Burchard paced in the aisle, furious that the captain, who he thought was his friend, could even suggest that he had magic. Old memories flashed through his mind.

"Burchard!" his mother called.

A young boy with a mop of curly blond hair, not more than five, came running to the house, carrying a squirming puppy.

"Momma, can I keep him?" he asked quietly, eyes hopeful. His mother was about to answer him when she gazed down at the puppy. Big, dark gray, with golden eyes and huge teeth.

"Wolf!" she screamed and yanked at Burchard's arms, causing him to drop the puppy. His mother picked him up and ran back into the house screaming, "Wolf! Wolf!"

He thought he heard the puppy yelp but wasn't sure as his mother carried him farther and farther into the castle, away from his puppy. Finally, she set him down and kneeled in front of him.

"How could you do that, Burchard? Endanger all of us with a wolf?" she said angrily, shaking him.

"It's just…it's just a puppy," Burchard whispered, trying to keep himself from crying. Heavy footsteps came in behind them, and Burchard gulped in fear.

"You brought a wolf into this house. Why?" said General George Wolfensberger in his quiet, scary voice.

Lip quivering, Burchard turned to face his father. "The puppy is my friend."

"The puppy is a wolf…you cannot be friends with a wolf. They are wild animals and not trustworthy." His father paused, and a strange look crossed his face. He grabbed Burchard's chin hard and turned his face this way and that. "Are you a mage, boy?"

Burchard shook. "A…mmmm…mmm…. mage?"

The General looked at his wife. "We need to have him tested."

A shiver went down Burchard's spine as he tried to shake off the old memories. The testing had been physically and mentally brutal. Because they had thought he had animal magic, they tortured him to try to get him to shift into one. Then, when that didn't work, they went to work on the wolf puppy.

He turned and headed back down the aisleway toward the captain. "I assure you, Captain Thomas, that I am not a mage. The General made sure of that long ago."

He watched the captain digest that tidbit of information as he finished applying the poultice to the horse. In Etria, for as long as Burchard could remember, mage testing was accomplished by pushing a child suspected to be a mage until they performed magic. Usually, heightened emotion was the trigger. Because having a mage in the family usually increased their status in the eyes of the king, families went to great lengths to be sure that child was a mage. Burchard had made a vow to himself after his testing that he would never allow anyone to be tested like that, not if he could help it. Nine years later, he still wasn't sure how he would accomplish that—other than if he were blessed with children of his own, to not permit them to be tested in such a way.

Captain Thomas coughed. "I will leave you instructions for how to make more of the poultice. You'll need to change it out once a day for a week. Stall rest only. After the week, you can begin hand-walking, two laps around the training yard twice a day for two weeks. Then, we'll see. I would advise finding a horse you can borrow for the time being. I'm sure your knight master is going to need you to be able to ride." The captain led the horse into a stall and removed its bridle before stepping out. He offered the bridle to Burchard.

Burchard took it. "Thank you."

The captain nodded, gathered his things, and departed. Burchard watched the captain leave and then finished putting away his riding gear in the room at the far end of the stable that was set aside for such things. Slinging his pack over his shoulder, he headed out of the stable and walked face-first into someone much taller than he was.

"Sorry," he muttered and was greeted by a familiar chuckle. Taking a hasty step backward, Burchard looked up. His knight master, a tall, lanky man with short-cropped brown hair and a graying beard, peered down at him with bright green eyes.

"Sir Peter," Burchard said with a bow.

"I heard you had trouble with bandits today," Sir Peter Windemere said casually.

Burchard bit back his initial response. Sir Peter was much more easygoing than his father, but he'd been serving under him for barely a month and didn't feel confident in their relationship yet. "Yes, sir. Captain Thomas helped patch up my horse," he replied, hoping Sir Peter would move out of the way so he could go get cleaned up before the dinner bell rang.

"Tomorrow morning, we are supposed to practice with Sir Daniel and Squire Ruschmann," Sir Peter informed Burchard as he stepped to the side so the squire could pass.

Burchard let a small smile escape as he moved past Sir Peter toward their barracks. His knight master would not get reprimanded for being late, but Burchard definitely would. "They're here?" Still smiling, he recalled the last conversation he had with Ruschmann, when his friend had mentioned they could be coming north when he saw him this past spring, but he hadn't had any word since then. Although Ruschmann Blackwell was a year older than Burchard, Burchard had found that he had more in common with him than he had with his own brothers. They had spent many evenings together practicing sword work or going over assignments the three years they were pages together.

Sir Peter nodded and turned, heading toward the barracks they were assigned to. "Yes. I don't know how long they will be here for, but it should be least a few days. There have been some small skirmishes at the Stinyia border with rebels, and I believe Sir Daniel is headed there." Burchard was about to ask another question when Sir Peter held his hand up to stop him. "No, we haven't gotten any orders yet. It is only a matter of time though."

Burchard opened the door to the barracks and followed Sir Peter in. He went straight for his bed and small chest of drawers. Burchard pulled out a clean tunic, pants, and undergarments.

"You'd better hurry!" Sir Peter called from farther back in the room.

Sighing and wishing he had time for a bath, Burchard hastily yanked off his boots and stripped, dropping his stinky clothing in a heap and pulling on the clean clothes. Then, Burchard walked to Sir Peter's space. The knight had the same bed, a slightly larger chest of drawers, and a desk.

"The water is still warm. You should at least clean the dirt off your face."

Burchard took the washcloth off the rim of the bucket and dunked it before scrubbing his face. When finished, he looked in the mirror. Bright blue eyes peered back at him. His blond hair was matted and in need of a comb or a haircut.

Gong!

"We're out of time," Sir Peter said, standing up. Burchard glanced at his knight master, unspoken question in his eyes. "You're presentable enough. He knows you had to take care of the horse."

Burchard didn't comment, not feeling nearly as confident as Sir Peter that his father wouldn't chew him out for his appearance and clear lack of a bath.

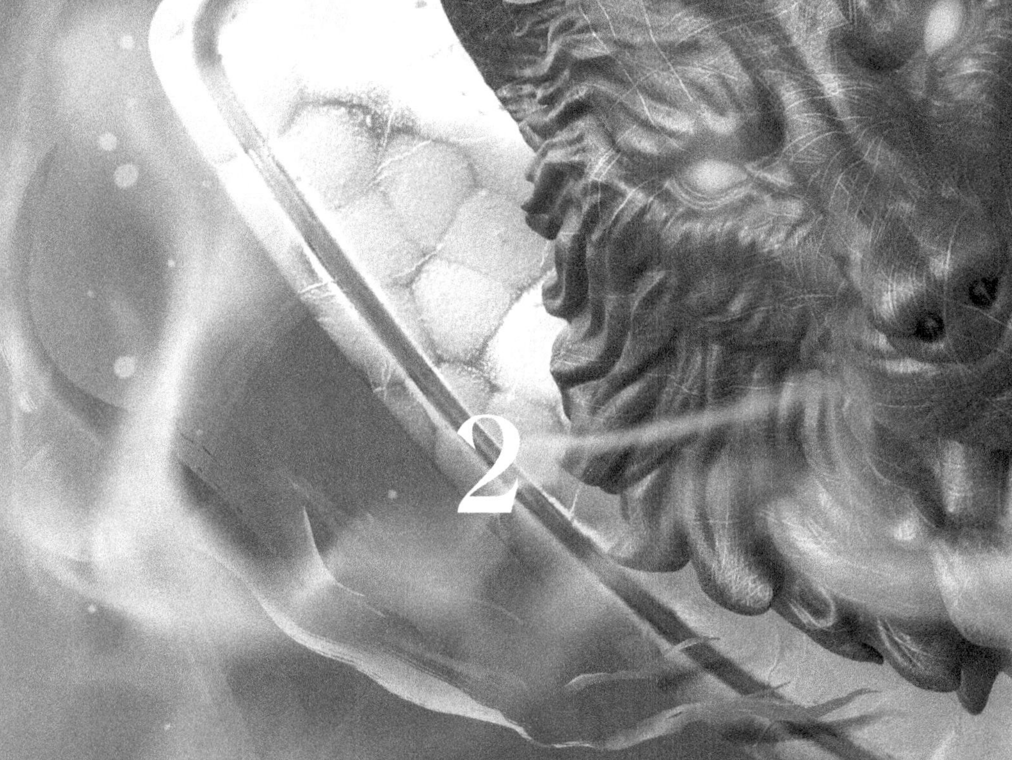

2

Burchard followed Sir Peter into the dining hall within Alderth Castle. The dining hall was situated in the center of the castle. High overhead were large wood beams. Huge metal circles hung from the beams, holding oil lamps that provided the light for the room. The castle staff would lower and raise them using a pulley system that was somehow hidden within the beams. In the center of the dining hall was the main table that ran the length of the whole room. The loud rumble of the officers' voices made it difficult to pick out any individual. Weaving through the crowd, Sir Peter led them toward the head of the table where the General was sitting. The seats at his immediate right and left were open, while the others were full. As they approached, Burchard caught his father's eye and gave him a brief salute. General Wolfensberger nodded in acknowledgement and waved his hand to indicate the empty seats were for Burchard and Sir Peter.

Sir Peter slid into the seat on the left, leaving the one on the right for Burchard. Burchard pulled out the seat, bowed to his father, and then sat down quietly. He was not surprised when his father began speaking to Sir Peter, ignoring him completely. As they launched into a discussion of the day's events, Burchard found himself listening while trying to be patient for when the food would arrive.

"I've heard a few rumors that Walter Pell and the Firebirds have resurfaced," Sir Peter said conversationally to the General, piquing Burchard's interest.

The General waved a hand in dismissal. "Don't believe everything you hear, Windemere. I was there the day their encampment was attacked ten years ago, and it was confirmed that Walter Pell and the last of his Firebirds died that day. I was second in command for that campaign, and we had a mage with us to ensure our victory."

Burchard raised his eyebrow. *Mages can't ensure your victory! What is my father talking about?* Sir Peter caught his eye in a warning to stay silent.

Sir Peter replied in a sad voice, "Yes, but at what cost to Etria? I heard about that battle, and it was a devastating loss. I hope you are right that Walter Pell is dead, because if he is involved in any way with the Stinyian rebels, then we have our work cut out for us."

The General's eyes blazed with annoyance. "As I said, Walter Pell is dead. Mind you remember who is the general at Alderth Castle and who is *just* a knight."

At that precise moment, servants started to bring out platters of food and set them on the table, helping to break the tension. Because of his favored position near the general, Burchard was able to get one of the first cuts of the venison and other dishes.

He was about to take a bite of a particularly juicy piece of venison when his father decided to direct his attention to him. "Tell me more about the bandits you encountered today, squire."

Burchard set down his fork and gazed solemnly at his father. "General, I did not notice anything particularly remarkable about the bandits. They seemed most interested in acquiring my horse and stealing anything I had of value. Is there some specific attribute you want to know about?"

The General tugged at his lip in thought before responding. "No, there is not a specific attribute. There have been an increased number of bandit attacks lately, but it still appears as though they are random. If I can acquire evidence indicating that the bandits are becoming an organized unit or that it is instead a group of rebels with a leader…then I have permission from King Roland to do what I can to eradicate the problem. However, with the very real threat of Stinyian rebels trying to gain a foothold at our northern border, I cannot afford to waste my men on a wild goose chase."

Burchard opened his mouth to reply, but Sir Peter caught his eye and shook his head. Blowing out his breath, Burchard took the unspoken advice of his knight master and did not say what was on his mind. Instead, he picked up the piece of bread on his plate and began to eat it. His father's comment was a reminder of how everyone in Alderth Castle was already on alert to move out at a moment's notice due to the threat Stinyian rebels presented. Meaning he must eat every chance he had; otherwise, he could be caught hungry out in the field.

As the General's attention returned to Sir Peter, Burchard turned to see who was on his other side. Much to his surprise it was Lady Gladys, daughter to Colonel Lincoln Frost. The colonel was a few seats down.

Burchard put a smile on his face and bowed from his seat. "M'lady, to what do I owe the pleasure?"

Lady Gladys rolled her eyes and slapped at his arm lightly. "Why are you being formal?" Burchard tipped his head toward the General, watching as she caught his meaning. "Squire Burchard, how was your day?" she asked in her most ladylike voice.

Burchard started to smirk but caught himself. *Is this another one of his tests? To see if I can screw things up?* Leaning in toward Lady Gladys, he replied, "I delivered a letter to a farmer and my horse got hurt, so I had to walk back." Taking a deep breath, the smell of the venison tantalizing him again, he slowly cut his slice into smaller, more manageable bites, not sure what else to say to Lady Gladys. Thankfully Lady Gladys was willing to keep up the pretense of proper etiquette and followed his lead, eating her venison.

Burchard had been stunned last week when the colonel showed up with his daughter in tow. He hadn't been the only one who shared his thoughts on the matter. General Wolfensberger was not pleased to have a fourteen-year-old noble girl within Alderth Castle and did not hesitate to voice his feelings vehemently to Colonel Frost in the courtyard for everyone to hear.

Colonel Frost did not seem to share the General's concerns enough to alter his plan of having his daughter reside at the castle, which Burchard had to admit he found intriguing. *What about Lady Gladys makes her father unafraid about being surrounded by knights?* Although the castle staff comprised adults as well as boys and girls ten years old and up, females of noble birth were held to certain expectations, and being the only noblewoman in a castle with over one thousand knights could be risky business.

Since her arrival, Burchard had tried to go out of his way to ensure that Lady Gladys was treated well by the knights within the castle, the same way that his older sister Anne would do when a daughter of a nobleman visited Wolfensberger Castle.

"Is your horse OK?" Concern lowered Lady Gladys's voice an octave.

Burchard shrugged. "He'll survive. Captain Thomas, one of the medics, cleaned up the wound and—"

Suddenly, the dining hall doors burst open, and a filthy young man with matted black hair plastered to his face, dark-brown skin, and mud-splattered leather armor stumbled into the room. A well-worn scabbard swung at his side, holding his sword.

Burchard leapt out of his seat, recognizing fellow squire Ruschmann Blackwell immediately and forgetting any obligations he might have to Lady Gladys. "Ru!" he shouted as he ran toward his friend as fast as he could, shoving anyone blocking his path out of the way. He skidded to a halt in front of Ruschmann and grabbed his friend by the arms, ignoring the slippery feeling of the mud under his hands.

Burchard felt his pulse quickening as he took in Ruschmann's appearance and what it meant. "What happened? Where's Sir Daniel?"

Gasping for air, Ruschmann shook his head. Someone reached out and offered a mug of something. Burchard grasped it and held it to his friend's lips.

After what felt like hours but was only moments, Ruschmann pushed away the mug. "Sir Daniel sent me here to come get help. We were on our way here when a group of Stinyian rebels attacked us."

Burchard could feel a body brushing against his back. He bristled at the close contact, then chided himself; whoever it was just wanted to help Ruschmann.

The General spoke, causing Burchard to jump slightly. He hadn't realized it was his father behind him. "How many rebels?"

Ruschmann closed his eyes for a moment. Burchard watched his friend, unsure if he had been injured too or was just tired. When his eyes opened, Ruschmann gazed over Burchard's shoulder to the General. "There were twenty, or at least there were when I left. We were outnumbered but our squad seemed to have more training than the Stinyians. I'm not sure how long Sir Daniel's men are going to last, though. They were in rough shape when he ordered me to leave. We need to hurry."

Burchard kept his attention on his friend, his gaze wandering over Ruschmann, searching for hints of an injury. Other than dirt and a few smears of blood, Ruschmann appeared unscathed.

Hesitating for a moment before speaking, Burchard offered his hand to Ruschmann. "Come with me. I can take you to see the medic." Behind him, he could hear his father giving orders to those around him and people leaving the dining hall to gather their weapons.

Much to his surprise, Burchard's friend shook his head. "I need to go with them. I cannot abandon Sir Daniel."

Burchard started to protest, but Ruschmann squeezed his arm. "You would feel the same way if it was Sir Peter. Besides, this is not my blood."

Taking a deep breath, Burchard nodded. "Then I will come with you."

"No, you will not," said a firm voice behind him.

Burchard's shoulders slumped. He pivoted so he could face his father. Afraid to meet his eyes, he focused on his father's shoulder.

"You do not have a horse; therefore, you cannot go," the General grudgingly explained.

Burchard bit his tongue to prevent himself from saying something that would get him locked in the stocks again.

The third day he had been at Alderth Castle, his father had questioned what he was doing when he dropped his saddlebags in front of the barracks to save himself from having to pack them from the barn. The General had told him to pick them up, and Burchard had refused to obey the direct order in front of two squads of knights. The General had then dragged him by the arm across the courtyard and put him in the stocks for the whole day.

Instead of responding, he bowed and departed the dining hall. He knew there was a good chance he would get in trouble for leaving without a formal dismissal, but he decided it would be safer than staying and speaking his mind. The last thing Burchard wanted to do was compromise his best friend's ability to save his knight master by being the cause of a delay.

Outside of the dining hall, Burchard glanced around the dimly lit stone hallway before slipping out one of the castle side doors and into the courtyard. He jogged over to the dark barracks that he had been assigned to. Hurrying toward his belongings in the darkness, Burchard was almost to his bed when he stumbled on his own feet and fell to his knees.

He scrambled on the floor to get up and over to his bed. If he wanted to go with Ruschmann and the knights on the rescue mission, he had to grab his gear and find a horse, fast.

Finally at his bed, Burchard reached underneath and snagged his scabbard with his sword and his chain mail. While not the ideal place to store those items, it was the best he could come up with given the amount of space he was allowed. He set the sword on the bed and stood up, sliding the chain mail over his head, grunting as its weight settled over his shoulders. He picked up the scabbard and buckled it onto his waist.

Back outside, he took off at a run for the stable. His father had said he couldn't go because he didn't have a horse. While his usual horse was indeed injured, spare horses were always in the stable. Although Burchard preferred to use his personal mount, he decided he would rather support his friend than worry about which horse he was riding.

Captain Thomas stepped out of a stall toward the end of the barn and saw Burchard. He smiled. "I thought I might see you in here tonight. Coming to get one of the spare horses?"

Burchard shrugged and went to the stall opposite of where Captain Thomas had been, where a brown horse with a white face was standing. "I'm going to take Chip."

Captain Thomas quirked an eyebrow out him. "You are *choosing* to ride Chip? Voluntarily?"

Burchard chuckled. "Why does everyone think she's so awful?" He stroked her white nose gently before making a beeline for the tack room. He picked up his saddle and Chip's bridle and headed back toward her.

"She has bucked off every rider who has ever been on her," Captain Thomas explained.

Burchard smiled politely and set his saddle down on top of a hay bale outside of Chip's stall. "She tried that…it didn't work. Trust me, we understand each other."

Opening the stall door, Burchard entered quietly with several brushes in his hand. Chip pinned her ears back at first. Burchard shook his finger at her before stepping to her shoulder and beginning the grooming process. As he expertly worked the curry comb into her fur, Chip sighed, and he could feel her muscles relaxing under the attention. Next came the stiff body brush to get all the loose hair off. Once grooming was complete, he pulled a sugar cube from his pocket and offered it to her. She eagerly consumed the sugar cube, leaving Burchard's hands a slobbery mess.

Rolling his eyes, Burchard hastily wiped his hands on his pants, then reached over the stall door to retrieve his saddle. Once again, he took slow, deliberate steps toward her. Instead of pinning her ears back, she just flicked them toward him. Burchard murmured soothing words to her while he got the cinch tight and then retrieved the bridle.

Once tacked up, Burchard led Chip into the aisleway before swinging up into the saddle. "I'll see you later." He gave Captain Thomas a slight wave before clucking to Chip and heading out of the stable at a brisk walk. Running through his list of supplies in his mind and hoping he packed everything he would need, Burchard almost rode right into another knight. Chip tossed her head and snapped her teeth when he steered her to the side just in time.

Relief coursed through him as he realized if they had been a minute or two later, he would have missed the group departing. The knights were starting to stream out of the gates. Waiting for his turn to head out, Burchard glanced around at the assembled knights. He noticed that unlike most of the assignments he went out on where they were ordered to be equipped a certain way, this time the knights were wearing an assortment of gear. Some decided to don full plate armor, while others just wore chain mail like Burchard. All told there were about fifty knights headed out to rescue Sir Daniel and his squad. Burchard spotted Ruschmann at the front of the group but decided to hang back to ensure his father, who was standing on the wall above the gate, wouldn't notice that he was with them.

Once they cleared the castle gate, the group surged into a gallop. Another advantage of being at the back of the group was that Chip wouldn't accidentally kick anyone. She had made a habit of attempting to kick or bite anyone, human or horse, stupid enough to be within striking range when Burchard was riding. *I suppose it's better than getting bucked off.*

As he settled into the steady rhythm of Chip's gallop, Burchard glanced back. His father stood on the wall, watching.

Shaking his head, Burchard returned his attention to following the knight in front of him. The group slowed to a brisk walk and veered off into the forest. Sounds of a battle were audible now that they were close enough. Burchard wrapped one hand around the hilt of his sword, checking to ensure it would easily slide out of the scabbard when the time was right.

"You came," murmured Ruschmann, startling him.

Burchard hadn't heard Ruschmann's horse, Cricket, approach. He gave his friend a sharp look. "You thought I wouldn't?"

Ruschmann pushed the hair out of his face with a grimace. "I remember what you said happened last time you disobeyed the General's orders to stay within the castle. You were whipped. I didn't think you would risk being punished to help me, not when he favors such extreme punishments."

Blue eyes locked with brown ones. "I will never abandon you. Regardless of what my father says or does." Blowing out a breath, Burchard continued, "These knights, do you really think they care about us? We're *only* squires. We're expendable. I know you haven't had the opportunity to spend much time at Alderth Castle, but I have. I hear what they say."

"Surely your father doesn't think you're expendable too?" Ruschmann replied in disbelief.

Burchard laughed harshly. "I have an older brother and a younger brother, and they both obey orders without question. So yes, I would say the son who won't blindly obey is likely considered expendable."

Ruschmann pursed his lips in thought but stayed silent. Burchard was about to speak when a dark shadow darted out of the trees straight for the two of them.

"Move!" he hissed. Sliding his sword out of its scabbard, Burchard dug his heels into Chip, causing her to rear. The move had the desired effect. The dark shadow stopped in the small patch of moonlight, revealing a wild-eyed, blood-spattered man with messy white hair, a broadsword, and leather armor with metal bands around his arms. Growling, Burchard jumped off Chip and swung his sword at the man, who was clearly not Etrian. Expecting the man to just drop, Burchard was surprised when his strike was parried instead.

Adjusting his feet, Burchard shuffled backward a step and swung his sword in a high strike a second time. Sparks flew as the swords connected. The rebel grinned at Burchard, showing a mouth with missing teeth. Burchard took a deep breath and instantly regretted doing so as the smell of rotting teeth and dead animals wafted from the assailant. Wrinkling his nose, he ducked a wayward swing before pivoting and striking again. This time his sword connected with the man's left arm, slicing open the unprotected bicep just above the metal band.

Unable to stop himself, Burchard winced in sympathy, knowing firsthand how much that cut had to hurt. Shaking himself, he tried to focus on his task, eliminating this non-Etrian. He settled into the rhythm of blocks, strikes, and parries, marveling at how even after being wounded, the attacker just kept going, oblivious to the pain. Somewhere behind him in the forest, Burchard could hear the ringing of swords from the other knights engaging the enemy. Both Burchard and his attacker paused to catch their breath for a fleeting moment. At that moment, Burchard had one thought. *I hope Chip and Ru are OK.*

Burchard shifted his stance, running different movements through his mind, trying to determine the best way to end this fight. He knew it was only a matter of time before he began to tire, and this much-larger opponent would gain the upper hand. Suddenly, he had an idea. As the rebel took two running steps toward Burchard, Burchard tucked into a forward roll and popped up on his feet behind his opponent. The rebel was caught off guard, and his forward momentum carried him to the tree that had been at Burchard's back. Smiling, Burchard leapt forward and drove his sword into the man's neck.

Yanking his sword out, Burchard spun, thinking he heard something. *Nothing. There's nothing here but me and the rebel's body.* A shudder ran through him as his thoughts returned to the body. He leaned over just in time as he retched up what little bit of dinner he had consumed earlier.

"Ugh," he muttered to himself as he tried to wipe off his mouth, annoyed that his stomach betrayed him. He had seen action before. *But have I killed anyone?* The thought dangled, taunting him. Even worse, he didn't know the answer.

Hands shaking slightly, Burchard bent over and grabbed a handful of leaves to clean the blood off his sword as best he could. Ears straining, he thought he could hear the distant sound of swords clashing. With one more glance around him, hand on his sword hilt, Burchard cautiously headed toward the sounds of fighting. He had no idea where Ruschmann had gone either. He had thought when his friend found him that they would end up staying together, but after he leapt off Chip, he had not been able to keep track of where Ruschmann went.

Burchard walked for what felt like hours. *It could be just a few minutes,* he chided himself. The forest in this area looked mostly the same, full of large, ancient oak trees. Most of the small animals seemed to have disappeared with the proximity of the fighting, not that he blamed them. *It must seem crazy to some to want to run into a battle or conflict instead of away from it. Yet this has always been my dream.* All he had to guide him was the sounds of the fighting. Wondering if his imagination was getting the better of him, Burchard stumbled sideways when something ran into him from the side. His knees hit a hard rock hidden by the thick layer of leaves. Groaning, Burchard rolled to the side just in time to avoid being skewered. As he rolled to and fro, Burchard dropped his sword. Growling in frustration, he finally found the leverage he needed to get off the ground and out of the way. Sweeping his sword off the ground, he blocked the next strike just in time. A hair later and he'd have been dead.

Sweat beaded on his forehead, threatening to drip into his eyes. Burchard stepped to the left and began a combination move of his own. Knowing he didn't have the strength to match the clearly well-trained foe in front of him, he decided to use what he did have: speed. His thoughts drifted back to the first conversation he'd had with Sir Peter.

Burchard had just finished his practice round with Ruschmann and looked up. A knight was standing at the rail, watching him with interest.

"Can I help you?" Burchard asked uncertainly. Usually, knights didn't pay any attention to third-year pages.

The knight chuckled and, to Burchard's surprise, offered his hand. Burchard shook the knight's hand, still uncertain about what was happening.

"You have potential, you know," Sir Peter said quietly.

"Potential, sir?" asked Burchard.

Sir Peter chuckled. "Sorry…I am Sir Peter Windemere. Yes, you have potential. Have you ever heard of a sword master?"

"Of course!" Burchard said, grinning and wondering why anyone aspiring to be a knight wouldn't know what a sword master was.

"Have you ever met one?" Sir Peter inquired.

Eyes narrowing, Burchard wondered if this knight was trying to trick him. "No, they're all dead."

Sir Peter shook his head. "You're wrong. They're not all dead. Most, but not all."

Burchard bit his lip, holding back a response.

Sir Peter shrugged and then shook his head, as if remembering why he was there. "Have you ever tried using speed to your advantage? I noticed that Page Ruschmann is larger than you are. It seemed at times like he almost got the upper hand because he has more weight behind him. When you are fully grown and trained you will have the strength to not have to rely on speed when going against a larger opponent. Until then…it is a great tool."

Burchard blinked as he resurfaced from his thoughts, realizing at that moment how right Sir Peter had been. Speed was his best tool. Hastily, he brought up his sword to parry his foe's strike. Sidestepping to the left provided the opportunity he needed to get underneath the other man's guard. Smiling wolfishly, Burchard feinted before sweeping his sword into the rebel's side. The feint worked, and his sword connected with the chain mail. The attacker stumbled backward, gasping. Not wanting to waste the opportunity, Burchard stepped in close again with short, quick strikes. Each one hit the desired target. Instead of parrying or blocking the attacks, the man stumbled backward, face going white. When his broadsword fell to the ground, Burchard leapt forward, sword pointed at the man's throat.

"Yield!" he shouted.

The man closed his eyes and nodded. "I yield."

Burchard grinned and then realized his mistake. *I have a prisoner…now what?* Burchard glanced around the area and then let out a loud whistle, hoping Chip was nearby and would come to his call. Sometimes the mare would deliberately ignore him, as though proving that she was as terrible as her reputation claimed. Twigs snapped, and he heard a soft whinny. Chip trotted over to Burchard.

"Good girl," he murmured, stroking her neck with one hand while keeping his focus on his prisoner. Searching one handed through his bags was not efficient, but he was afraid to take his eyes off the rebel for fear he would run away. Finally, he came across a coil of rope. Yanking it out of the saddlebag, he gave Chip one more pat before returning his full attention on his prisoner.

"Turn around and put your hands behind your back," Burchard ordered in what he hoped was an authoritative voice.

His prisoner complied, and Burchard used the rope to tie the rebel's hands before leading him to one of the smaller but still formidable oak trees. He wrapped the rope around the oak's trunk before securing the end of the rope to the rebel. Satisfied that the rebel wouldn't be going anywhere unless he had help to escape, Burchard returned to Chip's side. With one more glance at his prisoner, Burchard mounted up and clucked to Chip. They trotted off into the forest.

3

Burchard rode into a small clearing with an old rock-lined firepit in the center. Etrian knights milled around or talked quietly in small clusters. The medic who had ridden out with the fifty knights to rescue Sir Daniel was busy attending to several wounded lying on blankets under a makeshift tent. Burchard dismounted and found a place to tie Chip away from the other horses. When he turned around to find someone to tell about his prisoner, he bumped into none other than Ruschmann.

"I was worried you died," Ruschmann murmured, hugging Burchard awkwardly.

Burchard pulled back, surprised by the hug and that his friend thought he would die that easily. "It will take more than a single rebel to finish me off. I did capture one though. Maybe my father will want to interrogate him. How is Sir Daniel?"

Ruschmann shook his head. "It doesn't look good. The medic is trying to stabilize him so we can transport him back to Alderth Castle and better healing supplies."

"Did we lose anyone, or just injuries?" Burchard asked, worried.

"Just a few minor to moderate injuries, aside from Sir Daniel." Ruschmann opened his mouth to say something else when Sir Martin Forsyth, one of General Wolfensberger's commanders, walked over to them. Burchard's face fell at the sight of Sir Forsyth. He knew that no matter how much he had hoped his father would not know he had disobeyed a direct order, that hope was now gone. Sir Forsyth would surely report his presence to the General.

"Squire Ruschmann and Squire Burchard," Sir Forsyth spoke formally. Burchard gulped and thought this could not be good if he wanted to talk to both of them. "We will move out shortly to head back to Alderth Castle. However, the medic, Lord Hampton, is concerned about the surgical suite being ready when we arrive. He feels it is possible to save Sir Daniel, but only if no additional time is wasted upon our arrival at the castle. Which means I need the two of you to depart with haste to Alderth Castle and alert them. Captain Thomas will know what is required; just tell him it is the left leg."

Burchard glanced over at Ruschmann and elbowed him hard before his friend could speak and say something stupid. "Yes, sir." Burchard saluted Sir Forsyth and turned sharply on his heel before running to Chip, fervently hoping that Ruschmann was right behind him and not getting both of them in trouble with Sir Forsyth.

Just as Burchard swung his leg into the saddle, he heard the jingle of another horse. Ruschmann rode up beside him.

"C'mon, let's go," Burchard said. Without waiting for a response, he kicked Chip into a canter, afraid to gallop through this part of the forest, but also afraid of not giving Captain Thomas a much-needed heads-up. Thoughts churning, Burchard allowed Chip to navigate through the trees. When they reached the road, he kissed and gave Chip her head, and they quickly sped up into a gallop. Ruschmann was next to them, Cricket eagerly running with Chip stride for stride.

I'm going to be in so much trouble, Burchard thought, realizing he was running straight to Alderth Castle and his father. The orders Sir Forsyth had given made it impossible to avoid facing the General.

Sooner than Burchard thought possible, they galloped through the open gates of Alderth Castle. He heard a shout from above them on the wall. As they entered the courtyard, both horses slowed without being asked. Swinging his leg over the saddle, Burchard jumped off Chip, and Ruschmann quickly followed suit. Leaving their horses standing in the courtyard, Burchard sent a swift prayer that Chip would not harm anyone before he returned from delivering his message.

Leaping up the steps two at a time, he reached for the castle door. Just then, the huge, dark wooden doors with thick metal straps burst open, knocking Burchard backward. He tumbled head over heels down the stairs. Each step he hit, he tried to slow his momentum, but his fingers, slick with sweat from the ride, slid uselessly against the stone stairs. He tried to protect his head as much as possible, but by the time he reached the last couple of steps, his body was so bruised he could no longer protect himself. His head hit the last step hard, and everything went black.

Burchard opened his eyes and stood up. A shiver ran down his spine as he looked around and realized that he was no longer at Alderth Castle. He was somewhere else. *Am I dead?* he wondered. Laughter bubbled up inside of him at the thought that he had always been worried about dying in battle, and yet here he was, dead from being hit by a door.

Assuming he was indeed dead, Burchard decided it wouldn't hurt to explore. Looking down, he couldn't see his feet at all. Thick white fog covered the ground, thinning out some as it reached his knees. Shuffling his feet around, he felt as though he was on hard, compacted dirt, much like the courtyard of Alderth Castle. Turning his attention to his surroundings, he was surprised to see tree-like shapes rising out of the fog, but not quite discernable. Soft light coming from somewhere cast wherever he was into an eerie black-and-white landscape, void of all colors.

Putting one foot in front of the other, he cautiously walked forward, heading toward the trees. At first, it felt like he was walking through thick liquid, resisting his forward movement. But as he continued moving determinedly, the resistance eased up until it was gone altogether.

How odd, he thought. He also noticed there was no sound in this place. Or nothing was making any audible sounds. *Can I make a sound?*

He opened his mouth, preparing to shout, when a misty white shape appeared in front of him.

I wouldn't do that if I were you, it said, startling Burchard as he realized the voice was in his head. The figure was not actually speaking through its mouth. Burchard tried to work his jaw to reply, but the misty creature shook its head, stopping him. *Think what you want to say. Don't say it aloud…or you might wake it up.*

Eyes narrowing in annoyance, Burchard blew out his breath and attempted to project what he wanted to say into his thoughts. *What will wake up?*

The misty figure shook uncontrollably and started to disappear.

Wait! Burchard shouted in his thoughts, fear coursing through him that whatever this misty being was would leave him alone to deal with some creature of nightmares.

The misty form became solid again, its features clearer this time. Much to Burchard's shock, its face was not human, but wolf. He closed his eyes and then reopened them. The misty wolf thing was still there in front of him, cocking its head from side to side.

Who are you? he thought in a voice he forced to be calm.

Who are you? the misty wolf responded.

Debating how to reply, Burchard decided perhaps if he offered his name first the misty wolf would reciprocate. *I am Burchard Wo—*

A shriek escaped his lips as the wolf creature leapt forward and bit down on his arm. The bite didn't hurt, but his arm felt colder than ice. A tear escaped as the cold radiated toward his shoulder.

Saying your full name in this place gives it power over you, the misty wolf said with a warning growl.

Burchard glared at the misty wolf. First it asked him who he was and then it bit him for saying his name, which made no sense whatsoever.

Call me Eos, the misty wolf said quietly.

Eos, Burchard thought, trying to keep his words only in his mind and not as a projection. Why does that sound oddly familiar?

Burchard was about to ask Eos if they'd met before when suddenly he started to shake. But it was almost as though someone was shaking him.

What is going on? he asked, concern clear.

Goodbye, Burchard. I will see you soon, Eos said.

Everything went black.

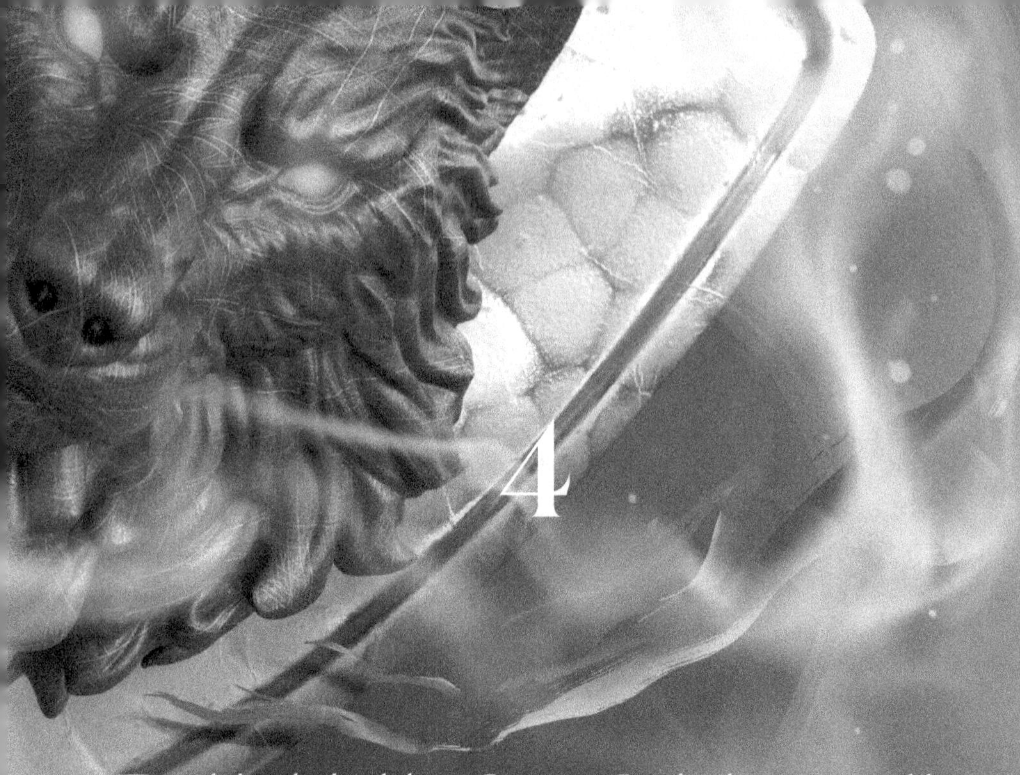

4

Rough hands shook him. Groaning, Burchard was surprised he felt what could be a bed underneath his prone body. He slowly opened his eyes, wincing as cold still pierced through the arm Eos had bitten.

A familiar face with a full pewter-gray beard and black hair with gray streaks in it peered at him with a worried frown. "You're awake!"

"I'm alive?" asked Burchard in a whisper before realizing it was his father's face hovering that close. *He's worried about me?*

"You took quite a tumble down the steps," his father replied somberly, his hands folded in his lap.

The memory of what happened came crashing down. Burchard struggled to push himself up out of bed. "The wounded!" It came out as more of a croak than the intended shout.

Gently, the General pushed on Burchard's shoulders until he stopped fighting and lay all the way down. "You and Ruschmann arrived in time, and Sir Daniel is recovering well. He's just at the other end of this room, in fact."

"Was there a wolf?" Burchard asked.

The General looked at his son sharply. "There are no wolves here, save for the one on my standard. You need to rest. In a few more days, you should be able to return to light duty."

"Days?" Burchard mumbled, his eyes wide.

Instead of responding, the General stood up and made a motion with his hand. "I am needed elsewhere, son, but perhaps Ruschmann can fill you in on what has happened and can answer your questions." With that, the General departed.

Taking a deep breath and wincing as his bruised ribs protested, Burchard gazed at his best friend waiting by the foot of the bed. "I have so many questions. How long have I been asleep for?"

Ruschmann gave him a hesitant smile. "Three days."

"Three days!" Burchard yelped.

"Yes…but please calm down. As the General said and I think you recall…you were hit by the door, and you fell down all of the *stone* stairs. Before that, we were in a skirmish. Wounds take time to heal."

"I thought I was dead," Burchard whispered.

Ruschmann gave him a quizzical look. "Dead? Why would you think that?"

"I was in a strange, misty place," Burchard explained with a shrug. He opened his mouth to say more, but the words wouldn't come out. He started to hack instead. Ruschmann handed him a glass of water. Burchard took it gratefully. After taking a few sips, he opened his mouth to try again and once again began coughing. *Strange. It's almost as though I'm being prevented from talking about it.*

"Are you OK?" Ruschmann gave him a concerned look.

Burchard nodded. "Yeah, I'm fine…so if I've been asleep for three days, what's happened?"

"Nothing terribly exciting, I assure you." Ruschmann paused. "The General ordered me to report to Sir Peter while Sir Daniel is recovering. Mostly I have been running errands for him."

"Did they find my prisoner?" Burchard asked.

Ruschmann laughed. "Yes, they found the prisoner. I think your father has forgiven you for leaving without permission since you are the only person to have captured one of the rebels."

Burchard looked away, not sure if he was willing to believe Ruschmann. His father did not easily forgive, especially with matters involving Burchard. The only way he would know for sure would be to confront his father about it. Burchard knew he sometimes did stupid things, but he was not sure he wanted to remind his father that he had disobeyed him.

Ruschmann's calloused hand on his arm drew his attention back to his friend. "Your prisoner has provided some very useful information. It appears the bandit attacks, including the one you experienced when you delivered the letter to the farmer, have been Stinyian rebels trying to create chaos. I believe the General now has the evidence he has been searching for to justify attacking the Stinyian rebel base."

"Good. Hopefully we will finally see some action," Burchard said excitedly.

"You've already seen action, and look where you ended up," chided Ruschmann.

Rolling his eyes, Burchard retorted, "Yeah, action by door. There is nothing you could do that would keep me from going."

A cough sounded from behind Burchard's bed. Burchard twisted, trying to see who it was. His knight master, Sir Peter, was standing there. "You may be right that Ruschmann cannot prevent you from going, but the General or I most certainly could order you to stay here."

Eyes widening, Burchard looked at Sir Peter in shock. "You wouldn't do that!"

Sir Peter tsked. "No, I wouldn't, unless I thought it was for your own good. However, what your father might decide to do is not in my control. I would advise that if you want to be in the group of knights that goes after the rebels..." The knight stopped speaking and looked at both squires squarely in the eyes. "...both of you need to be on your best behavior. While squires are a critical part to any group of knights, no commander would allow any individual they felt would compromise the objective to participate. The last thing any knight wants to do is play babysitter to a squire who is in over his head."

Burchard lowered his eyes in acknowledgement of what his knight master was saying. He would have to prove not only to his father but to the other knights that he was worthy of being sent with them into Stinyia. It made sense. Even if his father was the type to just let him go because he was in charge, Burchard would never have accepted a handout, not without proving to everyone he deserved to be there just as much as the other squires.

Taking a deep breath, Burchard was surprised to find himself yawning.

"I'm sorry. I have worn you out with all this talk. I'll see you tomorrow." Ruschmann gave Burchard's hand one last squeeze before walking out with Sir Peter.

Burchard's eyes began to droop when he heard someone slide into the chair that Ruschmann had been sitting in. He forced himself to open his eyes and saw Lady Gladys.

"M'lady," he said, struggling to push himself back upright to greet her properly.

"Hush, Burchard," she said and put a gentle hand on his cheek. "You're still healing."

Burchard gave her a tired smile, and his eyes started to flutter shut of their own accord. As he sank back into his pillow, he swore he felt Lady Gladys's lips on his cheek, but he could not get his eyes to open to verify.

5

It took several days before Burchard was deemed well enough by Lord Hampton to leave the healing rooms and return to his bunk at the barracks. Burchard was relieved to be out of there. As much as it had been nice to not worry about his father or anyone else critiquing his every move, he was itching to get his sword back in his hand. He couldn't remember very many times in his life when he had not had a sword of some sort strapped to his side. Even his earliest memories of himself, he had a wooden sword in his belt. Instead of a stuffed toy, he had slept with a wooden sword in his bed. His father had thought the behavior amusing and had encouraged Burchard to develop his interest in swordsmanship from a young age. His mother had not been pleased but had no say in the matter.

Burchard shut the door to the healing rooms and took a deep breath, relishing being outside again. The side door was the quickest way into the healing rooms and was used often when there was an emergency instead of carrying a wounded man through the entire castle. It also gave him a chance to go unnoticed since the door was on the side of the castle, away from the knights' daily bustle.

Sir Peter was leaning against the side of the barracks when Burchard rounded the corner. He gave his knight master a quick bow. "Good morning, sir."

Sir Peter smiled. "Good morning, squire. Why don't you put on some suitable clothing and grab your sword. I'll meet you at the training yard in ten minutes." Without waiting for a response, Sir Peter pushed off the building and headed in the direction of the training yard.

Grinning to himself, Burchard took the steps into the barracks two at a time, thrilled Sir Peter was as eager as he was to get a sword back into his hand. He quickly changed out of the undyed shirt and pants that the healer had put him in and into a thick pair of brown wool pants and a dark green shirt. He pulled on his soft leather boots, followed by his belt with the scabbard. He gave his sword a quick once-over before heading back out.

As Burchard approached the training yard, he could hear the clang of swords as other knights and men-at-arms practiced. Sometimes the yard would get quite full, making it difficult to have enough space to maneuver for anything other than the most basic of drills. Much to his relief, there was a small group of knights being led by Sir Martin and the rest of the yard was empty. Behind the training yard was a small archery range, which was full of the castle's archers practicing.

Burchard walked straight up to Sir Peter. "What's the plan?"

Sir Peter smiled at Burchard's eagerness. "To take it slow. You've had over a week off; I don't want you to get hurt because we rushed into complicated sword maneuvers."

"Does that mean I'm just doing drills solo?" Burchard asked in a flat tone. He had been hoping for a challenge.

"You can warm up with slow drills, but I was planning on sparring with you. We just will keep it slow and stick with basics. If it goes well today, maybe you can practice with Ruschmann tomorrow. I have had him under my wing while Sir Daniel is recovering. The extent of his wounds was far greater than yours. I imagine it'll be another week or two before Sir Daniel is cleared by Lord Hampton," Sir Peter informed Burchard.

Intrigued by the news that he'd get to spend more time with Ruschmann, at least for a little while, he did three slow laps at a jog around the training yard before stretching. When his stretches were completed, Burchard moved to a spot a far enough away from Sir Peter that he wouldn't hit him with the sword, but close enough for the knight to critique his moves. He unsheathed his sword and held it loosely in his right hand. *High, middle, low*, he instructed himself. Two sets of strikes followed by two sets of blocks. Then he swapped his sword to his left hand and repeated. He was going slow as he had been told. At first, he thought it was silly to go slow, but as he began his fifth round with his right hand, he could feel his body tiring. *I guess even a week of bed rest can really set me back.*

Apparently, Sir Peter could also tell he was tiring. "Finish this round, and then you'll take a break."

Burchard nodded. When he was done with his left hand, he slid his sword back into the scabbard and snagged a canteen from the fence post.

From behind Burchard came coughing. It would start, pause, and then start again. Turning, Burchard tried to hide his dismay when he saw his older brother, Reginald, or Reggie as he was known to most. Reggie was sixteen and had curly black hair that was cut right below his earlobes. They shared the same blue eyes and nose. Where Burchard was lean, Reggie was built much more solidly, with broad shoulders and a thick torso. He was almost a carbon copy of their father in his younger years.

Unable to stop himself, Burchard stiffened, and his hand dropped to his sword hilt. "Squire Reginald," he said formally.

"I want to practice with you," Reggie announced.

Burchard took a step back so he could see Sir Peter's face. His knight master's expression was carefully blank. As the General's favorite and oldest son, Reggie could do whatever he wished when it came to Burchard, and their father would turn a blind eye to it.

Although this was the first time Burchard had encountered Reggie since he'd become a squire, Sir Peter had met him before.

Mouth tight, Sir Peter nodded. "I will allow it as long as you promise to take it slow, squire. Your brother was just released from the healer's care."

Reggie smirked at Burchard. "I promise I won't damage him."

Burchard barely caught the whispered "too much" at the end of his brother's sentence. Burchard kept his face neutral, refusing to react to his brother.

Burchard put the cap back on his canteen and unsheathed his sword. Since the day before Reggie left to start at Trinity Page and Squire School, they had been rivals. Reggie had asked Burchard to practice with him one last time before he departed for Trinity. Burchard had eagerly obliged. Just at the end of their round, he had disarmed Reggie in front of their father, who arrived home at that precise moment. Reggie had been beaten by their father for the first and only time in his life because he had allowed his younger brother to disarm him. Six years later, he still hated Burchard for it.

Two days later, after Reggie left for Trinity, the General had returned to Wolfensberger Castle, and eight-year-old Burchard got to feel the brunt of his father's anger for disgracing the ten-year-old by disarming him. The whipping Burchard had been given made the beating Reggie had gotten look mild in comparison. Ever since that day, he had to be careful to not spar with Reggie to the point where he would win. Otherwise, he was punished. His father's logic had never made much sense to him. Why would he care that his younger son was a better swordsman?

Burchard swung his sword a few times before stepping into position in front of his brother. His face was carefully schooled into a mask. Reggie raised his sword and crossed it lightly with Burchard's.

"One…two…begin," said Sir Peter from his position on the sidelines. To Burchard's surprise, Reggie started off with a simple drill. They continued that way for several minutes. Burchard settled into the rhythm and allowed himself to relax. Suddenly, Reggie gave him a wicked grin before slamming his sword down much harder than his previous strikes. Burchard's arms vibrated from the impact. Not expecting the force of his brother's strike, Burchard found himself giving up ground. Reggie shifted to the side, spun, and did a backhanded strike. Burchard scrambled to get his sword up in time.

Frustration bubbling up, Burchard could feel his body protesting at the strength of Reggie's blows. He struggled to keep his face blank and to meet Reggie, but all he could do was block. He couldn't get his own strikes in. He spared a glance toward Sir Peter, wondering if his knight master would rescue him or not. Sir Peter gave a slight shake of his head. *I guess it's up to me.*

Burchard frowned. He had been warned to take it easy, but Reggie was doing his best to make him look bad. He returned his attention to his brother, deciding to push back. As Reggie swung his sword in a high strike from the right, Burchard spun out of the way, then leapt toward his brother from the side, doing a middle strike before his brother could regroup.

Reggie glared at him. Burchard focused on his brother's face and sword, taking a step to the left, then found himself falling forward. His brother had tripped him. Face in the dirt, Burchard flushed deep red as he felt his brother's sword caress his neck. If that wasn't enough, Reggie also planted a foot in the middle of his back.

"Yield," Reggie said.

Burchard couldn't move enough to respond without getting a mouthful of dirt.

Reggie ground his foot into Burchard's back again. "Yield!" he demanded.

Burchard could hear footsteps. "He would yield if you gave him space to lift his face up, squire," Sir Peter said from above Burchard in a low, angry tone.

Burchard could only imagine the look that Reggie was giving Sir Peter. Probably a sneer, but the foot did let up. "I yield," he said. The foot completely removed itself from his back.

Burchard decided to stay on the ground, until he was certain his brother had left. Then, he slowly pushed himself up.

"Are you OK?" asked Sir Peter quietly.

Burchard shrugged. "I've been worse," he responded, not really answering the question. His muscles felt like they were on fire. He tried lifting his sword so he could put it back in his scabbard, but he could barely move it. Burchard was surprised when he felt his fingers being peeled from his sword hilt.

Wordlessly, Sir Peter put Burchard's sword back in his scabbard. "Let's get you a bath and bed."

With a gentle hand on his arm, Sir Peter guided him slowly toward the officers' bathhouse. Burchard was too tired to question his knight master about whether it was a good idea to take him there.

6

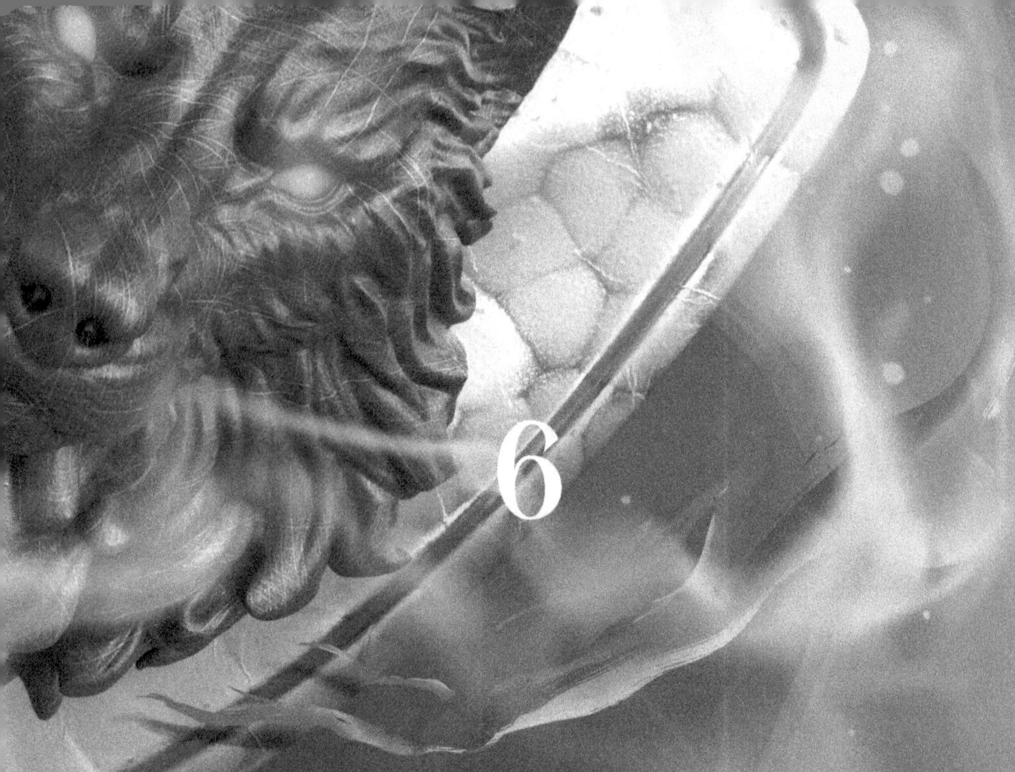

Two days after Burchard's sparring with his oldest brother, he still felt worn out. The healer had told him to make sure to take everything slowly. The first two days he could do short sequences of training exercises a couple of times a day and walk around the perimeter of the castle. He carefully avoided going anywhere his brother might be, altering his practice routine so that he was done before his brother had even eaten breakfast. Then, when Reggie made his way out into the practice yard, Burchard headed for the kitchen to see if Cook needed help with anything.

He pushed open the door to the castle kitchen and had to pause. The room bustled with people. Servants carried trays from the dining hall into the kitchen. Cook herself was going from station to station making sure the preparations for lunch were to her exact specifications. Burchard was afraid to move any farther into the room lest he bump anyone and cause a mess. He wasn't sure how long he stood there before Cook noticed him. She waded effortlessly through the servants and grabbed him by the arm, guiding him to the back corner, where Lady Gladys sat at a table.

"Stay here until things calm down more," Cook ordered and disappeared before Burchard could respond.

"Hi," he said softly, not sure what to do with himself. He clasped his hands together on top of the table.

Lady Gladys smiled. "I have some cards if you'd like to play."

Burchard shrugged. "Sure."

She pulled a deck of cards from her pocket and fanned them out face-up. "See this one?" she said and pulled out a card with a large gold crown and the number twenty-one on it. "This is the highest card." Next, she selected one that had a baby on it and the number zero. "This is the lowest card."

Burchard studied the cards she'd pulled out and some of the others still in the fan. "What do we do with them?"

"I was thinking of keeping it simple. There's a game I was taught that I like to call War. We each get half of the deck and flip over one card at a time. The person with the highest card takes both cards. The winner is determined when one of us runs out of cards," Lady Gladys explained as she slid the cards back together and shuffled the deck.

"War sounds simple enough. I'm willing to give it a go," Burchard informed her.

Burchard waited patiently, watching how at ease Lady Gladys was with the cards, as though she had spent many hours playing. As she dealt the cards, he noticed how worn some of them were, the edges a little ragged. When she finished, she handed him the stack closest to him.

"Any last questions?" she inquired.

He shook his head. "Nope, I think I got it."

"One, two, three!" Lady Gladys said, then they both flipped their cards. His card was the baby with a zero, and hers was the big gold crown with a twenty-one. She slid the two cards toward herself. "Ready?" Burchard inclined his head and she counted again. This time his card was a shield with an eighteen and hers was a knight with a twenty.

They continued for three more card flips; every time, Lady Gladys won. "Are you sure you shuffled properly?" Burchard asked, eyebrow arched.

Lady Gladys giggled. "You watched me the whole time."

Burchard pressed his lips together. They still had most of their stacks left. It was *possible* that the results could end up more balanced if they continued. "OK, let's keep going."

Burchard was on the last card in his hand. The rest of the flips had been more equal in who won or lost. Peering at the stack in front of him and the one across the table, he wasn't really sure which one was bigger. He flipped over his last card a hair faster than Lady Gladys did hers. It was a horse with a three, and Lady Gladys's card was the same.

"Now what?" he asked uncertainly. They hadn't discussed what was supposed to happen if they both put down the same card.

"Since we're both out of unused cards, we need to shuffle our piles of the ones we have won." Lady Gladys picked up her cards and shuffled them.

Burchard watched the motions her hands were making and decided to give it a whirl. He split his cards in half and, using his thumbs, lifted the edge of both halves. As soon as he began what he thought was the process of flipping them, all his cards flew into the air and fluttered around them, landing up, down, and stuck in things. He started to laugh and Lady Gladys soon joined him. How silly he must look sending all those cards into the air.

Sides still heaving, Lady Gladys helped him collect the cards. "I will shuffle them for you so that doesn't happen again."

"Brilliant idea," Burchard replied with a grin.

After both of their decks were properly shuffled, Lady Gladys blew out her breath. "Now we each put three cards down. I," she said, then placed the first card face down. "Declare." She placed the second card. "War." The third card she put face up. It was a compass rose with a four. "Your turn."

Burchard nibbled on the inside of his lip before placing his cards. "I…declare…war." His third card was a crossbow and had a five. He let out a whistle. "That was close. Do I get *all* of these cards?"

Lady Gladys nodded in confirmation. Burchard gathered up the cards into a neat stack before they continued their game.

Burchard lost track of the time. He jumped when Cook returned and set down two bowls of stew a safe distance from their cards.

"What's this?" he asked, reluctantly drawing his eyes away from the cards to look at Cook.

"Lunch. You two have been over here playing cards for a couple of hours now, and I thought you would appreciate the opportunity to eat," Cook said calmly.

"Hours?" Burchard said with a gasp.

Cook chuckled. "Yes, but I know you're in here to avoid your brother, and since the healer wants you to take it easy…it's not like you have any responsibilities to attend to at the moment."

Burchard opened his mouth and shut it. *Cook is right. I don't have anywhere else to be.*

Lady Gladys slid her bowl of stew closer to herself. "What about my responsibilities? I was going to make the meat pies for dinner tonight…" Her voice trailed off when Cook shook her head.

"You, my dear lady, are here because you want to help. None of your tasks are required. I thought you would enjoy having some time with Burchard. Once he is cleared for training again, you won't have much time together," Cook explained.

Burchard felt a blush creeping up his cheeks. "We're not…we're not…" he stumbled over the words.

Cook chuckled again. "Yes, yes, I know you're just friends. But since Lady Gladys is not a boy, she can't exactly go train with you and continue your friendship that way. Take this time while you have it." She paused. "Besides, not all friendships with people of the opposite sex have to be romantic."

Out of the corner of his eye, Burchard saw Lady Gladys squirm as Cook kept speaking. "It is good to have a variety of friends who come from all walks of life." With that, Cook turned on her heel and headed back to one of the large stoves.

Burchard was still blushing. Instead of looking at Lady Gladys, he decided to just eat his food. Thankfully, she followed suit. They sat in companionable silence and ate their stew. When they both finished, Burchard stood up and took their bowls to the wash basin, then returned to the table.

"Did you want to play more cards?" he asked, standing at the edge of the table, debating if he should sit back down or not.

"Sure," Lady Gladys said and shuffled the deck.

The door from the kitchen into the main part of the castle banged open. Burchard turned to face the door and saw Colonel Frost standing there peering at each person in the kitchen.

Lady Gladys groaned. "I guess I will need a rain check. My father must need me for something."

Burchard nodded in understanding. "Well, I had a good time today. Thank you for teaching me how to play War." He bowed and then headed out the kitchen door closest to them that would let him go outside.

As he wandered around outside the castle, Burchard mulled over what Cook had said, about how you can be friends with almost anyone if you want to. *I doubt that is something my father believes. He always seems to detest anyone who is not a noble or a knight, as though interacting with a servant for too long will somehow contaminate him in some way.*

It took Burchard four more days to fully recover after he sparred with Reggie. Each morning after breakfast when Reggie headed to the training yard, Burchard made his way to the kitchen where Lady Gladys was waiting with a friendly smile and her deck of cards. After the second day, Burchard realized how nice it was to have these few hours each morning, to not think about training but to just be fourteen. He knew it wouldn't last, but he wanted to enjoy it for what time he did have.

When the healer cleared him, exactly one week after his sparring round with Reggie, Burchard was pleased to hear his brother had been sent out on a two-day scouting assignment with two squads of knights.

The two squads of knights Reggie was accompanying were not the only ones sent out over the next several days. Alderth Castle had been bustling with activity once King Roland had given the General approval to attack the Stinyian rebels. Messengers arrived daily, and scouts frequently came and went. Luckily Burchard's father was too busy planning the upcoming battle to pay much attention to him.

Unfortunately, Burchard's regular horse was not recovering well, so Chip had become his full-time mount. Captain Thomas still thought he was crazy to ride her, but Burchard didn't care. He and Chip had an understanding that worked. He didn't mind that everyone was afraid to get too close to her. It meant most would leave him alone when he was riding, which suited him perfectly.

Under Sir Peter's watchful eye, Burchard and Ruschmann were able to practice mounted sword fighting after lunch in the field outside of the castle. Although Burchard wished he still had time to see Lady Gladys more, he was excited to work further on mounted fighting techniques. When they weren't practicing mounted swordsmanship, their riding lessons focused on other important skills such as how to ride with a wounded companion and how to dismount while their horses were moving, both intentionally and not. Burchard preferred making the choice to dismount over having Sir Peter pushing him from Chip. He had to admit, though, he was quickly figuring out how to stay balanced when he landed regardless of how he had come off. With the threat of the Stinyian rebels at the forefront of everyone's mind, Burchard was glad to know continuing to develop his skills was still a priority.

The third afternoon, as Burchard and Ruschmann were riding out toward the field, Sir Peter met them halfway. "Sorry, squires, but we have new orders. Captain Hugh Grayson just returned with information on the location of a rebel camp and the General wants us to be in the group going to investigate."

Burchard pursed his lips. *Captain Grayson was leading the group Reggie went with.* "Is Captain Grayson's squad coming with us?"

Sir Peter shook his head. "No, he was able to provide enough information that Colonel Frost should be able to lead us to the correct location."

"Colonel Frost is leading us?" Ruschmann asked.

"Do you have a problem with that?" Sir Peter demanded, eyes narrowing.

Ruschmann blew out his breath. "No, it's just he's Lady Gladys's father."

Sir Peter raised an eyebrow. "What does Lady Gladys have to do with orders the General gave us?"

Ruschmann replied, "Nothing, forget I asked."

Burchard glanced at his friend, wondering what that had been about. Normally Ruschmann didn't question who was taking the lead when they went out with a squad of knights. He shrugged, deciding it didn't matter. "Are we departing soon, or can we still practice?"

Sir Peter sighed. "I came out here because the General wants us to leave immediately. He is concerned the rebels will change positions and we won't be able to find them again if we take too long. We leave within the hour." The knight turned his horse back toward Alderth Castle, and both squires followed suit.

"How long should we anticipate being gone for?" Burchard inquired as he began running over a list of things he should bring with him.

"At least overnight, possibly a couple of nights. It depends on how quickly we find them and how long it takes to eliminate their presence," Sir Peter answered.

Burchard stayed silent for the remainder of the ride to the castle. He quickly led Chip into her stall, pulled off her bridle, and gave her a scoop of oats. He hung the bridle on the hook outside her stall door and made a beeline for his barracks. He figured the mare would be happier with departing again if she had a chance to eat her dinner early instead of doing without it.

When he reached his bunk, he pulled several empty packs from under his bed. He packed one spare set of clothing, deciding that if he had to, he could just wear the clothes for multiple days. He was more concerned with adding extra weight if he needed to move quickly than about having clean clothes. Food was a different matter. Luckily, Burchard had learned quickly after his arrival at Alderth Castle the benefit of having a go bag of food readily available. His was filled with an assortment of dried meat, nuts, and dried fruit. Food that would offer him sustenance, and he would not have to worry about it spoiling.

Next, he checked his weapons. His sword was already on his waist in its scabbard, but he also grabbed his long knife, his bow, and a quiver of arrows. *I should wear armor*, he reminded himself. He peered around his space. He saw the edge of what he was hoping was his chain mail poking out from under the bed. Bending over, Burchard grabbed it and tugged. It wouldn't budge. He tugged again; still nothing. Growling at himself, he wrapped both hands around the piece of armor and gave one final yank. Burchard found himself flying backward. He hit the dresser and fell in a heap.

Laughter came from somewhere behind him. Burchard blinked his eyes slowly, willing everything to stop spinning. He had hit the dresser harder than he expected. Taking his time, Burchard stood up and turned to face the source of the laughter. "Ruschmann," he growled.

Struggling to compose himself, Ruschmann took a moment before responding. "That was quite exciting! What was your armor stuck on?"

Burchard rolled his eyes. "It doesn't matter. What matters is it is the chain mail shirt I was hoping it would be." He unbuckled his scabbard and set it to the side before scooping up the chain mail and sliding it on. Once it was on, he snagged his scabbard and secured it around his waist.

"Is that everything?" Ruschmann asked.

Burchard reviewed his packing list in his mind and then peered carefully at each of his bags. "Yes, that's everything."

"Let's go then, before someone has to come find us," Ruschmann urged.

They both knew how much the knights liked to pick on the squires, and Burchard saw no reason to be late and encourage even more torment. Having not spent any time under Colonel Frost's command, he wasn't sure how much influence the colonel would have over the behavior of the knights they would be traveling with.

Burchard gathered up his two bags, bow, and quiver and followed his friend out the door and into the stable. The knights they would be joining were in various stages of readiness. A few were sitting on their horses waiting patiently; others were in the stable or heading that way. Burchard let himself into Chip's stall and proceeded to tie his gear onto her saddle. Once everything was secured, he snagged the bridle off the hook and gently put it onto her head.

"Let's go, Chip," he said softly, before leading her out of the stable and toward the edge of the group of knights. Most of the knights were mounted, so Burchard checked his saddle girth strap again. Confident it was secured so his saddle wouldn't slip, he put his foot in the stirrup iron and swung himself into the saddle.

Ruschmann followed his lead, keeping Cricket close, but not so close as to provoke Chip into doing something mean to him.

"Where's Sir Peter?" Ruschmann asked.

Burchard peered around the group and realized Ruschmann was right. Sir Peter wasn't here. Neither was Sir Daniel. "Are they sending us without our knight masters?"

Ruschmann frowned. "That seems like a strange thing to do."

Just then, Sir Peter and Sir Daniel came over to them. Both were wearing heavy coats and pants but showed no signs of preparing for departure. Burchard opened his mouth, then hastily shut it when Sir Daniel began to speak. "We are not going with you. General Wolfensberger wants us to go with a single squad to the south for more scouting." He paused. "I know it will be strange with neither one of us there, but we know that you are both capable of following orders and will do fine under Colonel Frost."

Sir Peter nodded in agreement. "Stay together, and obey the orders you're given. We'll see you in a few days."

Burchard wanted to say something to Sir Peter, but just then, Colonel Frost gave the command to depart. Burchard waved at his knight master instead and decided he would follow their instructions to stay with Ruschmann and obey orders.

That shouldn't be too hard, right?

7

Three hours later, Burchard was barely able to contain his anger. As soon as the group had gotten out of sight of Alderth Castle, the knight closest to the two squires, Sir Victor Bushman, had ordered them to fill up his water canteen at the creek on the side of the road. Burchard had done the task without comment. However, one by one all of the knights except for Colonel Frost made their way to the two squires and gave them orders. Some of them were simple, like filling up a canteen; others did not make much sense, like tying a shirt over their eyes.

At the three-hour mark, Chip and Cricket were not only carrying the squires' gear but that of about fifteen of the knights as well. Sweat trickled down their necks from the extra effort of carrying that much added weight for so long.

"Sir Daniel told us to follow orders," Ruschmann gently reminded Burchard.

Burchard growled. "I am certain this is *not* what he meant by that."

"What exactly do you intend to do about it? If you ride up there and tell Colonel Frost, it will just make matters worse. The knights will punish you behind his back," Ruschmann said softly to keep the knight closest to them from overhearing them.

"I want to fight them," Burchard declared.

Ruschmann shook his head. "Yes, I get that, but what you want is a fair fight. If the knights are stooping this low to bully us, there's no way they will fight fair."

Burchard opened his mouth to reply when he realized that Colonel Frost was riding at his side. He inclined his head. "Colonel, what can we do for you?" When he lifted his head up, he saw the colonel studying all the extra gear on his saddle.

"What is the meaning of this?" Colonel Frost demanded.

Burchard was about to speak when Ruschmann reached over and pinched his arm hard. "Ouch!" he yelped.

"I see," replied Colonel Frost. "Halt!" The order was passed all the way to the front of the column. "Squires, dismount."

Burchard exchanged a confused look with Ruschmann and dismounted. Colonel Frost also dismounted. He led his horse several paces a way, murmured something in its ear, and then walked back over to the squires. Instead of speaking to them, the colonel untied the extra bags from their saddles, which were obvious from their haphazard attachment. When he was done relieving the horses of their extra gear, there was a huge heap in the road. Still without speaking, the colonel returned to his horse and mounted.

"Let's go!" he commanded.

Burchard exchanged a look with Ruschmann. *He's just going to leave their gear in the road?*

Ruschmann shrugged, almost as though he could read Burchard's mind. Both squires mounted up and their horses quickly fell into line at the end of the double column. Burchard could hear the knights ahead of them muttering angrily. It almost seemed as though they were going to drop back again for a confrontation, when suddenly the column veered off the road and onto a narrow deer trail, forcing them into a single-file line.

Burchard let out a breath that he hadn't realized he was holding. He knew Colonel Frost must have a solid idea of where they were going, and the squires were content to just follow at the end of the line without drawing unnecessary attention to themselves. They slowed to a walk and continued to follow the trail, weaving in and out of trees and small rock outcroppings. He could have sworn they were also losing elevation, but without stopping, he could not be certain. When they reached a clearing, everyone halted. It was not large, and it made rather tight quarters getting all sixty horses together. Once everyone was within the bounds of the clearing, the colonel dismounted and moved around the group, giving orders softly.

"Squires, you will stay here to look after the horses while the rest of us go after the Stinyian rebels. I want to you to follow me for a moment," the colonel explained. He led the squires to the edge of the clearing and gazed into the forest.

"If you look through the trees, you can sort of make out that there is a larger outcrop of rocks," Colonel Frost said, and pointed to where Burchard could make out some dark gray shapes. "The rebels are supposed to be just on the other side. If things go well and they are indeed there, it should not be too difficult to dispatch them, and then I will return with the knights, and we can find a suitable campsite for tonight."

"What if they aren't there?" Burchard asked. He knew from tales that Sir Peter had shared that often even the best laid plans went wrong.

"As long as there are signs that we can use to track their whereabouts, my intention is to pursue them on foot. With the number of dead leaves underfoot here, it is difficult for the horses to be quiet. Much easier to minimize the noise we make if we do not have them. Now, while you are staying here, I expect you to be ready. If we do encounter the rebels, it is possible that some could sneak away and try to steal our horses," Colonel Frost explained.

Ruschmann and Burchard nodded. They had been told to obey orders, and although Burchard knew they would both prefer to be with the knights when they found the rebels, he knew that this order they were being given was reasonable and necessary. As Colonel Frost walked away to presumably finish his preparations, Burchard could have sworn he heard mutters and curses from the knights about missing certain supplies that they needed.

I guess some of them had important items in those saddlebags they loaded us with, Burchard realized.

A few sharp words from Colonel Frost, and the knights stopped talking and formed up around him. Burchard checked his sword in the scabbard and his long knife. He was debating if he should grab his bow or not. Ruschmann hadn't brought his bow.

"When they leave, what do you want our strategy to be? It's us and sixty horses," Burchard inquired.

Ruschmann took his time turning in a full circle, evaluating the clearing as well as the space just beyond it. The trees here were mostly tall pines with short, spindly branches, but there were three oaks. Burchard waited patiently, wondering if his friend would have the same idea or something else.

"Since you brought a bow, I think it would make sense for me to take your bow into that tree." Ruschmann pointed to the tallest oak tree, which was as wide as Burchard was tall and had a large branch about ten feet off the ground that looked like it could easily hold both of their weight. "Then you would position yourself at the base of the pine tree. Those positions will allow us to maximize the amount of area we can see and provide you cover if needed."

Burchard smiled. "I also came up with a very similar plan. Let's get in place." He offered Ruschmann the bow and quiver and watched as his friend slid both onto his shoulder, then headed over to the oak tree. As Ruschmann began climbing, Burchard turned away and walked to his position.

Burchard started with his sword held loosely in his right hand, body open and relaxed. After about an hour, he could feel himself getting stiff from the lack of movement. He was certain that Ruschmann couldn't be faring much better with his perch in the oak tree. They were also starting to lose light as the sun sank lower in the sky. Soon it would be too dark to see much at all. He was debating suggesting that they swap so Ruschmann could at least move around a little when he heard the clang of metal and snapping branches.

Instantly on the alert, Burchard slid back into position with the tree at his back. He could hear the horses starting to shift, the gear still on them making whispering sounds with the movement. There was a loud crashing sound and suddenly he could make out the glint of metal weapons. The shadows forming around the trees made it a challenge to count how many men were coming their way, or what exactly was happening. He was afraid to slip closer to see better, worried that if he was noticed, the advantage of surprise he had would vanish.

Burchard didn't have to wait long before a man in leather armor swinging a large axe was running straight for him. Burchard couldn't decide if the man knew where he was or was just running eagerly because the Etrian horses seemed unprotected.

Rolling his shoulders, Burchard positioned himself to attack from the side. As the rebel ran past him, Burchard swept his sword down, across the rebel's back. The rebel let out a howl as the sword sliced cleanly through the leather. Not wasting any time, Burchard lunged forward, bringing his sword up in a block just as the rebel pivoted and chopped at his head with the axe. Sparks flew as the blades met. Burchard shuffled sideways, disengaging their weapons, and swung his sword in a low arc, aiming for the knees. The rebel made the mistake of trying to jump over the sword and instead tripped, causing the blade to slice deeply into his unprotected hamstring.

Burchard yanked his sword away from the rebel as he collapsed and twisted just in time to miss being cleaved in half. While he had been busy with the first rebel, another one had tried to sneak up behind him. Regaining his balance, Burchard assessed this new rebel. After a couple of swings, he noticed the man tended to favor his left leg, as though something was wrong with his right. With that tidbit of information solidly in his mind, Burchard began his attack—a combination of high and low strikes focusing on the left side, forcing the rebel to rely on his weaker right leg. When Burchard initiated the second combination, the rebel stumbled, and Burchard's uppercut, which was supposed to have landed on the chest, went cleanly through the rebel's neck. The severed head went flying through the air.

Burchard gasped in horror and felt bile rising in his throat. Before he knew what was happening, he was bending over and retching, narrowly missing his own booted feet. Taking deep breaths, nostrils flaring, he fought his body's instinct to continue heaving. The last thing he needed was to be caught off guard because he beheaded someone.

Just as Burchard lifted his head, a rebel toppled over sideways at his feet with two arrows through his chest. Burchard gave a half-hearted salute in the direction of Ruschmann's tree, then focused his attention on the rebels running toward him.

Where are the Etrians? he wondered. *Colonel Frost had fifty-seven men with him.* His thoughts were cut off when not one but two rebels with swords came spinning toward him. They executed some fancy twists and turns. Burchard smirked. He was familiar with that tactic of trying to confuse the opponent with fancy footwork. It was one Reggie favored.

Burchard launched himself toward them, yanking out his long knife, focused on the rebel on the right. At the last moment he twisted and did a mid-strike with his sword in his right hand followed with a high strike with his knife in the left. He then spun and jabbed with the knife at the rebel on the left. The rebels scrambled to keep up with his moves, and the knife connected both times, poking large holes in their leather armor, sending out spurts of blood in its wake.

Burchard glanced up at Ruschmann in the tree before returning his attention to the two rebels. He made a quick jab to the left with his sword and then one to the right with his knife. Both rebels fell. Three more came toward him, but they fell with arrows in their necks. He realized that Ruschmann was likely to run out of arrows soon. Hopefully, his friend would have the good sense to come join him on the ground.

Where are the Etrians and Colonel Frost? he wondered again, before chiding himself to stay focused on his task—killing as many rebels as possible to prevent his own death or the loss of the horses.

One axman running toward him showed evidence of having been in a fight, with smears of blood on his armor and a slice across his forehead. The rebel axman grinned, and Burchard grinned back. Quicker than the eye could see, Burchard entered a combination with a swipe to the right and a sweeping uppercut to the neck, followed by a short chopping motion. The rebel blocked the first and second steps of the maneuver but was not quick enough to prevent the third strike from slicing deeply into his shoulder and getting caught on his collarbone. Blood sprayed, and the rebel slumped to the side, groaning. Burchard stepped over him, knowing the rebel would not be a problem anymore.

Then, he glanced up at Ruschmann and saw his friend descending the tree with an empty quiver. Rebels kept coming in small groups of two or three, but it was a long time before they finally saw some Etrians. Two Etrians appeared and sprinted to the squires.

Burchard raised his eyebrow and peered over at Ruschmann. It seemed odd to him that the Etrian knights would want to rely so heavily on the squires they had earlier made it clear they detested. But the rebels were hot on the heels of the Etrians and gaining speed from running down the hill, not leaving much time for thought.

The Etrian knight lurched forward as he came within reach of Burchard, who caught him just in time, preventing the knight from skewering himself on his own sword. He tugged on the knight, dragging him over to a tree.

"Are you OK?" Burchard asked.

"Not really," came a mumbled reply.

Burchard glanced at the knight sharply and realized it was Colonel Frost. "Colonel?" He let his eyes go back to the rebels heading their way.

Colonel Frost took a raspy breath. "I don't know if the others are coming or not. There were many more rebels than expected. We were overrun. Sir Richard Stone is right behind me and will have to take you back to where the others are to look for survivors," the colonel continued. "Then, we must run."

Burchard closed his eyes briefly. *Why would the colonel be willing to give up so easily? What has scared him?* He made sure that the colonel had a water canteen before walking back over to Ruschmann, sword at the ready. Sir Stone reached them at the same time.

Moments later, the axmen reached them too. The rebels were no match for three of them working together. *Which begs the question, what happened with the group? What else went wrong?* Burchard didn't feel comfortable posing that question to Sir Stone.

When it became clear no more rebels were coming, Burchard and Ruschmann faced Sir Stone.

"We need to go after the other knights to see if there are any survivors. It is likely less than half of our men," said Sir Stone.

"That's it?" gasped Ruschmann.

Sir Stone nodded grimly. "Unfortunately, yes, that's it."

Burchard stared up the path from where the rebels had come. "Do you think more will come?"

Sir Stone shrugged. "I don't know. None of this mission has made much sense. We should see what Colonel Frost wants us to do."

The two squires nodded and followed Sir Stone over to the colonel. Burchard suppressed a shudder as he realized his face and arms were covered in rebel blood.

"Sir," Sir Stone said with a curt bow to the colonel. "What are our orders?"

Colonel Frost coughed and took a sip of water. "If you are confident the rebels are defeated, then you can go look for the remaining Etrian knights. Make sure you take some extra horses."

Sir Stone nodded. "Do you want one of us to stay with you?"

Colonel Frost shook his head. "No, I'll manage. If you're really worried about me, you can get me the crossbow from my horse."

Burchard turned and quickly retrieved the crossbow and satchel of bolts, returning before Sir Stone had even finished talking to the colonel. "Here you go, sir."

Colonel Frost took the crossbow and settled it on his lap.

Awhile later, both squires and Sir Stone were riding through the forest and past the outcrop of rocks to where the main skirmish had taken place. Once they passed the line of sight from where they had been stationed with the horses, they could see bodies of Etrians and rebels. It was obvious the Etrians had done the best they could in the situation. Around each knight were piles of rebels. But clearly it had not been enough to overcome the rebel force.

Sir Stone dismounted and began inspecting the Etrians, making sure that each fallen one was indeed dead. Eventually, they made it to another small clearing that was backed by some large boulders about the height of a man. Burchard could hear moaning. There was a hiss of metal as three swords slid out of their scabbards. The two squires allowed the knight to take the lead and stayed mounted.

When Sir Stone came back over, his face was grim. "We have ten survivors."

"That's it?" exclaimed Ruschmann.

"I don't think we have enough horses. I need both of you to go bring more," Sir Stone ordered.

Burchard could see the wisdom in Sir Stone's suggestion. They had brought four spare horses and could easily bring four more. "We will be right back."

The squires cantered back to Colonel Frost. *I can't believe there's only ten. That means fourteen survivors out of sixty in our group. The odds are terrible. I wonder how many rebels there were. Why is the*

General's information always wrong? He kept his mouth shut, not wanting to raise his concerns to his friend, not now, when they still didn't know what they could be facing.

Colonel Frost was where they had left him, propped up against the tree, sipping some water. "Did you find them?"

Ruschmann coughed. "We did, but…um…"

"Spit it out, squire," Colonel Frost ordered.

"There's only ten survivors," Burchard said softly.

"Ten!" gasped the colonel. "How is that possible?"

Burchard spread his hands. "I have no idea, but that is how many we found."

Colonel Frost smiled sadly. "You should take the horses you came for and head back."

"How'd you know?" mumbled Ruschmann.

Colonel Frost shrugged. "I just do. That's one of the things about being an officer. You learn how to read people and situations."

An hour later, Ruschmann and Burchard returned to Sir Stone. The knight had managed to get four moderately wounded knights situated on the horses, but the remaining knights seemed to have more severe injuries.

"I'm going to need your help for the rest. It was more than I could manage solo."

Burchard walked over to Sir Michael Cormorant, one of the knights who had bullied the squires with the gear bags. "Sir Cormorant," he said softly, but did not get a response. The knight wobbled from side to side as he edged closer to the horse that Burchard was holding. He was able to stabilize the stirrup on the opposite side while Sir Cormorant mounted with Ruschmann's help.

Next, they went over to Sir Phillip Ravenwood, whose eyes were unfocused.

"We are going to help you mount, Sir Ravenwood."

The knight bobbed his head in what Burchard hoped was agreement. Ruschmann wedged himself under Sir Ravenwood's arm, supporting the knight as he limped to the horse. It took both of them to lift and shove Sir Ravenwood into the saddle.

Eventually all ten wounded knights were mounted. Some had had to be tied to their saddles, and both squires were riding double with a wounded knight.

The group cautiously worked its way back to where Colonel Frost was waiting. By the time they reached him, it was almost pitch-black. Burchard was not sure how they were supposed to continue in the darkness.

Colonel Frost was on his horse when they arrived. "Good, you're here. Now let's tie the rest of these horses together and get going. I don't want to stay here. It's too dangerous." The colonel paused. "However, I want the two squires to go back to Alderth Castle with a warning and request for a healer."

Burchard asked, "Are you sure? We can help you."

The colonel replied, "Yes, I'm sure. I just want you to eat a snack and then go. You'll take four of the extra horses. I know you're tired, but this is imperative."

Instead of protesting again, Burchard kept his mouth shut. Sir Peter had told him to follow orders. They were being given orders, and with how exhausted he was, he was not in the mood to protest.

"Yes, sir!" both squires replied in unison.

Covered in dried blood and dirt from head to toe, Burchard and Ruschmann let their horses walk with their hooves almost dragging through the Alderth Castle gate. The four horses they were ponying were not much fresher than Cricket or Chip. The squires had galloped as long as they could sustain it, then took short breaks of walking mixed with galloping. It had been a brutal pace, but Colonel Frost had insisted they make haste and Burchard did not want to let him down. Out of the corner of his eye, Burchard could see a flurry of activity at their arrival. He assumed a runner has been sent to his father.

Sure enough, General Wolfensberger emerged from the large main castle doors, apprehension clear on his face. As they reached the steps, both Burchard and Ruschmann bowed to the General from their saddles.

"Squires, where is everyone else?" General Wolfensberger questioned.

Ruschmann wobbled in his saddle. "Colonel Frost and the rest of the knights are coming. They were going to find somewhere to camp for the night. There's twelve in the other group. But everyone else…everyone else, sir, is dead."

The General's eyes widened in surprise. Burchard's fingers slackened on the reins as he felt someone tugging on them, afraid to turn toward whoever it was for fear of angering his father.

"Squire, dismount," said the familiar voice of Captain Thomas. Burchard felt his body being gently tugged out of the saddle. "Is there anything else you need to tell the General?"

Burchard nodded and took a few steps toward his father. "General, sir. Colonel Frost wanted you to know we were badly outnumbered. The information you were given was incorrect."

"How many rebels were there?" asked the General tersely.

Burchard blew out his breath. "Unfortunately, the colonel did not tell me that before ordering us to leave. Just that it was more than he had expected. From the bodies we found, I would hazard to guess at least three or four to one were the odds, maybe greater."

The General snarled something under his breath that Burchard was not able to hear.

"Come on, let's get you some food and bed," said Captain Thomas. With a gentle hand under the elbows of each squire, he led them away.

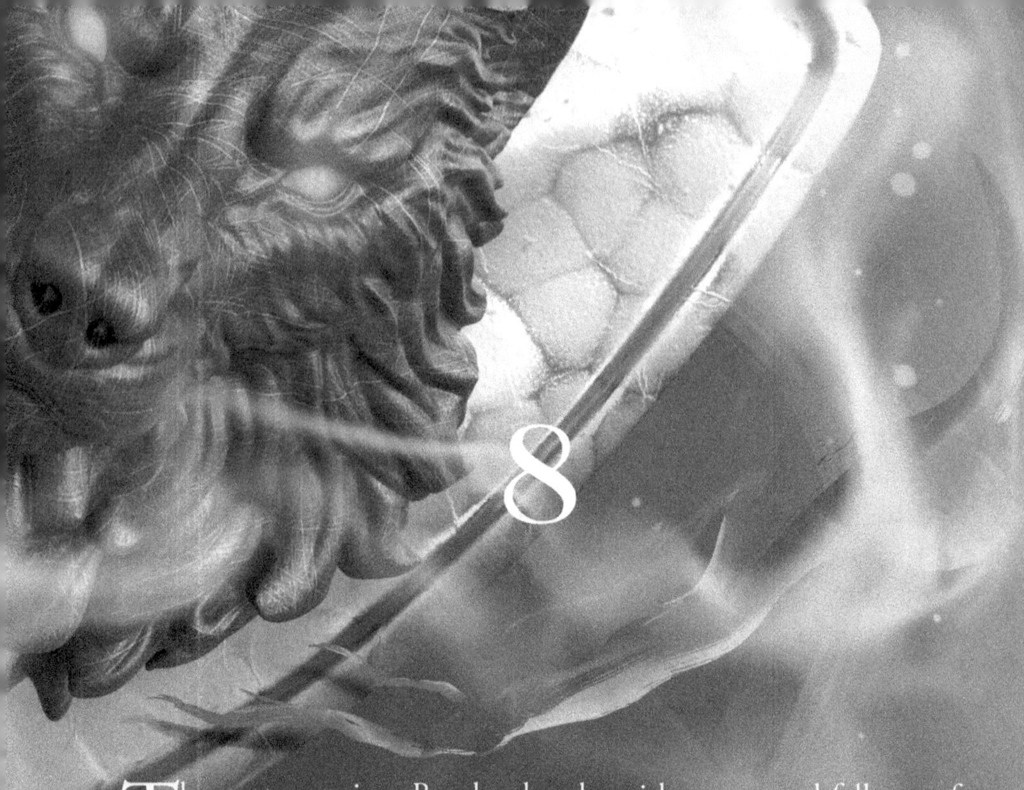

8

The next morning, Burchard woke with a start and fell out of his bed. He disentangled himself from the blankets, stood, and stretched. He could hear something from outside the barracks. Hastily, he pulled on pants and a tunic and went to the door, opening it slightly. He gasped as the sunlight hit his eyes, and he realized it wasn't morning. It was closer to lunch. The sun was high overhead. Blinking to get his eyes to adjust, he observed the people in the courtyard.

A group of knights with spare horses tied to their saddles seemed to have just returned. *Colonel Frost must be back!* he thought, taking a few steps down the stairs before he realized he had forgotten his boots. Smacking his forehead in annoyance, Burchard dashed back to his bunk for his boots and tugged them on before running full speed into the courtyard.

"Colonel!" he shouted. Colonel Frost turned stiffly in the saddle and waved.

Burchard skidded to a halt in front of the colonel's horse and held the reins steady while he dismounted.

"Thank you for sending help. Captain Thomas was able to get everyone patched up enough for us to ride here," said Colonel Frost.

Burchard nodded and opened his mouth to say something again when General Wolfensberger walked over. "Colonel Frost, glad to see you in one piece," the General said in a cold voice. "Let's go into my office so we can discuss what happened."

Without another word the General turned on his heel and led the colonel in the direction of his office. Burchard watched them depart for a moment before turning his attention to the others in the courtyard. He volunteered to help, ferrying the extra horses into the barn where grooms were waiting to untack and feed them.

An hour later, when the last horse was settled in its stall, Burchard realized he hadn't eaten. By then, his stomach was making loud gurgling noises, letting everyone know he was hungry. Burchard made his way to the kitchen, hoping Cook wouldn't mind feeding him in there. He wasn't sure he was ready to face whatever criticism the knights in the dining hall might deign to throw his way.

Pushing the door open, Burchard was surprised to see Ruschmann had beat him to the kitchen. His friend was sitting at the table in the corner with Lady Gladys. They both smiled at him and beckoned him over.

"Thank you, both of you, for bringing my father home," Lady Gladys said warmly.

"We didn't do anything," Burchard mumbled, blushing.

Lady Gladys clicked her tongue. "You came here exhausted to make sure that help would reach them in time. In my book, that deserves thanks."

Burchard looked away and saw Cook heading their way with a platter of bowls of stew. "You two didn't eat yet?"

Ruschmann laughed. "We did, but that was a few hours ago. We thought we could join you with a second bowl whenever you woke up."

"Oh," Burchard said softly. He slid into his seat and Cook set down his bowl of stew and a piece of bread hot out of the oven. He took a bite of the bread before remembering his manners. "Thanks," he said to Cook. She waved him off and went back to the stove.

The three friends spent the rest of the day playing cards. Burchard was glad to have some time to relax after the chaos of the day before.

After dinner, when the two squires were helping the kitchen staff clean the dishes from the evening meal in the dining hall, Sir Peter came in.

Ruschmann noticed the knight first. "Sir Peter," he greeted.

Burchard raised his eyes from his task for a moment and gave his knight master a brief nod before returning to scrubbing the large copper pot. The kitchen was fairly empty for the moment, so when Sir Peter started speaking, it was easy to hear him.

"Tomorrow we will resume our training. By then, there should also be more information about what the General's plan is to tackle the rebels going forward and what role, if any, the two of you will have." Sir Peter paused. "Make sure you get plenty of rest tonight," he gently reminded them, before snagging a roll out of a basket and heading into the castle.

The next morning, Burchard was walking toward the dining hall when the General intercepted him. "Squire, a word."

Burchard carefully kept his face blank and followed his father down the hallway, presumably out of earshot of anyone within the dining hall. He stopped just a hair before he ran into his father's back.

The General turned and gave him a dark look. "I was informed that you left the gear of several of the knights in your group in the mud on the road when you were under Colonel Frost's command. Is this true?"

Burchard inhaled slowly through his nose. "Sir, Colonel Frost chose to relieve me of the extra gear I was carrying. I was not permitted to retrieve it from the road."

"I see. Were you given a direct order by Colonel Frost?" the General asked softly.

Burchard spoke carefully, knowing that if his father didn't believe him, he would likely get put in the stocks or whipped, or worst case, both. "Yes, he ordered Squire Ruschmann and me to leave the gear and for the group to continue on its way."

"Were you aware that gear critical to the outcome of the fight was left on the road?" the General demanded.

"No, sir. When the bags were given to us to carry, we were not informed of their contents. The orders Sir Windemere and Sir Tiniel gave us were to obey any orders given, whether by Colonel Frost or one of the other knights. To my knowledge, we followed the orders explicitly," Burchard explained.

"Very well. I will confirm what you have said with Colonel Frost." The General turned on his heel and walked down the hallway, the cadence of his boots echoing on the stone long after he was out of sight.

Burchard let out his breath. *Whew, that was close.* He turned slowly back toward the dining hall and his breakfast.

The two squires and their knight masters fell back into their training routine over the next two days. Hand-to-hand combat, sword work, and archery in the mornings with mounted practice in the afternoons.

On the third day, a rather cold and dreary morning, Sir Peter walked up to both squires as they were heading out of the barracks toward the training yard. "Change of plans for today. The General wants the two of you to go on an overnight scouting assignment to check out the area to the northeast."

"Northeast? But the rebels are in the north*west*," protested Burchard.

Sir Peter held up his hands. "I am just relaying the orders."

"Which squad are we going with?" Ruschmann asked.

Sir Peter shook his head. "You're not going with a squad. It will be just the two of you. No one else is available."

Burchard gazed at his knight master in uncertainty. "Where are you going to be?" The General had been sending him and Ruschmann to do occasional scouting with other knights, but never by themselves. He wondered what had happened to make the General change his tactics.

Sir Peter sighed deeply before answering. "I am going on patrol with two squads. I will be gone for a full week. When you return, Sir Daniel should be able to take over your training, Burchard."

Burchard nodded in understanding. "OK. Is there anything in particular we are supposed to be looking for?"

"The General mentioned that there have been whispers of something happening in the northeast also. I don't think he believes the whispers, but he wanted to be certain since the king sent an inquiry specifically asking about the northeast," Sir Peter explained. "But as far as anything in particular, I would just recommend being prepared to encounter bandits. If there is evidence of any movement in that area, make note of it and include it in your report. You need to leave before dawn tomorrow morning."

"Very well. I will go start packing, then," Burchard said with a bow.

9

Early the next morning, in the pearly gray light just before dawn in the Alderth Castle courtyard, Burchard tied his last bag onto Chip's saddle. Running through his list in his head, he was certain he had remembered everything that was important. If it hadn't made it on the list, then it mustn't be important enough for this scouting trip.

Ruschmann glanced up at him from tying his last bag as well. "You ready?"

Burchard grinned. "Yep."

The yard was just beginning to wake up. The cook's rooster crowed, followed by soft nickers of the horses in the stables and the bleats of the goats. Burchard glanced around and then swung his leg up into the saddle. Guiding Chip with his legs, he urged her into a brisk walk out the side gate.

They rode in companionable silence till the sounds of the waking castle were no longer audible.

"I think we're chasing ghosts," Burchard said, starting to relax.

Ruschmann shrugged. "Ghosts or real people, at least we get out of the castle for a few days. Our first assignment on our own. We better not mess it up."

Burchard chuckled darkly. "I don't think I've ever *tried* to mess up any of our assignments. The General just doesn't always appreciate what I do."

"This should be easy. Take notes if we find any evidence of rebels or bandits in the northeast. We are only supposed to be gone for one night, so we go as far northeast as we can in one day, camp, and then ride back," Ruschmann said.

"Well…sort of." Burchard thrust a scroll at Ruschmann.

"What is this?" Ruschmann asked, taking the scroll. He dropped his reins and unrolled it. It was a rough map, showing Alderth Castle and the area surrounding it, plus a blue line that was almost a circle.

"That is the route we're taking," Burchard explained.

"I thought we were just going to the northeast," Ruschmann muttered.

"We are. But Sir Peter thought it would be more thorough if we did a circle and covered more ground than just a straight line there and back. My father was not very specific; therefore, Sir Peter took it upon himself to ensure we would provide as much useful information as we could upon our return. We are not traveling for any longer than before. Just not quite to the same place. Trust me. This is a good plan," Burchard said.

"I do trust you. But how do you know we are even going the correct direction? This is a circle drawn in the middle of the forest," Ruschmann questioned.

Burchard sighed. Sometimes his friend was really dense. "If you looked at the drawing at all you would see that we go through Radvall Mill, Leosor Hollows, and then Camp Tooth. There are some marked paths between them. Although I think when we go by the mill and the hollows, we probably want to stay off the path."

Ruschmann peered at the map again, finally seeming to notice the very tiny words that named the places mentioned. "Aha, whoever made this seems to think everyone expects words to always be that tiny. I didn't even notice the words when I first looked."

"OK, now that we have established we both know where we're going, would you like to get there faster than a walk?" Burchard inquired.

Ruschmann grinned and kicked his horse into a canter, quickly leaving Burchard and Chip behind. Chip didn't need any encouragement. She eagerly picked up the pace until both squires were riding stride for stride in a ground-covering canter.

When they were within a mile of Radvall Mill, Burchard and Ruschmann slowed their pace and slipped off the well-worn path they had been following. Radvall Mill was a small village, although calling it a village was probably too generous. There were three families that managed the lumber operation. They did business when they had to with Alderth Castle, filling the quarterly orders; otherwise, they discouraged anyone from the castle from visiting.

Burchard was not overly concerned that they would get attacked, but he also didn't want any complaints to get back to the General that the families at the mill were being harassed by two squires. Giving Radvall Mill a wide berth was in everyone's best interest. The trees they passed were young, but the older trees had been harvested—several years ago, from the look of it. Burchard knew that much like farming, a strategy was involved in harvesting lumber to ensure that the forest could continue to provide for many years to come. He had seen areas around Wolfensberger Castle that had been completely cleared, and they were not growing back as expected. In theory, it didn't matter. Since Wolfensberger Castle's two villages were used primarily for growing crops, including hay for livestock, additional cleared land was useful for expanding the fields.

Burchard let out his breath when they crossed into denser forest and could no longer see Radvall Mill. He glanced over at Ruschmann and saw that his friend was also relaxing now that they had passed the mill. They grinned at each other, when suddenly their horses lurched to a stop. Lucky for them, their practice riding sessions with Sir Peter meant their bodies were better trained to maintain their balance on the horses, even when startled.

A large man with bright red hair and a beard stood before them, carrying an ax on his shoulder. "What is your business at Radvall Mill?" he asked roughly.

Burchard cleared his throat before replying. "Just passing through, sir."

The man gave both squires a thorough examination before replying. "It looks as though you must be headed *somewhere*. Squires are not usually sent to the mill."

Before Burchard could respond, Ruschmann blurted out, "We're on a scouting assignment."

Burchard stifled his groan. From the looks of the man in front of him and the questions, he seemed to be one of the mill's residents, but Burchard couldn't be sure. He'd never been to the mill before. Which meant they would be obliged to make note of the encounter in their report. Telling everyone they came across they were on a scouting mission was certain to cause them trouble, especially once word got out that they were just two squires traveling alone.

"A scouting assignment?" said the man, although it was clear he was talking to himself. His eyes seemed to be focused on the horses, not on the squires.

Twigs cracked, and another man appeared seemingly from nowhere, although Burchard was sure he just had been too focused on the first one to remember to pay attention to anyone else trying to sneak up on them.

"Sean, what are you doing?" growled the new man, who looked very similar to the other one—in fact, almost identical. With a pointed glance at the squires, he turned his back to them, blocking their view of the first man.

"Seth," Sean replied. "I was just finishing up with the last tree on this side, and I heard these two squires jabbering. Figured I'd see who was trying to sneak through our forest."

With Seth's back to Burchard, it was difficult for him to see how Sean's explanation had affected him. He spared a peek at Ruschmann, who shrugged. Burchard tried to remain patient, but he was itching to get on their way.

"I see," replied Seth, before stepping to the side and turning around to face Burchard and Ruschmann. "Is there a particular reason you lot are sneaking around our forest instead of coming through the village?"

Burchard decided he should reply before the encounter escalated. "Sir," he said with a bow from his saddle. "We were not assigned any business with Radvall Mill and decided it would be…" He paused, searching for the right word. He wasn't sure saying he thought it would be quicker to avoid the village would be wise. "The most direct route to our destination is going through the edge of your lands, which is what we were doing before we came across Sir Sean." Burchard decided treating them with respectful formality would likely be the best course of action.

Sean studied Burchard for a few moments without responding, then reached into a pouch on his belt and pulled out a folded piece of parchment. "It is fortunate you came this way. I presume you will be returning to Alderth Castle?"

Burchard nodded in confirmation.

"Good. I have this letter for General Wolfensberger. It is regarding the next lumber order. If you can deliver it to him, that would help immensely." Sean stepped close to Burchard and offered him the letter before stepping back just in time to miss Chip's attempt to bite his arm.

"Sorry," muttered Burchard. He tucked the letter into his front saddlebag.

"Don't worry about the horse. I have been known to bite strangers when they got that close too," Sean said with a grin. "Oh, and just in case the General wants to know who gave you that letter to be sure it's official and whatnot, I'm Sean Radvall and this here," he said with a wave at Seth, "is my twin, Seth Radvall. Our uncle

Samuel Radvall runs the mill." Sean took another step back toward his brother. "We need to get back to work before we lose what's left of the light. I'm not sure where you're headed, but I would not go up to the hollows if you were planning to. Some bad business is happening in that area, and no one I've sent up there has come back."

Burchard bit his tongue, preventing something stupid from spilling out. Taking a deep breath, he said, "Thank you, sir. We appreciate the warning. I will keep your letter safe and see that it is delivered."

Before Burchard could say anything else, both Sean and Seth Radvall melted back into the trees without a trace.

He shared a look of bewilderment with Ruschmann. "Let's go." Clucking, he urged Chip into a trot, eager to get out of the forest belonging to Radvall Mill.

10

After riding for about an hour in silence, Burchard couldn't stand it anymore. He just needed to say what was on his mind. "Sean Radvall…he mentioned bad things happening at 'the hollows.' Do you think he's referring to Leosor Hollows or somewhere else?"

"You have the map. Can't you check it?" Ruschmann pointed out.

"I have the map memorized. There aren't any other places labeled 'hollows,' but who knows if what the locals name things is what the king names them. I also have no idea how current the map I have is," Burchard responded.

He watched as Ruschmann picked at a twig in his horse's red mane. "What is going on with you and Lady Gladys?"

Burchard felt his face heat up. "What do you mean?' He kept his eyes focused on the trees in front of him.

"Well, she spent a lot of time at your bedside when you were injured, and I've seen the looks you share at times," Ruschmann teased.

"We're just friends," Burchard said defensively.

Ruschmann snorted. "Does she know that's how you feel?"

Burchard tipped his head to the side so he could look at Ruschmann. "No. Or I mean, I don't think so. It's not like we go around talking about our feelings."

"Perhaps you should before she gets the wrong idea and you break her heart," Ruschmann said loudly.

Burchard sighed. "We're fourteen. I'm not going to break her heart. Besides, when did you become so knowledgeable about girls?"

"You and I spent a year apart last year. Sir Daniel and I had a chance to go up to Port Riverdale, which is a larger city than Ironhaven is at Burmstone Palace. I met lots of different people," Ruschmann said and got a misty look in his eyes.

"What you're saying is that you have a girl waiting for you at Port Riverdale?" Burchard asked in disbelief.

Ruschmann nodded. "Yes."

"Do you realize how silly that sounds? We both belong to noble houses, which means our marriages are likely to be arranged. Why bother getting involved with anyone like that when you know what's certain to be in your future?" Burchard demanded.

Ruschmann shrugged. "What's wrong with living the way I want while I still have a chance to? We are only granted one life, Burchard. I don't want to realize one day that I could have had a better one if only I'd lived it for me, not for someone else's agenda."

Burchard nibbled on the inside of his lip, contemplating Ruschmann's words. His friend wasn't wrong. In some ways, what Ruschmann was suggesting was already what he was doing. Standing up for what he felt was right, even if his father disagreed.

They rode in silence for a while, the fall light starting to fade and casting deep shadows around the trees. Burchard was pretty sure they could reach Leosor Hollows before it got completely dark.

Shadows were growing long, making it difficult to see the details of the forest surrounding them. Burchard heard a noise, and Chip paused in response to the subtle shifts he made in the saddle. He drew his sword and swung just in time as a large great horned owl flew right over his head, talons out. With the close proximity of the owl to his head, the swing missed, but the owl screeched while banking and came back for another pass. Before the owl could reach him, an arrow grazed his cheek, causing him to almost drop his sword in surprise. Growling, he swiped his left hand at his face and it came back covered in blood.

He adjusted his hand around his sword, wondering where on earth Ruschmann was. *He was just behind me a few moments ago.* The owl came back for a third pass. This time Burchard put both hands on his sword, preparing to strike and take it out once and for all. As the owl swooped down, he began moving his sword in an arc, when a sharp pain pierced his arm and his sword fell from his hand. Glancing down, Burchard realized there was an arrow sticking out of his arm. *Who are these people attacking us?* He saw the barest outline of a cloaked figure standing next to a large oak with a longbow drawn and another arrow aimed right for him. At this distance, whoever it was would have to be an absolutely terrible shot to miss him, even with minimal light.

The owl abruptly flared its wings and glided to the branch above the stranger. Its dark golden eyes followed his every movement.

"Why are you here?" the stranger said.

At precisely the same time, Burchard growled, "If you're going to shoot again, just get it over with."

The stranger's hood fell back. Based on the voice, Burchard thought it was a young woman, but the minimal light made it difficult to discern much else. Her long hair flowed over her shoulders, no longer hidden by the hood.

"The owl was just informing you that we were here and you drew your sword first. I was only defending myself," she said in a surprisingly musical voice.

"Your owl was going for the kill. It is my right to defend myself," Burchard said, straightening in the saddle. With his left arm dangling at his side, the arrow protruding from it, he could feel the blood dripping down his fingers and onto the leaf-covered forest floor.

She tilted her head, considering him, before giving a sharp whistle. Another figure came out from a rock outcropping, pushing Ruschmann before them at sword point. *I wonder where Cricket went.*

"You are trespassing," the figure said in a deep male-sounding voice.

"This is King Roland's land. I am a squire of Etria; therefore, I am not trespassing," Burchard said quietly, keeping his focus on the woman with the bow.

To his surprise, she laughed. Burchard just stared at her, not sure what to think.

"The king does not own this land," she informed him.

Out of the corner of his eye, Burchard saw Ruschmann stumble forward, onto his knees, as the figure shoved his friend at sword point. Ruschmann pulled his gaze from the archer as he fell, which was when Burchard realized that the big man who had captured Ruschmann wasn't a man at all, but a centaur. Startled by that realization, Burchard felt himself swaying. He braced his legs more tightly against the saddle, not wanting to give these people, whoever they were, any indication that he was not capable of rescuing his friend by himself. Burchard bit his cheek hard to keep from reacting, drawing blood.

Centaurs don't exist. Maybe I hit my head again?

"We will have to agree to disagree on who owns the land we're standing on," Burchard murmured. *I guess my father was right. Something was definitely going on in the northeast.* "Can you tell me who you believe this land belongs to?"

"No, I cannot tell you who this land belongs to, not yet," she replied.

"Is there anything you can tell me? Your name?" Burchard asked, at the end of his patience. Burchard watched as the archer glanced at the centaur, who gave a subtle nod. He had thought she was in charge, but apparently that was not the case.

"My name is Jade, and this is Damos. We are druids," the archer replied. "You are Squire Burchard Wolfensberger, middle son of General George Wolfensberger, and your companion is Squire Ruschmann Blackwell, born in Wanonia and adopted into the Blackwell family."

Burchard blinked a few times as she revealed details that were not common knowledge. "How do you know who we are?"

Jade shrugged. "I imagine the same way I know this land doesn't belong to Etria."

Burchard ground his teeth together. He didn't think rolling his eyes would be a wise move, but clearly Jade and Damos weren't willing to tell him anything useful. "Do you have a healer?"

"When we get to camp, Damos will heal you," Jade said. "Now let's get going."

Burchard watched as Damos nicked Ruschmann with the tip of his sword, encouraging him to walk in front of him. Jade brought up the rear, stepping just a hair behind Burchard, who was surprised to still be allowed to ride. He kept silent while praying Chip would not decide to kick Jade and get him in more trouble than he was already in. They walked in silence for quite some time through the trees. In addition to the growing darkness, fog was rising, making it even more difficult for Burchard to see where they were going and had come from. If he had the opportunity to escape, he doubted that he would get very far.

I still don't know much about these people. Damos is a centaur who can heal, and Jade is clearly a skilled archer with an owl pet.

They walked through a narrow gap between some boulders and a clearing opened before them with a large cave at its back. *Leosor Hollows*, Burchard realized when he saw the cave. He knew there were several large caverns that were linked together in the area by smaller tunnels. Wanting to get a better look around without being overly obvious, he tipped his head forward, allowing his hair to slide over most of his face as he peered around. He saw evidence that a larger group had been there recently, but only one small fire was closest to the cave mouth.

A firm hand gripped his leg. "Keep moving," Jade ordered.

Burchard sighed and lightly bumped Chip with his legs. His arm was sticky with blood and was starting to really throb. Hopefully Damos was a proficient healer.

"Dismount and leave your horse over there," she instructed, waving an arm to a post at their left. "Then come and sit by the fire, and Damos will look at your arm."

Burchard followed Jade's instructions, finding a spot by the fire where Ruschmann was already sitting. Damos stood waiting, but Burchard couldn't get a read on him. In the firelight, he could make out some more details of the centaur. He seemed to have olive-colored skin that was mostly hidden by a leather coat, dark blue-black hair, and golden eyes. His horse parts were also blue-black. He wore a wide belt with a small axe and an empty scabbard hanging from it.

"Take off your coat. It needs to be mended or scrapped," the centaur ordered. Burchard carefully slid the coat off, looking mournfully at the shredded sleeve. His shirt underneath was caked in drying blood. "Shirt too."

Burchard obeyed and pulled off his shirt. Since Damos was standing and Burchard was sitting, he heard Damos's whistling breath as he saw the scars on his back.

"Who did that to you?" Damos demanded angrily.

Burchard was surprised at the reaction and wasn't completely sure what the centaur was talking about. "Who did what to me?"

"The scars on your back. You were whipped," Damos snarled.

The comment clearly piqued Jade's interest as she stopped preparing a meal and came over to peer at his back too. Burchard felt a very feather light touch on his back, just barely grazing his scars.

"The General," Jade said softly.

Burchard clamped his mouth shut and kept his eyes on the fire. If Jade had a way of seeing who had held the whip, then good for her, but he was not going to tell anyone who had whipped him or why. He felt Jade step away.

A heavier hand settled on his shoulder. "I will heal your arm now," Damos said in a deep voice. Burchard sucked in a breath. When he let it out, he could feel the tendrils of magic wrapping around his arm. He glanced at it, unable to help himself, and was surprised to see green and gold threads encasing his arm. As he watched, the gash the arrow had made in his arm knitted itself together and shrank. When Damos finally let go of his shoulder, all that was left on his arm was the barest of scars and dried blood.

"Thank you," Burchard murmured.

The centaur shrugged and carefully moved away from him and over to Jade. Burchard glanced at Ruschmann, who was gazing at him with a difficult-to-read expression. He arched his eyebrow, wondering if his friend was going to say something. Instead of speaking, Ruschmann scooted closer to Burchard so their shoulders were brushing.

"Have you ever seen magic like that before?" Ruschmann asked.

Burchard shook his head. "No. To my knowledge, Etrian mages who heal use their magic inside someone's body so you can't see it. Or at least non-mages can't see it."

"What do you think it means?" Ruschmann asked.

"Only that the magic Damos has is different than what is normal for Etrian healers. Since I am not a mage," Burchard said with a pointed look, "I don't know everything there is to know about them."

Ruschmann bumped his shoulder. "Yes, but you do know something. Since we first met, you have always made it clear that you believe it is important to not only be an expert at skills you have but also to have knowledge of those you don't. I am *sure* you have more to share."

Burchard rolled his eyes. "Fine, I will tell you some of what I know. In Etria, Wanonia, and Stinyia, elemental magic is the most common type of magic. Fire, air, water, and earth. Some mages are more specialized within those categories, such as metal or stone.

Although less common, they can wield two elements. Even more rare is weather magic. However, there are places beyond those three I mentioned, and they have other kinds of magic that might use elements, but I would hesitate to call it elemental magic. Shadow, nature, and death are three I know of."

"Death?" Ruschmann questioned.

"Yes, you know—raising the dead," Burchard explained.

"That's not a fairy tale?" Ruschmann said with a quiver of fear in his voice.

Burchard laughed, but it came out more like a bark. "I have not spoken to anyone who has death magic, so I cannot be sure, but I did find some firsthand accounts, and from what I could tell, yes, it is a very real type of magic that is primarily used to raise the dead."

"Let's not run into anyone who has death magic, OK?" asked Ruschmann.

"Sure, no problem," Burchard replied, out of habit more than anything. He knew as well as Ruschmann did that they had no way to predict if they would run into a mage, let alone a death one.

"What about creatures?" Ruschmann asked, somewhat to Burchard's annoyance.

"If that is your way of asking about centaurs…I don't know anything. Nothing I've ever read has indicated they exist. It also makes me wonder, if centaurs are real, what other *creatures* exist that we believe are fairy tales?" Burchard said thoughtfully.

As he waited for a response, his mind drifted to a story he had read years ago about a centaur.

On a dark stormy night in the desert, Baccagio the centaur, axe in his right hand and sword in his left, faced the giant, Foom. Lightning flashed and Baccagio and Foom entered a deadly dance. Each flash of lightning illuminated the battle. Baccagio was the last centaur standing against Foom. If he died, then Moon City at the edge of the desert would be left unprotected.

Baccagio staggered backward, his front left leg crushed with a deft sweep of Foom's club. Blood seeped from many cuts down his flanks too, but Foom was injured as well. Baccagio closed his eyes. When he opened them, he whinnied and charged straight for Foom's stomach. The giant hesitated and Baccagio's sword and axe struck true. The giant howled in pain and toppled backward. Baccagio knew giants did not die easily. He hobbled over on three legs to Foom's head, wrapped both hands around his sword hilt, and chopped downward, severing Foom's head and ensuring the giant would never be a threat to Moon City again.

Burchard sniffed the air, and his mouth watered at the tantalizing spices pulling his mind from the story and back to the present with the druids and the fire. Jade walked over with a bowl of something in each of her hands.

"A lot of things exist that you don't believe are real," Jade said as she handed Burchard his bowl. "Dragons, unicorns, and elementals are a couple that come to my mind. I would highly recommend, though, that you don't refer to centaurs as 'creatures.' They are people, just like we are. I'm sure that you like keeping all your body parts, so it's best to not offend a centaur."

"Thank you for the warning," Ruschmann uttered, taking his bowl from Jade.

Burchard accepted his bowl. The steam came off in waves. He cautiously took a bite, worried about burning his tongue. It was almost too hot, but as he chewed his first bite, he closed his eyes in appreciation. It was stew with a mix of meat and vegetables and a grain he couldn't identify. Burchard blew gently over his bowl.

While he was waiting for the stew to cool, he pondered Jade's words about the different types of beings that existed. *She seemed so certain that dragons and unicorns are real. I wonder if she's seen them before.* "Is the story of Baccagio and Foom real?" he mused more to himself.

Damos must have heard him, "Yes, Baccagio and Foom and the battle at Moon City all happened."

Mulling this new information over, he took a tentative bite. Burchard was relieved that his stew had cooled enough so he could enjoy it. With slow, deliberate mouthfuls, he consumed his meal.

Jade and Damos might be whatever the Radvalls were warning us about, but although we are their captives, I am not sure they mean us harm. His thoughts paused. *If they don't want to harm us, what do they want? I must ask when we're done eating.*

As the last traces of the sun disappeared completely, the camp was sent into an eerie darkness. The fire cast strange-looking shadows on the rocks around the cave entrance. Jade collected their bowls and put them in a stack near where she had made dinner. She then sat down next to Burchard. The owl fluttered down and settled on her shoulder.

"We need your help," Jade announced.

"You have a funny way of asking for help," Ruschmann blurted out.

Jade ignored the comment and continued speaking. "There is a camp of rebels north of here, and they managed to capture our people," Jade said, waving her arm to indicate her and Damos. "We were not here when it happened, which is why we did not get captured, but the two of us cannot free them alone." The owl clacked its beak in disapproval. "The three of us," Jade amended.

Burchard gave Jade an assessing look. "The *three* of you caught us off guard and captured us. How is it you expect Ruschmann and me to turn the tables on a group of rebels?"

"You will be the distraction," Jade replied.

"No," Burchard said without even thinking about it.

"You two are the perfect distraction. Stinyian rebels would love to get their hands on Etrian squires who just happen to stumble into their camp by mistake," Jade said with a smirk.

"What you want is to trade, not our help. The rebels will capture us while you free your companions. How is that a good deal for us?" Burchard bristled.

Damos appeared out of the darkness. "I can guarantee you won't get captured."

"I don't believe you," Burchard replied, lightning quick.

"You are a gladius domini. They are no match for you," Damos explained.

Burchard opened and shut his mouth. He had no idea what Damos was talking about.

Jade supplied the answer to his unspoken question. "A gladius domini is a sword master."

"Etria *does* have that title, but I cannot earn it until after I become a full-fledged knight," Burchard protested.

Damos sighed. "The Etrian structure for its warriors is designed to train average people at a rate that by the time you have completed eight years of training, a young man should be able to hold his own against average enemies with a sword. You are not average in skill." Damos gave Ruschmann a sideways glance. "Neither is he, though he is not a gladius domini…not yet. There are perhaps twenty rebels in the camp. They have my five centaurs in a pen like you would keep horses in," he growled. "I should be able to break through the spell on the pen if you are able to distract them long enough. Once the spell is broken, if you need help finishing off the rebels, then we will help you."

Nostrils flaring, Burchard took a deep breath. Damos had just dumped a lot of information on him all at once. The most important, though, was that the centaur needed the distraction to undo a spell and felt that he and Ruschmann could distract and likely fight twenty rebels without any issues. Burchard was not as confident in his ability to go against twenty as Damos seemed to be. To him, it sounded like a death wish.

"Damos, you have said what you will be doing. What is Jade going to be doing?" Ruschmann asked.

"She will be in a tree providing cover for you if you have to fight. Liala will also help as she can," Damos replied.

"Who is Liala?" Ruschmann asked uncertainly.

"Liala is the great horned owl," Jade responded.

Burchard stretched his arms over his head, wincing as the freshly healed scars were pulled taut, then he lowered his arms and cleared his throat. "I don't understand why you felt the need to capture us to ask for help. Why couldn't you announce your presence the normal way?"

Damos closed his eyes momentarily before opening them and locking gazes with Burchard. "I was worried you would attack us."

Burchard laughed. "Us attack you?"

Damos shrugged. "Jade has been able to learn enough about you and your reputation, aside from the fact that you are gladius domini. We must get the centaurs back. I could not afford to gamble that you would not attack us outright. I apologize."

Burchard let out his breath, not sure how to respond. *They were worried about what we would do! How odd.* "We were at Radvall Mill this afternoon, and they mentioned something about staying away from the hollows. Do you know what they were talking about?"

Damos cocked his head to the side and ran a finger over the top of his axe. "Radvall Mill?"

Jade joined the conversation. "I think he means where they are cutting down the trees, closer to Alderth Castle."

"Ah. We have been discouraging anyone from coming around here. Liala keeps watch and usually can scare people off without us having to intervene directly. But there are other places in this area, I believe, that some refer to as hollows…certainly there are more caves than this one," Damos said, gesturing behind them at the cave mouth.

"There are?" Ruschmann said in disbelief. They had both studied the map, and there was no other mention of more caves than this one.

"Of course. Can't you feel them?" Damos said in an offhand way, then sighed. "Right, you don't have magic and cannot feel the earth. You would not know what druids know."

"Is that a skill all druids have? Feeling the earth?" Ruschmann asked, awe lacing his voice.

Damos nodded. "Yes, or at least to an extent. It is a latent druid ability. When we are within a certain range of natural features, we can feel their existence. It is particularly useful when we're traveling to a new place and need to find water and shelter." The centaur paused. "But we are getting sidetracked. I was trying to apologize for our tactics. As you mentioned, it wasn't the best choice, but that is now in the past. If you can accept my apology, then we can move forward."

"Apology accepted," Burchard and Ruschmann said in unison.

Burchard tugged on his lip, considering his next words. "Is there a particular reason why you wanted it to be us to help you? And how did you know where we would be?"

Jade and Damos shared an unreadable look before Jade spoke, "You are likely unaware, but your attempts at being quiet as you move through the forest are not very successful. We could hear your approach long before we decided to apprehend you."

"Really?" gasped Ruschmann.

Sir Peter taught me how to move quietly. I wonder why it's not working, Burchard pondered.

"Yes, you really were quite noisy. At least to a druid. Maybe to the people you are around on a regular basis, your movements were not as noticeable," Jade explained.

"What about why you wanted us to help you?" Burchard pressed.

Jade twisted the end of her hair. "Most Etrians do not take kindly to outsiders. Our hope was that since you are not full grown, your opinions on the matter might be different than most of your brethren."

"You've never come across my brother then," blurted Burchard before clamping his mouth shut. Jade giggled, then schooled her face into a more blank expression. Burchard struggled to do the same before continuing. "Now you're making it sound as though it was just luck that you came across us instead of some other Etrians. Yet you knew who both of us were before we introduced ourselves. I will ask again. Why did you want our help?" He bit his lip.

Jade glanced to Damos, as though seeking his permission to answer the question. "We were given some information that you would be the ideal candidates to help us rescue the centaurs."

"Given by whom?" Ruschmann asked, his voice an octave higher than normal.

Jade's mouth pressed in a thin line. She shook her head, unable or unwilling to answer.

"Have you been spying on us in Alderth Castle?" Ruschmann asked incredulously.

Damos took a step forward, face tense, tail swishing. "No. But we are able to gather information from animals and plants with our deep connection to nature and the gods. For the time being, you will have to accept this as our explanation. Perhaps after we rescue the centaurs and you have fully earned our trust, then I will provide the details you want."

Burchard watched as Damos unclenched his fists and let his fingers dangle loosely at his sides. The sharp movements of the centaur's tail also ceased. "When are you proposing we rescue them? It's dark."

Damos nodded. "Yes, I know. I think it would be in everyone's best interest to do the rescue in the morning. I know the cover of night holds some advantages, but I do not think your distraction will be as successful if they cannot see you."

Burchard covered his mouth with his hand, stifling a yawn. "Sleep would be welcome."

Damos led the two squires partway into the cave. Their bedrolls and bags of gear had been brought inside at some point. Burchard yawned again and decided he was too tired to care about how his gear made it. He quickly laid out his bedroll and slid inside. As soon as he shut his eyes, just wanting a brief moment, he was fast asleep.

Burchard found himself standing in an area filled with white fog. He couldn't see much else. He took a few steps forward. Unlike last time, it felt like soft grass under his feet. He knelt and ran his hand over it, confirming that it was indeed grass.

As he was mulling over why there was grass and not dirt, the large white wolf appeared. Burchard was still kneeling, and she walked right up to him, their eyes level. Burchard shivered at the intensity of her gaze. She turned and walked a few paces away before sitting down and facing him. He breathed a sigh of relief.

You must help the druids tomorrow, Eos said matter-of-factly into his mind.

Why? Burchard replied, slowly standing up.

Eos just stared at him until Burchard had to look away. *There is no real reason for you to decline.*

I suppose not, muttered Burchard.

The wolf bared her teeth. Burchard couldn't decide if it was supposed to be the wolf's version of a smile or a more sinister expression. *Then it is settled. You and Ruschmann will help the druids rescue the centaurs tomorrow.*

Can you tell me the outcome? Burchard asked, wondering if that was even possible. He still couldn't decide if he was in some very strange dream or if this conversation was really happening.

The wolf tilted her head to the side. *The outcome will make itself known to you tomorrow.* Burchard pursed his lips at her non-answer. *Just trust your instincts,* the wolf said softly, then slowly faded away.

Burchard walked over to the spot the wolf had sat in.

He took a step forward and found himself thrashing around in his bedroll. He hit something soft with his legs.

"Hey!" yelped Ruschmann.

"Sorry," muttered Burchard. He scooted away from his friend and tried to get the blanket to loosen its hold around him. It took him a while to get settled, but eventually he drifted back to sleep.

11

The next morning, under the direction of Damos, the squires left their horses at the camp at Leosor Hollows and walked to the rebel camp, which was less than a mile away. Damos had felt like the horses would make it more difficult to create a believable distraction of two lost squires wandering into the rebel camp by mistake. Burchard glanced over at Ruschmann. To his dismay, they had been liberally covered in mud and leaves. His shredded coat was back on as it added to the desired look of needing help. Taking a breath, Burchard threw his arm over Ruschmann, and they took stumbling steps toward the camp. It was slow going but would buy Damos enough time to get into position where the penned centaurs were.

"Ho there!" came a shout.

Ruschmann waved his arm at the rebel who had shouted at them, and they continued to approach.

"State your business!" a gruff voice called.

"We're lost and need supplies!" called Ruschmann. The two squires staggered abruptly to the side before falling in a heap.

Burchard had to keep himself from elbowing Ruschmann to get him off. He knew this was all part of the ruse and buying time for Damos, but their stumble had put Ruschmann in a rather awkward position on top of Burchard. Burchard's view of the path into the camp was blocked by Ruschmann's head, but he could hear the guard's feet on the hardpacked dirt. A booted foot bumped Burchard's foot. He had to bite his tongue to keep from kicking it.

"Lost, eh?" the guard asked.

Ruschmann disentangled himself from Burchard and tilted his head back to look at the guard. "Yes, and in need of food and water, if you would be so kind," Ruschmann said in a shaky voice.

"Get up, and I will see what I can do for you," the guard said before moving away from them.

To Burchard's relief, Ruschmann stood up and offered him a hand. Together, they followed the guard. It took Burchard a few steps to remember he was still supposed to be in character, a lost and hungry squire. He fervently hoped no one in the camp was watching. Damos had been unclear how much time he needed to undo the spell. Which meant Burchard and Ruschmann had to sell the lost squire act for as long as possible.

Gazing out of the corner of his eye, Burchard was not pleased with what he saw. The camp that was supposed to house a mere twenty rebels had several neatly organized rows of small tents, like those the Etrian knights are issued. There was a large tent at the center, though not quite as large as the one General Wolfensberger preferred when out in the field on a campaign. Burchard shared a worried glance with Ruschmann. While knowledge of this camp was definitely something they would be including in their report, his concern was deepening for how well the plan to rescue the centaurs was going to go. Facing twenty unorganized rebels was one thing. Facing multiple squads led by a commander? Even a gladius whatever Damos had called him was not going to be enough.

The flap of the large tent opened, and Burchard's jaw dropped open in shock. A short man with bright white hair and a full beard wearing plate mail walked briskly toward them. A growl escaped from his lips. Ruschmann reached over and gave his hand a quick squeeze. Burchard couldn't tell if that meant his friend also knew who was walking toward them or if he was just trying to comfort him.

"I have been told that the pair of you are lost and in need of some food and water," the armored man said in a voice that rang across the camp. "I am Lieutenant Commander Walter Pell, leader of the Firebirds. Please come into my tent for some refreshments, and you can tell me how you came to be lost." The lieutenant commander turned on his heel and went back into the tent.

Burchard bit his tongue to keep himself from gasping. *Just the other day my father said Walter Pell was confirmed dead! How is he here?* After his father had mentioned Walter Pell, Burchard had asked Sir Peter about him and was told that the lieutenant commander had been one of the more well-known Stinyian knights because of his ruthlessness on the battlefield. The two squires followed, still trying to maintain the pretense of being lost, and swayed and wobbled in a meandering line into the tent. As soon as they were in, the flap closed behind them. The temperature in the room dropped. Burchard could see his breath in the air and he noticed frost creeping up the sides of the tent. He let his hand drop casually to his sword hilt and knew Ruschmann was doing the same.

"Now, please tell me what you're really doing here, Squire Burchard Wolfensberger," the commander ordered.

Keeping his face as blank as possible, Burchard replied, "We are lost."

"If you lie again, you won't like the consequences," the commander warned.

"We were given an assignment to scout the area northeast of Alderth Castle and happened across your camp. Since General Wolfensberger requires a detailed report, we decided that we should find out who is in this camp. Squire Ruschmann came up with the idea to say we were lost." Burchard shrugged. Everything he said was true to an extent. "But…General Wolfensberger said that you're dead. How are you here?"

"I see." The lieutenant commander paused, ignoring the question about how he was alive. "It wouldn't happen to have anything to do with the centaurs I captured?"

Burchard allowed his eyes to widen in surprise. "Centaurs are just a fairy tale," he replied softly, shivering, half tempted to add, *So are you.* His hands were stiffening with the cold.

The lieutenant commander laughed. "They are far from a fairy tale. I have no idea what nonsense they are telling you in your Etrian school for pages, but clearly your education is severely lacking. Would you like to see them?"

Feigning eagerness, Burchard smiled. "Yes! Do they come in the colors of normal horses?"

"Come and you shall soon find out," the lieutenant commander said.

This time, Burchard noticed the small motions that Walter Pell was making with his fingers as the air warmed back up to regular temperature and the frost disappeared. He chided himself. The camp had to have at least one mage if the centaurs were being held in a pen contained by magic.

Walking stride for stride, Burchard and Ruschmann followed Walter Pell through the camp and toward a large pen with a heavy-duty wood fence. As they reached the pen, Burchard realized it was empty. The lieutenant commander howled in rage and spun toward them, sword drawn.

Not wasting another moment, Burchard deftly yanked his sword out with Ruschmann a few seconds behind. Walter Pell let out a shrill whistle, then charged them. Burchard leapt forward, meeting the knight's sword with a loud clang that rang throughout the camp. *If people didn't hear the whistle, they definitely heard the swords.* Sure enough, he could hear the pounding of booted feet as the rebels came running.

To Burchard's relief, Ruschmann stayed at his back, keeping an eye on the approaching men while Burchard engaged the lieutenant commander. As Burchard twirled and spun with Walter Pell, Ruschmann stuck to his position. Burchard was grateful for the hours they'd spent training together, allowing them to be so in sync with each other. He knew the moment Ruschmann stepped away from his back and engaged the rebels without having to look. *If I can take Walter Pell out of the equation, then maybe we will stand a chance.*

Burchard stepped to the left and rolled, sending him underneath the lieutenant's swing. He popped up behind him and did a sweeping cut across Walter Pell's back. Just as his sword touched the chain mail, Burchard was thrown backward in a blast of magic. He landed flat on his back, dazed.

Blinking rapidly to try to clear his vision, Burchard brought his sword up just in time to block a blow that would have cut his head off. As he thrust up with his sword, his attacker was thrown off balance, clearly not having expected to meet resistance. Burchard rolled his eyes and stood all the way up. He glanced to the side, uncertain of where Walter had gone, before returning his focus to the brown-bearded man in front of him. The rebel's sword swung wide; Burchard easily parried it and launched into an attack of his own. The rebel was slow to react and gasped in surprise as Burchard thrust his sword through the rebel's unprotected middle.

Burchard gave his sword a deft yank and spun, parrying the next blade coming for him. He could hear the clash of swords and knew Ruschmann must still be fighting. But Burchard was worried. *Two squires can't hold off one hundred veteran knights. Is this what Damos intended? To sacrifice us in exchange for rescuing his friends?*

Mouth in a grim line, Burchard continued to block and parry, getting in as many strikes as possible, but knowing he was only holding off the inevitable. Sweat dripped down his face. For a moment, he wished Walter Pell would chill the air again so he could cool off.

"Watch out!" shouted Ruschmann from somewhere behind Burchard.

Burchard spun, looking for whatever might be coming his way, and, to his dismay, saw a wall of rebels charging him. He set his feet. *I will make sure I take as many with me as possible,* he told himself firmly.

A split second before the first sword reached him, Burchard watched with growing apprehension as all of the rebels were struck by lightning till it was only himself, Ruschmann, and Walter Pell left standing. Burchard shot Ruschmann a questioning look, wondering if his friend could see something he couldn't. Ruschmann shook his head.

A big gust of wind blasted through the whole camp. It was so strong that it drove the three of them to their knees. Burchard tried to keep a hold of his sword, wrapping both hands around it to keep the wind from carrying it away. The wind stopped as suddenly as it came.

Clip. Clop. Clip. Clop.

The sound of hooves on the hard packed dirt rang out. Damos walked over to Walter Pell, followed by five other centaurs. Damos drew his sword and with one motion sliced clean through the lieutenant's head.

Burchard's face blanched and he fell forward, bracing himself on his hands as he retched up whatever was in his stomach from their last meal. He stayed there, hoping his stomach would settle, as his eyes were drawn to Walter Pell's head and body, which began to rapidly age and then decompose until all that was left was a pile of black ash. When he looked up, he found Damos glancing between him and the pile of ash with a curious look.

"What?" Burchard growled, wishing he had some water to rinse the bitter taste of bile from his mouth.

"Clearly you have no problem killing," said Damos with a wave of his hand to indicate the fallen rebels. "Why does this bother your stomach?"

"You didn't even give him a chance to explain himself. You just beheaded him," Burchard snapped, his throat still burning. He prayed he wouldn't throw up a second time.

The centaur crossed his arms across his chest, nostrils flaring. "The outcome would have been the same. However, I am not sure why he turned to ash."

Burchard stood up. "My father told me Walter Pell had been confirmed dead."

"I will have to make some inquiries about this. I am not familiar with Walter Pell or the Firebirds. From what I gathered they are part of Etria's history and not related to the druids or centaurs," Damos said.

"Now what?" Ruschmann asked, walking over to Burchard's side.

Burchard shrugged. If he had his way, they would finish their scouting assignment. They were already going to get back to Alderth Castle later than expected from this delay at Leosor Hollows. But besides "helping" Damos get his comrades back, he had no idea what would happen next.

Damos was having a hushed conversation with the other centaurs when Jade jumped off the top of the fence and strolled over to Burchard and Ruschmann. Burchard stared at the fence, wondering how long Jade had been perched there. *If she was there during the whole fight and I didn't even notice, I really need to work on paying better attention to my surroundings. Good thing she's on our side, or she could have easily put an arrow through me during the fight with Walter Pell.*

"I was in a tree protecting Damos's back while he undid the spell," Jade explained.

Burchard blew out his breath in relief. "Everyone in the camp is dead. The centaurs are freed. Can Ruschmann and I go?"

Jade glanced over her shoulder at Damos before returning her attention to the two squires. "I believe so. As we said at the campfire, we only waylaid you so that you could help us free the centaurs. Since that task is complete, I see no reason why you would not be permitted to leave."

Burchard clamped his mouth shut, bristling at her choice of words. *Permitted. As though we are under their command.* Ruschmann gave his arm a squeeze—a silent warning, Burchard mused.

"If you could let us know sooner rather than later if we can go, that would be much appreciated," Ruschmann said in a clear voice that carried across the camp.

Damos seemed to have heard the words since he turned away from the other centaurs and came over to the two squires.

"My apologies. Yes, you can leave if you would like. Just be warned, Walter Pell might have been stationed here, but this was not the only rebel camp under his control. There are others in the vicinity of the hollows," Damos said.

Interest piqued, Burchard wished that his map wasn't back at the druid camp. "Do you know where they are?"

Damos shook his head, sending his hair fluttering around him. "No, those camps are not as permanent as this one and move around fairly frequently." The centaur then reached into a pouch at his waist and pulled something out, offering it to Burchard. "A token of our gratitude. I owe you a debt for your help. I would not have been able to free them without your distraction." Damos bowed.

Burchard took the object without looking at it. He would have time to examine it later. "You do not need to owe me anything," he said.

"It is the way of my people, the druids, to repay our debts," Damos explained.

"Very well then," Burchard replied, then bowed. Ruschmann bowed a moment behind him. "We shall take our leave."

With that, Burchard and Ruschmann departed to retrieve their gear and horses from the druid camp.

12

An hour later, Burchard and Ruschmann were just mounting up at the druids' camp when Jade appeared. Burchard peered around her, wondering if the others were coming too, but she seemed to be alone.

Jade's dark brown hair was trying to escape from its braid; loose strands framed her face. She walked over to Burchard. "I wanted to say it took a lot of courage for you to keep fighting against Walter Pell and the rebels, even when you were so outnumbered."

Burchard felt his face heat up. "We are trained to face the enemy regardless of the odds."

Jade shook her head in disagreement. "Not many fourteen-year-olds would have held to their training when faced with those odds. Anyway, I wanted to give you this." She held out a small paper-wrapped package.

Burchard took it hesitantly. "A gift?"

Jade shrugged. "If you want to call it that, then I suppose it is a gift. It's just a token of my friendship."

Eyes narrowed, Burchard unwrapped the paper. He could feel her eyes on him as well as Ruschmann's burning into his back.

94

Burchard didn't like that Jade had chosen to single him out. Inside the paper was a bracelet woven from some kind of hair. The black strands weaved between red ones. As he gazed at the bracelet, it dawned on him that there were two bracelets that matched and that the hair was from Chip's and Cricket's tails.

"This is for Ruschmann too?" he asked.

Jade smiled. "Of course. I just thought you might like something to represent your friendship. The two of you are well suited for each other."

Burchard nibbled on his lip, not sure how to respond. "Uh, thank you." He gave her a slight bow, then slid the first bracelet onto his wrist before turning and offering the second one to Ruschmann. "We really must be going now."

Jade took a step back, giving them room to mount. "Good fortune on the rest of your trip," she said softly and then melted back into the trees.

The squires exchanged a look and then clucked to the horses and headed out. They decided to retrace some of their steps so that they could skirt around the rest of Leosor Hollows before finding a deer trail that seemed likely to lead them northeast.

Letting Ruschmann take the lead, Burchard pulled the token that Damos had given him out of his pocket. It was an intricately designed circular piece of metal. In the center was a large tree, its branches spreading across the top half. Around the base of the tree was a wolf, an elk, a large cat, and a unicorn. Bringing it closer to his face, Burchard realized things were also inside the branches of the tree. An owl and hawk and some other winged creatures he could not identify. In the bark of the tree were swirling designs.

"Ru, this medallion that Damos gave me," Burchard started, not sure what else to call the metal piece in his hand. "The craftmanship on it is unreal." He urged Chip up beside Ruschmann's horse and handed it over for his friend to study, before scooting Chip farther away. He had to admit the horse was getting better about being in close proximity to Ruschmann's horse without biting horse or rider.

Burchard watched as his friend examined the medallion. He didn't raise his eyes from his inspection while speaking. "Did you catch that Damos called them druids? Have you ever come across mention of a druid before?"

Tapping on his lip with his finger, Burchard considered the question. Typically, when he was reading about people from different lands, he was specifically looking for information on fighting styles and weapon preferences. The term *druid* did not feel familiar, but it was possible he'd come across it before.

"I'm not sure," Burchard replied.

"I thought you knew everything," Ruschmann countered.

Burchard laughed. "While I appreciate your confidence in my knowledge, I know far from *everything*. If we were back at Burmstone Palace, I would offer to search the library or inquire at Onaxx Academy, but we're not anywhere near Burmstone Palace. I am sure what few books Alderth Castle has are likely to discuss battle strategy or historic Etrian battles and not have anything to do with druids."

"Do you think anyone will believe us if we tell them we were waylaid by druids who are centaurs?" Ruschmann inquired.

Burchard considered the question. "I don't know. I doubt my father will believe us. He will accuse me of making up a story to cover that we were instead shirking our scouting duties. Sir Peter, though—he will."

"I hope someone believes us, or we're going to get in loads of trouble. This medallion might help us prove we're not lying," Ruschmann said and waved it around.

"No use in wasting time worrying about what my father will or won't do. We should just finish our task, make it to Camp Tooth, and then return. We *did* find rebels, which was the purpose of this scouting assignment," Burchard said firmly, then clucked to Chip, and they pulled ahead of Ruschmann at a quick trot.

There isn't much we can do if my father doesn't believe us about the centaurs. As long as he reads the report and takes the threat of the rebels we did encounter seriously, that is all that matters.

The sun was beginning to set when they reached the well-worn road going into Camp Tooth. Since the camp was built about twenty years ago to have a place to station knights to support Alderth Castle, the wall was made of wood, not stone, and about half as tall. As they approached it, Burchard heard the bell toll, then a creaking sound.

"They're shutting the gates," hissed Ruschmann.

"Let's run," Burchard growled, then dug his heels into Chip hard. The mare protested with a half-hearted rear before shooting forward in a full-out gallop. Ruschmann's horse met Chip stride for stride, and they ran for all they were worth to reach the gate before it shut all the way. Burchard could hear the horses' labored breathing and crossed his fingers, hoping that someone would notice them and hold the gate for them.

A shout from the wooden walls and the large wooden gates stopped moving. Burchard, followed by Ruschmann, burst through the opening, barely wide enough for one horse. As they reined in the horses, Burchard looked around in apprehension. The knights all had swords drawn. The gates slammed shut behind them.

One of the knights had armor that had been darkened. He slid his visor up but kept his sword out. Burchard gasped at his tattooed face and tightened his legs around Chip. Chip reared, striking out, but the dark-armored knight was standing just a handsbreadth out of reach.

The knight chuckled. "Not who you were expecting?"

Burchard let his hands go slack on the reins, hoping Chip would keep all four hooves on the ground. The knights closed in on them.

"What happened to Captain Volrain?" Burchard asked, hoping if he kept whoever this was talking that Ruschmann would come up with a plan.

"I ate him," the knight said in a deadpan voice.

"You what?" Burchard asked certain he'd misheard.

"He was quite delicious," the knight responded, licking his lips as though remembering a delicious meal.

Eyes wide, Burchard realized that this knight, man—or whatever he was—was serious. *How am I supposed to get out of this?* As he was contemplating how to respond, he was caught off guard when armored gauntlets roughly grabbed him and yanked him from Chip. Burchard twisted and bucked, trying to fight the gauntlets away, but they held firm no matter what he tried. When he was far enough away from the horses, the knight shoved him face-first into the ground with his arms pinned tightly behind his back. He couldn't even turn his head to see what had happened to Ruschmann.

He could hear booted feet approaching him and a creak as whoever it was presumably kneeled beside him. "You will take a nap, and when I'm ready, we shall have a discussion," the dark knight said.

Burchard wanted to see this knight up close, but before he could begin to struggle, his eyelids got heavy and he fell asleep.

Burchard opened his eyes and gasped in surprise when he saw he was lying on his back in the misty place, and Eos was standing on his chest, licking his face.

Wake up, she growled during a pause in her licking.

When he opened his eyes, she rocked back and sat down on her haunches. Oddly, though, he couldn't feel her weight at all, as though she wasn't even there.

But am I even here? he wondered.

You must wake up, the wolf growled again, her teeth clicking in agitation.

Burchard rubbed his eyes with his hands and blinked a few times. *I am awake.*

Eos hopped off him. *Good. Now you must hurry. We haven't got much time.*

Time for what? mumbled Burchard as he sat up.

Before he finds out I'm helping you. Eos pinned her ears back and bared her teeth. *You must escape from Camp Tooth. It is not time yet for you to face him. You must follow my instructions precisely.*

Burchard covered his mouth and stifled a groan before opening his eyes the barest of slits. *I had another strange dream.* He peered through his eyelashes and saw that Ruschmann was not in the same room as he was. Calling the space a room was being generous. It was not much larger than a broom closet. A couple of rings were strategically placed with chains running through them. Burchard shivered and ran a hand over his wrists, seeking reassurance that he was not shackled.

Standing up, he ran his fingers over the walls and door, looking for some way to escape. When he was making his second round, he suddenly remembered. Eos had given him instructions. *How do I know that was even real? But if it was not real, then what harm is there in following the directions? They just won't do anything.* Mind made up, Burchard turned around so his back was facing the door and, using his finger, drew an outline of a wolf's head on the wall. As he closed the line, the wall began to shimmer. The stone disappeared and was replaced with an opening, showing him the next room and a stunned Ruschmann.

"What is that?" gasped his friend.

"Don't worry about it," Burchard said and stepped through to his friend's cell. The wall he'd passed through shimmered and turned back to stone. There was barely enough room for the two of them.

This time he turned and faced the door. He drew another wolf head. The door shimmered and then disappeared, revealing a tunnel.

"Follow me," Burchard ordered, stepping through. Eos had told him that he had to do this quickly or he would get caught again. To Burchard's surprise, Ruschmann followed without comment.

They walked down the tunnel for what felt like hours. Burchard had no idea how much time had passed since they were captured. He recalled the dark knight saying they would take a nap and then have a discussion, but their cells hadn't had any windows, making it impossible to guess what time of day it was.

A little ways ahead, the tunnel led to a shimmering doorway. The other side appeared to be a dim forest. Burchard could hear a familiar nicker from somewhere in the trees. A few more feet and they'd be out of the tunnel. Just then, Ruschmann bumped into Burchard, and they both fell into a tangled heap.

"Why do you always fall on me?" growled Burchard in annoyance.

Ruschmann grumbled something unintelligible, and finally they disentangled themselves. The opening to the forest was shimmering more.

"I think it's going to close. Eos said we don't have much time." Burchard reached back and grabbed his friend's hand, and together they jumped through the opening into the forest just as it disappeared.

Tied a few strides away were both of their horses.

"How? And who on earth is Eos?" asked Ruschmann.

"Let's get going and I'll explain," Burchard replied, thinking, *If I can even get the words out this time*, as he jogged over to Chip, untied her, and mounted.

"Do we even know where we are?" Ruschmann asked, peering around before mounting his horse.

Burchard shrugged. "Hopefully far enough from Camp Tooth that we won't be followed." He clucked his tongue and Chip took off at a trot. Anytime he tried to steer her in a different direction, she would twist her neck and snap at his foot.

"Why is Chip being weirder than normal?" Ruschmann inquired.

Burchard choked. Ruschmann was right—Chip was being out of character. "Maybe Eos was able to show the horses where to go."

As soon as he stopped trying to change directions, Chip increased the pace, weaving through the trees at a fast canter. A few times Burchard was certain they were going to run headlong into a tree, but Chip shifted away from the tree just in time. He could hear Cricket breathing and was reassured that they were sticking as close as possible. With the crazy pace there was no way he could explain anything to Ruschmann, and his friend wouldn't be able to hear it anyway. *Maybe this is how I once again don't get to explain anything.*

The ground started to slope downward. Burchard had no idea where they were. None of the landmarks they had passed were familiar. He was wondering if he should insist that Chip stop so he could consult the map when the ground leveled out and a wide road was just in front of them.

The road didn't slow Chip down one bit. Both horses were side by side. Burchard exchanged a glance with Ruschmann. "Where do you think we are?"

Ruschmann opened his mouth to reply when they rounded a bend in the road, and the familiar towers of Alderth Castle were just visible over the top of a patch of dense fog. The sun was hidden behind the clouds, giving the castle a foreboding gray cast.

"Do we even know what day it is?" Ruschmann finally managed.

"No. I think today should be our third day gone, but I don't know how long we were at Camp Tooth. I don't think Eos was too concerned with making sure we know what day it is, only that we got out of there safely," Burchard said.

"What are we going to tell Sir Peter when we get back? You know we won't be able to do anything until we provide a report," Ruschmann reminded him.

"When we are alone with Sir Peter and Sir Daniel, I believe we should be able to give them the full story. But I think if I said anything about a magic wolf to my father, we would both get whipped." He grimaced, remembering all too well the feel of the whip on his back—something he hoped Ruschmann never had to experience himself.

The horses slowed to a walk just before they reached the gates.

"Ho there!" came a shout from the wall. As they went under the gate, Burchard could hear heavy footsteps coming down the wall stairs.

Sir Peter almost tripped down the last stair and stopped, staring at them in stunned silence. Finally, he spoke. "You're alive!"

Burchard looked down at himself and then at Ruschmann before returning his gaze to his knight master. "Yes, it would seem we are still alive."

Before Sir Peter could say anything else, both squires dismounted, and a pair of grooms came up to take the horses. Burchard pulled the letter from Radvall Mill out of his bag before motioning for the groom to lead Chip away.

Sir Peter came closer, inspecting both of them from head to toe. "General Wolfensberger declared you deserters two days ago. You've been gone for five days."

"Five days!" gasped Ruschmann.

"Yes. How long did you think you were gone for?" Sir Peter asked, giving them a curious look.

"Three days," supplied Burchard. *I wonder if Father was upset when he declared us deserters or if he was pleased to no longer have to worry about having us underfoot.*

Taking a deep breath, he followed Sir Peter as he led them inside the castle in the direction of the General's office. Sir Peter paused at the door and knocked. A muffled reply could be heard. The knight slowly pushed open the door. Burchard didn't blame him; since they couldn't understand the words that had been spoken, it was impossible to know if it had been an order to come in or come back later.

"I told you earlier not to disturb me," General Wolfensberger said gruffly, continuing to review the stack of papers on his desk.

Sir Peter coughed, causing the General to look up. Other than a slight widening of his eyes, which was quickly hidden, General Wolfensberger did not seem overly affected by the sudden appearance of his middle son.

"It appears they did not desert after all," the General said coldly.

Burchard sighed. His father never made anything easy for him. "General Wolfensberger, we are here to give you a report from our scouting trip." He paused. "I was asked to deliver this message to you from Radvall Mill." Burchard pulled the crumpled letter out of his pocket and bowed before offering it. Ruschmann also bowed.

The General took the offered letter with a sniff of disapproval. "Next time someone sends you with a letter, you need to respect the sender and take care of it, not stuff it in whatever spot is most convenient."

"Yes, sir," Burchard and Ruschmann said in unison.

The General set the letter on top of his stack of paperwork and turned toward the squires with his hands behind his back. "Give me your report. I don't have time to waste."

Burchard nudged Ruschmann, who pulled out their half-written report and handed it to the General. The General gazed expectantly at Burchard, who sighed, then launched into his explanation. "We began our scouting trip on the first day and made it to Radvall Mill with no sign of any rebel activity. In the vicinity of the mill, we came across the Radvall brothers. They beseeched us to bring you their letter. They also warned us of rebel activity near Leosor Hollows." He paused to give his father a chance to comment, but all the General did was wave his hand, indicating Burchard should continue.

Taking a deep breath, Burchard plunged onward. "Our plan was to camp at Leosor Hollows for the night since it is close to halfway. We were waylaid by a centaur and a young woman who wanted our help rescuing their friends in a nearby rebel camp. They were—"

"Centaurs are not real," the General said in an accusing tone.

Ruschmann stepped forward. "I assure you, General, this one was very real."

General Wolfensberger pressed his lips together till they formed a thin white line. Burchard could see the anger blazing in his eyes. *I better hurry up with my report before he blows up.*

Burchard coughed and continued. "We helped them rescue their friends, who were held in a large rebel camp that had over one hundred rebels led by Walter Pell."

A loud snarl emerged from the General's lips, causing everyone in the room to jump. "Walter Pell? That's not possible. He was confirmed dead ten years ago. I was there."

But did you see the body with your own eyes? Burchard wondered. With eyes lowered, he replied, "Very certain. He also knew who I was."

The General eyed the two squires with an expression Burchard could not interpret. "Lieutenant Commander Walter Pell just let you walk out of the camp with his captives?" he said in disbelief.

Once again, Ruschmann stepped in. "When we left, everyone in the camp, except for us and the centaurs we rescued, was dead. The centaur leader was a mage." Burchard was grateful for his friend trying to ease the tension. "They gave us a medallion in thanks."

Burchard dug around in his pocket with his fingers for a few moments before he found the medallion and offered it to his father. He had forgotten about it but was thankful Ruschmann had remembered because it was proof that they weren't making everything up. He watched as the General turned the medallion over in his hands and examined it, his face unreadable.

"You still haven't told me anything that would explain why you have been gone for five days," General Wolfensberger said as he offered the medallion back to Burchard.

"After we left Leosor Hollows, we headed straight for Camp Tooth. We knew at that point we would have to spend the night there or on the road but decided that would be acceptable given we *had* encountered rebels. I also wanted to make sure Captain Volrain knew about the rebels at Leosor Hollows. We made it to Camp Tooth just as the sun was setting and they were closing the gates for the day. But that's where things got strange."

Sir Peter blurted out, "Strange how?"

"When we entered Camp Tooth, all the knights drew swords on us. A knight in dark armor came forward and…he claimed he *ate* Captain Volrain. We were told that after we took a nap, we would meet with him," Burchard said, his voice shaking slightly.

"Did I hear you correctly? You were told that Captain Volrain was eaten?" Sir Peter said incredulously.

Ruschmann nodded fervently. "Yes! Our plan was to find out more when we had this discussion with him, but we never had the chance."

"Then how did you escape?" Sir Peter spoke quickly, then gave the General an apologetic glance.

Thankfully, Burchard thought that the General did not seem to mind the interruption.

"While I was asleep, the magic wolf Eos told me she was going to help us escape. When I woke up, there was a magic tunnel or something to Ruschmann's cell, and then out of his cell going somewhere. We took it," Burchard explained, giving Sir Peter a worried frown, unwilling to meet his father's eyes.

General Wolfensberger began pacing. Burchard couldn't decide if that was a good or bad sign, only that his father seemed just as unbalanced as he had been by the events that occurred at Camp Tooth. "Both of you believe that Camp Tooth is being held by some unidentified enemy who are cannibals?"

Burchard nodded in confirmation. "Yes, that is what we believe."

"I will need some time to decide what course of action I should take. But, the two of you need to be ready to go at a moment's notice. I want you there with whoever I send to investigate Camp Tooth," the General said decisively.

Sir Peter bowed. "We will take our leave so I can make sure they get as much time as possible to eat and rest before they depart again."

The General waved his hand in dismissal, his attention now on some papers on the desk. Burchard didn't need any more encouragement to know he should leave before his father changed his mind.

13

Sir Peter sat in an uncomfortable-looking wood chair in the barracks with an intense look, facing Burchard, who was sitting on his bed.

"Tell me again what the knight in dark armor looked like at Camp Tooth," Sir Peter ordered.

Burchard wanted to roll his eyes. This was the third time he'd told his knight master and he wasn't sure what the man hoped to accomplish by him continuously retelling the tale. Instead, like the dutiful squire he was supposed to be, he recounted everything he could remember about the time he was at Camp Tooth.

"Just as I suspected," Sir Peter said, and got up to rummage through his chest of drawers. He came back with a folded piece of paper. "Read this." He shoved the paper into Burchard's hand.

Burchard took it and carefully unfolded the worn paper.

The few survivors were raving about a knight in darkened armor with a tattooed face and knights eating people. I examined some of the bodies and it definitely looked as though they had been eaten by something. I cannot determine whether it was human or animal teeth that did the damage to the flesh.

Unfortunately, none of these cannibal knights was captured or killed. All I have to go on is a couple of firsthand accounts. Honestly, I am not sure what to think. There have been other attacks, in small villages and isolated farmsteads, that had the same body parts strewn about. No one is going to believe me if I tell them what I suspect is happening. That he has returned.

Burchard chewed on his lip, not sure what to make of the journal entry or whatever it was. He was about to hand it back when he noticed the small sketch of a knight with tattoos on his face at the bottom of the page. He dropped the letter with a shudder.

Sir Peter picked it up. "You recognize the sketch, as I hoped you would."

Burchard looked at him incredulously. "You want it to be that knight who eats people?"

Sir Peter clicked his tongue. "I would rather face an enemy we know than one we don't. Wouldn't you?"

"Well, when you put it that way…yes. But all we know is that it's likely the same person mentioned on your piece of paper. How does that help us?" Burchard asked.

"Why is it that you are patient when you are around your father and not with me? Never mind, don't answer that," Sir Peter said. "I know more about this tattooed knight than what is in this old journal entry. But it is the only sketch that I have found. Which is why I showed it to you. To see if you recognized it."

"I still don't see where this is going. How does us knowing who this cannibal knight is help with anything?" Burchard demanded. *The cannibal knight has been around for a while. So what?*

Sir Peter opened his mouth, then snapped it shut and took a deep breath instead. "You read where it said, 'That *he* has returned.' It's that 'he' I am concerned about. I have been working with the

General for longer than you've been alive. I understand if I want him to believe me when I say that the cannibal knights are unnatural, I better have a way of backing up my statement."

"Who do you think 'he' is referring to?" Burchard inquired.

"An old god of death and decay. There are legends about him and the commanders of his armies of the dead—legends that are better left buried," Sir Peter answered with a shudder.

Burchard gave his knight master a long look. It was obvious that Sir Peter believed this old god existed and that the cannibal knight in the dark armor was likely one of his commanders. "Why is this happening now?"

Sir Peter shook his head. "I have no idea, but it would be helpful to find out. You mentioned centaurs and druids. It is possible they know more. Did you ask them?"

"We ran into the cannibal knights *after* we had parted ways with the druids, so no, I did not ask them, nor do I know how to find them so that I can ask them," Burchard said with a sigh.

"Perhaps when we go back to Camp Tooth, we will find the answers we seek there."

Before Sir Peter could respond, the barracks door opened with a loud bang, letting in a blast of icy-cold air. Burchard looked at Sir Peter, wondering if he was expecting someone. The newcomer's feet treaded heavily across the worn wood floors, making the boards creak and groan.

"Sir Daniel," Burchard said with a bow from his seat. Peering at him, he realized that Sir Daniel was dressed for battle.

"Gather your things. We are moving out within the hour to Camp Tooth," Sir Daniel announced, before turning on his heel and heading back outside. The door banged shut behind him.

"I will put this away while you put your gear together. I'm expecting the plan will be for us to spend the night at the camp and return in the morning," Sir Peter explained before heading over to his bed.

Burchard stood up with a groan and went through a series of stretches. He was tired, and instead of resting, his father had ordered they go to Camp Tooth *now.* The order shouldn't have come as a surprise. Likely the General wanted confirmation that Burchard's story was rubbish so that he could turn to more important matters at hand, such as that Walter Pell had been at the rebel camp at Leosor Hollows.

Sir Peter gave Burchard a tired look when he appeared with Chip, just as the castle gates were opening to let the squad out. Burchard ignored the look and swung his leg into the saddle, taking the spot next to his knight master as they rode out the gate in a double wide column. He was trying to identify which squad they were with when he recognized his brother's red-and-white-spotted horse at the front of the column. From what he could tell it wasn't one of the usual squads—it was a bunch of first-year knights. Biting the inside of his lip, he tried fighting the growing feeling of dread in the pit of his stomach.

"Who has command of our group?" he said.

"Squire Reginald Wolfensberger," Sir Peter replied quietly.

Burchard bit down on his tongue hard, hard enough to draw blood. *There's all the proof I need that my father thinks we made up some fairy tale about what happened. If he thought the cannibal knights were real, he would never let Reggie lead, or send a group of inexperienced knights.* Lowering his eyes, he brooded over how to get his father to believe him about what had happened on their scouting mission. *Maybe if I feed Reggie to the cannibal knight, he would believe me.*

Chip tossed her head as Burchard accidentally tightened his hands on the reins. "Sorry, Chip," he murmured, stroking her neck.

At midday, they reached Camp Tooth. The gate was open; guards were on the wall. Burchard had expected his brother to at least send a scout into the camp to give everyone an all-clear. To his dismay,

Reggie led them right through the gate without pause. Burchard could hear Sir Peter's breathing hitch as they crossed through the gate. Glancing down, he realized his own hands were shaking. He willed himself to control the shaking, not wanting anyone else to see how much it was affecting him to be back in Camp Tooth. *I wonder how Ru is handling being back here.*

The clank of plate metal drew Burchard's attention from his thoughts. Gazing to the front of their column, he saw his brother and the knight who had been at his side dismount and approach the knight in darkened armor who seemed to be in charge. The knight in darkened armor removed his helmet from his head and relief washed over Burchard as he realized the man looked exactly like he should, no tattoos anywhere in sight. Captain Volrain was alive. Words were spoken that Burchard couldn't make out. Then, his brother's hand waved in the air, motioning for everyone to dismount. Knowing disobeying would only cause more problems with the General, Burchard kept his lips clamped shut and dismounted, then waited for their next orders, his face a blank mask.

He didn't have to wait long. Reggie walked over to him when he concluded the discussion with the knight in darkened armor.

"I have no idea why you spun that tale for Father, but there does not seem to be anything amiss here. We will spend the night, and I will be given a tour of the camp so I can inspect it." Reggie's lip curled in a sneer. "This was a waste of time." Then, Reggie turned toward Sir Peter and gave the knight a mocking bow. "I am sad to inform you that there is not enough space for you, Sir Tiniel, or the two squires. There is a clearing outside of the camp at the edge of the trees that should be suitable for your needs."

"Thank you for informing me. We will go prepare our camp now," Sir Peter said with a formal bow—completely unnecessary for a knight to a squire, Burchard mulled, but probably a wise decision given the squire was Reggie.

Sir Peter offered Burchard the reins for his horse. "Hold Mort for me, and I will go tell Sir Daniel."

Burchard nodded. Although annoyed his brother had not wanted to make space for them inside the camp, part of him was glad that he would not have to sleep within the camp walls. He could not shake the feeling that something was wrong here.

Sir Peter returned with Sir Daniel and Ruschmann following on their horses. Sir Peter quickly took Mort's reins and swung into the saddle with Burchard doing the same. None of the knights in the squad said anything as the four of them rode out of the gate and toward the indicated clearing.

The field they had to cross was larger than Burchard had thought originally. The sun was beginning to set as they unpacked their gear. The night would be cold enough to warrant a tent. Burchard found himself grateful that his knight master had told him to pack one, just in case.

"Are we building a fire?" Ruschmann asked. Burchard busied himself setting up the tent but was curious to know what the answer would be.

Sir Peter nodded. "Yes. Reggie was very specific in his directions. Everyone within earshot knows where we are, so I don't see what difference a fire will make, other than it would help us stay warm."

Burchard could hear the clicking of rocks hitting each other. Sir Peter was a stickler for putting a ring of rocks around a fire. Ruschmann wandered over and helped Burchard anchor the tent to the ground in case it got windy.

"Thanks," he murmured as Ruschmann hammered the last stake.

Ruschmann was about to respond when Sir Daniel began speaking to Sir Peter behind them. Sir Daniel's gruff voice carried to them. "I know you have records of these cannibal knights existing, but are you sure that your squire wasn't just making things up to pester General Wolfensberger? It is no secret that the general despises his middle son, or that Burchard constantly toes the line with the rules."

Sir Peter replied, "Yes, I am confident he was not spinning a tale. Didn't Camp Tooth feel off to you?"

Burchard waited for Sir Daniel's response, but it never came. He must have given some nonverbal reply.

Sir Peter began speaking again. "At least tell me you trust my instincts."

Sir Daniel's chuckle rumbled through their campsite. "Your instincts have saved my hide more times than I care to admit. Of course I trust you." A pause, and Burchard wished he could see what they were doing. "I just don't think our word and that of our squires is going to be enough to convince the General that he needs to visit Camp Tooth himself. Especially not with Reggie in here."

Unable to help himself, Burchard snorted.

"Why don't the two of you come here instead of lurking by the tent," Sir Daniel suggested.

The two squires approached the growing fire and sat across from the knight masters.

"Much better," Sir Daniel said.

"I don't want to provoke whatever is within those walls into an attack to prove my point though," Sir Peter said thoughtfully.

Sir Daniel nodded in agreement. "I know. I just wish we could get proof somehow."

"What if Ru and I look for proof? An object or something?" Burchard suggested.

Sir Peter shook his head. "No, it's too risky. What if you are captured again?"

"Do we just sit idly by while Reggie prances around then?" Burchard growled. Ruschmann placed a comforting hand on Burchard's leg.

"Yes, we must just watch and wait. If an opportunity arises, then we will take it. Let's eat and go to sleep," Sir Daniel said.

A while later, belly full of dried beef and fresh bread, Burchard was wrapped in his fur-lined bedroll. He fell asleep before he could say good night to Ruschmann.

Burchard opened his eyes and blinked. He was in the strange misty place. Eos padded up to him. To his surprise, she bared her teeth at him.

You must leave Camp Tooth immediately. No good will come of you being here again, Eos snarled in his mind.

I have orders that I must follow, Burchard said resolutely.

Disobey them if you must, but you must go back to Alderth Castle. Do not return to Camp Tooth. The wolf snapped her teeth, narrowly missing his fingers, as though that would emphasize her demand.

Before he could reply to Eos again, she disappeared. Burchard found himself standing alone. A shiver ran down his spine, and he took a tentative step forward. When nothing happened, he took a few more steps, gaining confidence as he went. Nothing appeared out of the fog to stop him.

Up ahead, he could see what seemed to be a large person emerging out of the fog. Burchard quickened his pace, wanting to speak to this new person. The fog dropped, revealing a knight in darkened, almost-black armor with its back toward him. Long gray hair cascaded down the knight's back, making Burchard momentarily wonder if the knight was a woman.

Slowly, the knight turned around, revealing a face covered in black tattoos of a skull. But it was the eyes that terrified Burchard, for there were none, just bottomless black pits.

Burchard tried turning to run, but his limbs were frozen in place. Terror coursed through him. He knew that this was what he had faced the other day in Camp Tooth and what his brother was now sharing a meal with, likely why Eos had been warning him.

"Burchard!" A rough hand shook his arm, the voice soft but urgent. "Burchard!"

Burchard forced his eyes open and jumped, knocking his forehead into Ruschmann's. Growling and rubbing his forehead with his hand, he sat up and started to speak, but Ruschmann shook his head and held his finger to his mouth. Mind still reeling from the dream and unsure if this was another dream or real, he decided to follow Ruschmann's instructions and stayed silent.

Then he heard it—the muffled sound of clanking metal. *Swords,* his mind supplied. He could also hear faint howling that seemed to be coming closer. Eyebrows raised in alarm, Burchard looked to Ruschmann, and his friend nodded. Cautiously, Burchard untangled himself from his bedroll and buckled his scabbard on. The noises seemed to be far enough away that Burchard thought they were safe where they were, but inside the tent, they couldn't see anything.

With a nod, Ruschmann, sword ready, pulled the tent flap open. The camp was shrouded in darkness; the fire had gone out, and the trees were blocking the moon. Burchard could not tell where Sir Peter and Sir Daniel were, but he hoped they were unharmed. The two squires edged out of the tent.

When they got far enough away from the tent, the familiar shapes of their two knight masters became visible. They were near the other tent with their swords at the ready too.

For a moment, it felt as if the darkness around them was pressing heavily on Burchard, almost as though it were trying to go through him. When the pressure let up, they were surrounded by knights in plate armor. It was hard to make out much else about them in the darkness. He also wasn't sure how many there were.

Unfortunately for Burchard and his companions, the knights did not seem to be as affected by the darkness as they were. One moment the four Etrians were surrounded; the next, blades were flashing through the air. Burchard brought his sword up just in time to block a strike from his left, forcing him to step away from Ruschmann. The knight struck but left enough of an opening for Burchard to parry. Step by step, Burchard gained ground on the knight, driving him away from the camp.

Until he realized that this had been a ploy to get him away from the others. When they reached the tree line on the back side of the camp, two more knights appeared from within the woods. All three of them glowed eerily, as though they had magic of some sort. The glowing permitted Burchard to see the tattoos on their faces. Not a full skull like in his dream but instead a half-mask, from forehead to the tip of the nose. As one, they charged him.

Burchard pivoted to the right at the last moment and swept his sword in an undercut. It slid off the knight's armor. Using the momentum of the sword to carry him, Burchard spun, swinging his sword in an arc toward the exposed gap in the armor at the armpit. Luck was with him, and he could feel as the sword sliced into flesh. Blood dripped down the knight's armor.

Distracted by the bleeding knight in front of him, Burchard almost didn't block the next strike that came from one of the other knights in time. He blocked and blocked, trying to get a measure of them and whether they were just trying to power through his defenses or if they were coordinating. It seemed like they were attempting to coordinate, and a few of their strikes did successfully connect. Burchard winced as one sliced through his heavy coat and nicked his arm. Running his mind through different training exercises Sir Peter had drilled him on, he came up with a plan.

He took a few steps back, then ran straight for the two knights and the gap between them. They momentarily froze as he squeezed through the gap. He pulled out a long knife, drove it into the armpit of the knight on his left, and twisted. The knight collapsed, and Burchard yanked his knife out, leaping out of the way, as the knight on his right let out an unearthly shriek before jabbing his sword toward Burchard's stomach. Burchard stepped to the side and swept his sword up into the opening the knight had unwittingly made. His sword struck hard against the plate armor. He spun to the left and parried, then stumbled as he heard what he thought was a wolf howl that sounded very, very close.

The knight grinned at Burchard, showing unnaturally sharp, pointy teeth, before launching itself at him. The knight's sword sliced through Burchard's left shoulder. As Burchard grunted in pain, the wolf howled again, and Burchard tripped over his own feet, falling to the ground with a groan. His left shoulder stung.

Get up, he commanded himself. *The others are fighting too.* Behind him, within the camp, he could hear the clang of swords. He hoped the others were faring better than he seemed to be. He rolled to the side as the knight's sword came slashing down. Scrambling to his feet, Burchard blocked the next strike, trying to regain his footing. The swords hissed as the blades slid along each other. The knight came at him with a low strike. When the knight grinned at him, Burchard swung to parry and reversed his sword, sweeping it up in an arc toward his head.

The sword skimmed his ear. Gasping as pain seared through it, Burchard fell to his knees as his vision swam before him. Forcing a deep breath into his lungs, he adjusted his grip on his sword, the soft leather a welcoming touch.

Crunch, crack.

Burchard turned slowly, vision starting to go dark again as a knight spun toward him, sword raised. A growl and a blur rocketed through the trees at Burchard's left side, launching into the air and straight into the tattooed knight.

Burchard adjusted himself, trying to shake off the pain and vertigo, knowing that he would perish either to the black dog or the knight if he didn't.

The knight stumbled under the impact of the dog and corrected himself clumsily. The dog leapt in the air and somehow was able to latch its jaws onto the man's armpit. Balancing on its hind legs, the dog shook its head, driving those teeth farther into the flesh. Not wanting to lose his chance and praying he wouldn't faint, Burchard levered himself up with his sword, then took a few steps toward the knight, swinging his sword to the right. Much to his surprise, the knight parried one-handed. The other two had been completely disabled when he had sliced that vulnerable area; he wondered what made this one different.

Sparks flew as the swords met again. The big black dog was growling and circling them, occasionally darting in to snap at the knight, but surprisingly leaving Burchard alone.

Burchard danced back and to the side before sweeping up with an undercut to disarm the knight. Just as he was about to complete the move, everything went black. He stumbled to the ground, groaning. Unable to make his eyes open, Burchard waited for the inevitable killing blow to be delivered by the knight. Instead, he heard a terrible scream followed by a yelp from the dog, and then silence.

"Burchard?" Sir Peter's voice called from far away. Burchard moved his fingers first before cracking his eyes open slightly. Sir Peter's concerned face filled his vision. "You're alive!"

Groaning, Burchard rolled to his side, wanting to get up. The dampness from the dead leaves soaked through his tunic.

"Slowly," his knight master warned.

Grunting but following the advice, Burchard slowly sat up and opened his eyes all the way.

The mangled body of the knight was about ten paces away.

"Where are the others?" Burchard asked, concern lacing his voice.

"I am not sure. The knights were effective at splitting us up and driving us away from the camp. I killed two," Sir Peter replied. "If you can manage it, we should see if they need help. Or I can leave you here."

Burchard shook his head. "No, I am not sure I can hold my own against another one of those knights right now."

Sir Peter nodded and started to walk off, presumably in the direction that he thought Sir Daniel and Ruschmann were in.

"Wait!" Burchard called.

Sir Peter came back. "What?"

"Where is the dog?" Burchard asked.

"Dog?" echoed Sir Peter. "There is no dog."

Muttering to himself, Burchard wobbled before he closed his eyes, waiting for everything to stop spinning, then cautiously opened his eyes again. "There was a big black dog…it helped me," he explained.

Sir Peter gave Burchard a look, like he thought his squire was losing his mind. Shrugging, Burchard focused on scanning the area for clues. He realized that at some point the sky had lightened with dawn and that he could indeed see. Everything wasn't just in dark shadows anymore. He finally saw blood on the bushes to the left and odd drag marks.

"There," he said pointing. Moving quietly so as not to spook the dog into attacking, he approached the bushes. When he was only a few feet away, Burchard could see the edges of black fur not completely concealed by the bush. Burchard cautiously crouched by the bush and spoke in a calm, quiet voice. "My name is Burchard. I am a squire of Etria. Thank you for saving my life. I want to see if you need help too." As he spoke, Burchard slowly parted the bushes, revealing a blood-soaked…wolf. Sucking in a deep breath, he shuddered at the old memories threatening to resurface again. *This is the present. It's not the same wolf. I am not an innocent boy anymore.*

Golden eyes gazed back at Burchard as he wondered why a wolf would help him. He reached out a steady hand toward the wolf's face for her to sniff. The wolf remained immobile. Gently, he ran his hands over the wolf, probing for wounds, just as he would do when his horse was injured. There was a large, deep gash on one of her hind legs and smaller cuts throughout. Glancing over his shoulder, Burchard saw Sir Peter staring at him with his mouth hanging open. Returning his attention to the wolf in front of him, Burchard remembered that he had packed bandages in a small mending kit.

He glanced at Sir Peter. "I have bandages, but they're in the tent."

Sir Peter gave him a frown. "Sir Daniel and Ruschmann finished off the other tattooed knights. You should be able to get the bandages without any problem, if you really think it is worth saving a wolf."

Burchard glanced from his knight master to the wounded wolf and back again. "Eos, another wolf, helped me escape from this place. The least I can do is help a wolf who also came to my aid in the same manner."

Sir Peter pressed his lips together and nodded. Taking that as approval, Burchard ran a hand lightly down the wolf's side.

"I'll be right back," he stated quietly to the wolf, then stood up shakily. Slipping inside the tent, Burchard rummaged through his packs for his medical kit and smiled grimly when he found it. Slinging the small bag over his shoulder, he slid out of the tent and back over to the wolf. Even with all the extra motions of getting in and out of the tent, the dizziness and vertigo finally seemed to be wearing off. He still took his time kneeling beside the wolf. Once her wound was clean, he expertly wrapped the bandage around it.

As he stood up, Burchard realized the clearing was filled with fog, making it almost impossible to see. Burchard looked around warily, hand on the hilt of his sword. Sir Peter was doing the same. The forest was eerily quiet, yet it was a different quiet than it had been right before the attack. A shimmering blue glow appeared, and a huge white wolf, larger than a horse, materialized out of the glow.

Burchard shifted slightly, trying to hide his nerves. He'd thought the injured wolf seemed large, but she was nothing compared to the one in front of him now, who looked familiar, but he couldn't quite place why. *It's not like I go around making friends with wild wolves.* As the giant wolf turned its attention directly on Burchard, he began to shake as nerves gripped him.

"Burchard Wolfensberger, I am Eos, goddess of the wolves. For the unexpected kindness you have shown to my granddaughter Fang, she will accompany you on your journey," Eos stated matter-of-factly.

Burchard's jaw dropped in surprise and awe. *Eos is a goddess? She has time for me, a lowly squire?* He closed his jaw hastily and tried to come up with an appropriate response but drew a blank. *What do you say to a goddess? I've never even been in the presence of royalty before…now I get a visit from someone even more important. What is going on?*

The wolf goddess looked at Burchard with her piercing eyes as though she could hear his rambling thoughts. "As long as you treat Fang with respect and honor, she will defend you."

Without further explanation, the shimmering fog got brighter, and the goddess faded.

Burchard took a step forward, hand reaching as though to stop her. "What about my father?" he asked, concern lacing his voice. General George Wolfensberger had no tolerance for disobedient squires or people who bonded with animals.

Eos's eyes were all that remained, but her voice came through the fog, "He will accept her…in time."

Suddenly, the fog was completely gone from the clearing, as though it had never been there.

Rough hands shook Burchard, and he leapt into the air, startled. "What the hell!" he growled, arms swinging.

"We need to go," hissed Sir Peter.

Burchard looked around, realizing that his knight master hadn't seen the wolf goddess even though she had been here in the camp with them. *Perhaps it didn't happen at all.*

"Oh, your wolf friend seems to be feeling better," the knight added as an afterthought.

Burchard glanced in the direction of the wolf before replying, "Her name is Fang."

"Fang?" echoed Sir Peter. "How do you know the wolf has a name?"

"The wolf goddess told me," Burchard said softly, bracing for Sir Peter to contradict him.

Sir Peter, eyebrows raised, gave Burchard an appraising look. "The Eos you mentioned who helped you is *the wolf goddess?*"

Burchard *ahem*ed in embarrassment. "I guess so. She just told me that's who she is. Did you see her, just now, when she appeared?"

Sir Peter shook his head. "No, I did not see her. But…that means the situation here is even more grave than I suspected. Let me get your wound wrapped, and then we can go find Sir Daniel and Ruschmann."

Burchard handed over his medical pack and stood quietly while Sir Peter cleaned and then bandaged the slice across his arm and the wound on the side of his head and ear. He was sure he looked utterly ridiculous with the bandage wrapped around his head, but the blood was no longer trickling annoyingly down his neck, and for that he was grateful. "Should we take the pack with us?"

He watched as Sir Peter debated his answer. "I think since you're injured already, we should try to move as quickly as possible without extra gear."

"The plan is that we're going to find Ruschmann and Sir Daniel, and then what?" Burchard asked, not sure what his knight master was thinking. *Running back to Alderth Castle or helping whoever was alive at Camp Tooth?*

"Then we will rescue whoever is still alive in Camp Tooth," Sir Peter said firmly.

"Just the four of us?" Burchard asked incredulously.

Sir Peter gave him a toothy grin. "We now have five."

Just then Burchard felt the wolf slide her head under his hand. He looked down and saw Fang's head tilted up, gazing at him. Her bandage was gone. Since she had initiated contact, he ran his hand across where the wounds had been. Shock lined his face as he felt nothing, no scars. It's as though the wounds were never there.

Clearing his throat, Burchard spoke. "Let's get going."

14

By the time Burchard, Sir Peter, and Fang reached Ruschmann and Sir Daniel on the other side of their campsite, the bodies of the tattooed knights had been moved into a pile. Both knight and squire had small slices in their clothing and were bleeding in a few places, but luckily they had fared better than Burchard and Fang.

"Who is the wolf?" Ruschmann asked in a high-pitched voice.

Burchard gave his friend a small smile, "This is Fang."

"Where are the horses?" asked Sir Peter, directing the question to Sir Daniel.

Sir Daniel shrugged. "I think they're somewhere in the trees. Why don't you have Burchard whistle for Chip? The others will follow her."

Burchard did as ordered and let out a piercing whistle. Fang whined at his side, and he belatedly wondered if the horses would come with a wolf so close. *I guess we shall find out.* Soon, they could hear the snapping of twigs and branches, accompanied by soft snorts. The four horses emerged from the forest and stopped a healthy distance away from Burchard and Fang. Eyes rolling so the whites showed, the four horses stood their ground, but would not move any closer.

"They look unharmed," Ruschmann announced, walking around the four horses and running an experienced eye over them.

"Good, let's go then. I am not sure what will happen once the sun has risen all the way," Sir Peter said, eyes going to the sky that was turning pale shades of pink and blue.

Swiftly, the four of them mounted. With an unspoken command, they took off at a gallop and headed for the open gates of Camp Tooth. Burchard glanced to his side and saw Fang, effortlessly keeping pace with the horses. He wondered how long she could keep up. He knew wolves could keep up a steady ground-eating pace for long distances, much like horses, but a sprint like this, he wasn't sure.

Sooner than he expected, the horses and wolf slowed as the wooden gates loomed ahead. It was eerily quiet. Burchard could feel Chip's muscles tensing, and he thought he could hear a low growl coming from Fang, but he wasn't sure. Turning to Sir Peter, he opened his mouth. "Do we—" A quick wave of Sir Peter's hand had Burchard clamping his mouth shut.

He kept one eye on his knight master and the other trained toward the gate and what awaited them. Instead of going through the gate, Sir Peter led them several paces away, then dismounted. He threw the reins over Mort's neck, and Burchard, Ruschmann, and Sir Daniel followed suit.

Burchard ran his hand across Chip's neck. "Stay out of trouble," he whispered to her before moving toward Sir Peter's position at the edge of the gate. He could feel Fang as she occasionally brushed against his leg, sticking close.

"We will stay together. Stay alert. We do not know what we shall be facing once we get through the gates," Sir Peter ordered. Sir Daniel inclined his head in agreement.

Silently, the two knights and their squires crept through the gates. Fang moved away from them, nose to the ground, as though she were looking for something. Burchard surveyed the camp. The knights who had come with them were easy to identify by their armor, which was chain mail instead of plate. He counted ten dead. The ground was splashed with blood in some places, but he could not spot any sign of who had been attacking or that any of the opposing force was killed. *How odd.*

When it was clear no one was in this part of the camp, Sir Peter motioned for them to fan out. In the middle was the residence Camp Tooth was built around, and below the main house were the dungeons that Burchard and Ruschmann had been held in. Methodically, the four of them inspected each building within the camp, until all that was left was the residence.

Unlike Wolfensberger Castle, which was built to withstand attacks, this building was short and sprawling, making it difficult to defend on its own but useful as a camp headquarters, providing plenty of space for war councils and storage for supplies. It was made of reddish-brown stone, different from the gray-and-black granite that was common throughout Etria. The main level was in the shape of a square with a garden in the center. The level below, which held the dungeons, went underneath the garden too, making it quite large.

Ruschmann opened the front door with a big push. The door banged against the wall, and Burchard grimaced. *Anyone inside knows we're here now.* Moments ticked by as they waited for someone to come running out, but nothing happened.

Out of the gloomy residence came a familiar voice. "Burchard." His eyes narrowed as he recognized Reggie's voice. "Burchard, help me."

Overcome with the need to save his brother, Burchard felt himself being drawn inside.

"Burchard," hissed Sir Peter in warning.

Burchard braced his feet, trying to keep himself from going farther into the house, but he could not keep himself from moving. He tried opening his mouth, but it would not open. He was being pulled and was helpless to stop it from happening.

"Burchard, help me, brother," Reggie's voice came again.

Burchard stopped fighting the pull and followed as bidden. Soon he could hear the clang of swords and fighting behind him, and he knew the others were not with him; he was on his own. Winding through the rooms, he came upon an open door to the garden in the middle of the house. His brother stood in the center, facing him. Reggie had several gashes along his arms and one on his left cheek. He held his sword loosely in his right hand, with the tip resting on the grass.

As Burchard crossed the threshold into the garden, the tugging stopped. He stumbled forward and almost dropped his sword. When he regained his balance, he peered at his brother through the blond hair that had swung into his eyes.

"Are you OK?" he asked, taking a few steps toward Reggie until they could almost touch their swords.

"Help me, Burchard," Reggie pleaded.

Burchard studied his brother's face, unable to decide if his brother was being serious and truly needed help, or if this was just another game.

"I am here to help you. Where is the rest of the squad?" He peered around, as though the missing knights would just materialize in the garden.

A cackling laugh from behind Burchard had the squire raising his sword and pivoting to protect his brother.

"You!" Burchard growled.

"I knew we would meet again," replied the tattooed knight with a grin. "My name is Ossa. My sister, who you will meet soon, is Umbra."

"Let my brother go," Burchard snarled, debating if he should make the first move against Ossa. He remembered Sir Peter's instruction: if he had the opportunity to choose when to attack, take it.

Mind made up, Burchard lunged for Ossa. Ossa brought up his broadsword, and they clashed in a mighty clang that shook the walls and sent sparks showering over the grass. Twisting his wrist, Burchard freed his sword from Ossa's and went for an uppercut. Ossa blocked and parried with a swift combination that forced Burchard to give up some ground, pressing them closer to Reggie.

He was tempted to swap sword hands but wasn't sure his wounded left arm would hold up against the heavier broadsword. The momentary pause as he considered his options was a costly mistake. Ossa flew at him with a left-right combination that Burchard wasn't able to block in time. The slices across his arms were not deep, but they stung and made it more difficult to react quickly. Backing up a few steps, Burchard hissed as he felt the point of a sword against his spine. Wondering how he let someone get behind him, he glanced over his shoulder and realized it was Reggie who was holding a sword to his back. Burchard lowered his sword.

Ossa grinned at him, sharp teeth flashing. "You didn't really think your brother would beg you to save him, did you?" Ossa's head tilted. "See, your brother, he wants the same thing I do—for you to get out of our way."

Burchard blinked in surprise. *Get out of Reggie's way? What on earth is Ossa talking about?* The doors to the garden shuddered. It sounded as though someone was using something to ram them. *Hopefully it's Sir Peter.*

Ossa clicked his tongue. "Your friends are not going to be able to rescue you. I took some precautions after you escaped last time."

Just then the doors blasted off their hinges, sending wood chips spraying over the garden.

The moment Reggie's sword slipped from his back, Burchard shifted away from Reggie and Ossa, bringing his sword up. A black blur hurtled toward them and launched itself at Ossa. Out of the corner of his eye, Burchard could see Sir Peter, Sir Daniel, and Ruschmann coming into the garden. His relief was short-lived as knights with darkened armor and tattoos on their faces came running through the doors too.

One of the dark knights made a beeline for Burchard. He had no choice but to take his attention from Fang and Ossa to defend himself. The clang of swords filled the garden. Occasionally, there was a strange swirl of shadows. Burchard swiped at his forehead with his left hand as sweat threatened to trickle into his eyes. Back at their tents, what felt like days ago, but he knew was probably only hours, a slice to the armpit had done the trick, so that was what he was trying to do with his current opponents. Unfortunately, these knights seemed more skilled than the others had been. He wasn't sure if it was because Ossa was here and somehow controlling them or if they were just a different kind. Either way, Burchard wasn't sure they were going to make it out of Camp Tooth alive.

Spin, strike, block, strike, parry, over and over. Finally, his adversary gave him the opening he needed. Burchard took the risk, swapping his sword to his left and driving it upward into the unprotected armpit. Black blood sprayed as the sword punched all the way through into the knight's chest. Burchard yanked on his sword, but it would not come out. He wrapped both hands and twisted, and finally it released, dripping black blood—or what he thought was blood.

He wasn't sure where Fang and Ossa were, but his attention was drawn to Ruschmann near the center of the garden, facing none other than his brother Reggie. Burchard took a few steps toward Ruschmann when another dark knight charged at him. Sighing in frustration, Burchard viciously chopped at the dark knight, a burst of energy bubbling within him. Just as he drove his sword into the knight's armpit, his eyes met with Reggie's. His brother gave him a malicious grin as he locked swords with Ruschmann, lifted his foot booted in plate armor, and slammed it into Ruschmann's unprotected ankle.

Ruschmann's inhuman scream of pain rang throughout the garden before he collapsed on the ground. Without thinking, Burchard let go of his sword and sprinted toward his brother as Reggie raised his sword to take the killing blow. Burchard barreled into Reggie's stomach, and they fell to the ground in a thrashing heap. Burchard punched with everything he had, fervently hoping one of the knight masters would help Ruschmann before another enemy killed him.

One moment Reggie was grappling with Burchard, the next his body went limp. Burchard let his fist drop and peered at his brother in concern. "Reggie?" he said hesitantly, his body tense, ready to defend himself if his brother was faking it.

"Burchard?" Reggie's answer was muffled as his eyes slowly opened.

"Do you still want to kill me?" Burchard asked.

Reggie gave him a quizzical look. "That depends on how long it takes you to get off me. What did you do? Eat a horse?"

Burchard scooted off his brother and offered a hand. Reggie took it and stood up, peering around the garden, still looking rather confused.

"How much do you remember?" Burchard asked.

Sir Peter walked over to them at that moment. Confusion lacing his voice, Reggie asked, "What do you mean?"

Burchard glanced between his brother and knight master. "I think Ossa—the dark knight Ruschmann and I met the first time we came here—had Reggie under some spell or something. We may not like each other very much, but we both fight for Etria, and that will never change."

Reggie let out a breath. "I remember arriving at Camp Tooth and sending you to make camp on the edge of the trees. Then, I did the inspection. After that…it gets hazy. I think I gave orders when the knights in the dark armor appeared. The next thing I remember is you punching me."

"This is all rather strange," Sir Peter said. "But now is not the time or the place to figure out what Ossa's purpose was to control Reggie. It would be in our best interest to round up any survivors from the squad and get on our way to Alderth Castle."

Burchard nodded in agreement. "What about Ruschmann? I don't think he can walk."

"You can carry him," suggested Reggie.

"You could help," retorted Burchard.

"No thanks," Reggie replied and walked away.

Growling to himself, Burchard went over to Ruschmann. *I should have known Reggie would go back to being his normal useless self as soon as possible.*

"I can help you," offered Sir Peter.

Burchard shook his head. "No, I can carry Ruschmann. Reggie only said it because he doesn't believe I can do it."

Sir Peter gave Burchard a concerned look. "I don't think I've ever seen you carry him," he said carefully. "Not that you can't, but you are already injured."

Burchard turned away from Sir Peter, not wanting to reply. *He's probably right.* Burchard helped Ruschmann stand up, and then, standing in front of his friend, he shifted his weight onto his right leg, placing it between Ruschmann's legs. Then, grabbing Ruschmann's right hand, he draped it over his shoulder. Squatting, Burchard slid his head under Ruschmann's armpit and positioned his friend's body over his shoulders, then slowly stood.

Ruschmann had stayed silent through most of it, Burchard glanced at him out of the corner of his eye. "You look a little queasy."

Ruschmann gave him a half-smile. "I'll try to not puke on you."

Burchard took a few steps, then felt something on his leg. He glanced down and saw Fang. Her fur had black blood in it, but she seemed unharmed. "Come on, let's go."

15

Grunting with the effort of carrying Ruschmann, Burchard was happy to see the horses standing within the walls of Camp Tooth, not outside the gates. Despite their best efforts, Sir Peter and Sir Daniel had not found any surviving members of the squad. Reggie couldn't remember what Ossa had done with them. Burchard knew it bothered Sir Peter to not know what had become of the Etrians, but no one wanted to linger at Camp Tooth any longer. Not when Ossa could return at any moment.

Sir Daniel was still in the lead. He snagged the reins for Ruschmann's horse and brought it over to Burchard. "Do you think you can ride?"

"Anything would be better than having Burchard pinching my balls," Ruschmann grumbled.

Burchard turned beet red. He had been trying not to pinch anything on his friend, but carrying him over his shoulders was the only way he could manage a load that weighed more than he did. He relaxed his grip on Ruschmann and slowly squatted. Ruschmann groaned and took his time dragging his body upright, still leaning heavily on Burchard.

"How are you going to get on your horse?" Burchard asked.

"You could boost me from my right knee instead of my foot. I think that would work. I can still use my left foot to push off," Ruschmann replied.

"OK. Ready?"

At Ruschmann's nod, Burchard counted to three, then boosted his friend into the saddle. Ruschmann swayed precariously before he found his balance.

Burchard stepped away. His limbs felt all noodly, and he wasn't sure if he'd manage getting into his own saddle without help at this point.

Fang pressed against his leg and gave his hand a lick. "Thanks, Fang," he said softly, running a gentle hand over her head.

Sir Peter handed Burchard Chip's reins. Burchard took them and dragged himself into the saddle before his legs could protest. He glanced over at Ruschmann, who gave him a wan smile. Reggie found his horse somewhere and was mounted next to Sir Daniel.

"Is everyone ready?" Sir Daniel asked. Without waiting for confirmation, the knight clucked, and they headed out at a brisk walk. Burchard was about to protest the slow speed when he realized that with all five of them injured to some extent, and Ruschmann unable to bear weight on his right foot, a brisk walk was the smartest pace. It would just take most of the day to get back to Alderth Castle.

Somehow Reggie ended up riding next to Burchard. Burchard peered at his brother through his lashes, not sure what his brother wanted.

"What are we going to tell Father?" Reggie said, startling Burchard out of his thoughts.

"The truth," Burchard said matter-of-factly.

Reggie chuckled without mirth. "You of all people should know that Father would not believe me if I told him I was being controlled by Ossa, a commander of a dark god, and that the whole squad was killed because of it."

"He's more likely to believe you than me," Burchard pointed out.

"I think all five of us can agree that what happened at Camp Tooth is a major concern. But how do we convince the General that he needs to turn his attention to something other than the Stinyian rebels?" Reggie continued.

Sir Daniel slowed his horse down so he was on Burchard's other side. "Your father is not a stupid man. He should take the loss of a squad of knights as a serious threat. Perhaps telling him that the rebels have joined forces with a dark mage will be sufficient. I hope for our sake that Ossa is not connected to the Stinyian rebels." He paused. "Burchard, you were trapped in the garden with him. Did he say anything to you that could indicate what his purpose is?"

Burchard tugged at his lip with his finger, trying to remember what Ossa had said. "He said he wanted to kill me. That the attack was targeting me specifically. I still don't get why a god or his commander would care about me. I'm just a first-year squire."

Sir Daniel fiddled with his reins. "I agree. It doesn't make much sense. Perhaps there is more to it, or…" He hesitated, clearly considering his next words. "Or it is just a way to draw the General into a direct confrontation. It is no secret he is the most skilled general within the Etrian ranks and has the ear of King Roland. Taking him out of play would have a huge impact on the war against the Stinyian rebels."

Burchard nodded. Sir Daniel was right. His father was a valuable piece of Etria's defenses, and his demise would be a big blow to the king. That must be what Ossa was planning.

Chip stopped moving, and Burchard felt himself tipping sideways. Hastily gripping the saddle to hold himself in place, he realized they had reached Alderth Castle. *I must have fallen asleep.* Rubbing his eyes with his hand, he saw that Fang was sticking close to Chip. Clearly the wolf and horse had come to some agreement.

Sir Peter walked over to Burchard. His horse was being led away by one of the grooms. "You need to get patched up properly. Then some food and rest."

"What about the General?" Burchard said softly, trying to wake up more.

Sir Peter shook his head. "He can wait. Sir Daniel will give him a brief report, and the rest of us will meet with him tomorrow. Captain Thomas will get Fang settled with some meat."

Burchard kept silent and focused on dismounting and staying on two feet. He wobbled back and forth a bit, using the stirrup for balance before he felt steady enough to step away from Chip. A groom came up to them and took Chip's reins, leading her into the stable.

"Let's go," Sir Peter said. With a light hand on Burchard's elbow, he guided the squire toward their barracks. Burchard was too tired to protest that they were going the wrong way.

When they got to his bunk, Captain Thomas, the medic, was there waiting. Sir Peter directed Burchard to sit in the chair. A small stool was brought over with a bowl of steaming stew. He could see the pieces of meat and vegetables floating in the thick brown sauce. A chunk of crusty bread rested next to it.

Captain Thomas smiled at him. "I'll patch up your arm while you eat, and then you can get some rest."

Burchard merely nodded in agreement and took a big bite of stew, sighing in satisfaction at the perfectly spiced venison. Focusing on his food, he was only vaguely aware of his wound being washed, stitched, and then wrapped in a clean bandage. The slice to his ear was cleaned and left unwrapped, not deep enough to warrant stitches.

"All finished. Perfect timing, too, since you're on your last bite." The medic began putting away his supplies. "I would recommend taking it easy with your arm for a few days to give yourself a chance to heal. No sword practice or hand-to-hand combat for three days, but you can ride or run without need for caution," Captain Thomas instructed.

Burchard nodded and set his bowl on top of the dresser. "I will follow your instructions." He was about to say more, but he could not stifle his yawn. Once the first one escaped, he kept yawning.

Captain Thomas gave his arm a squeeze. "Just go to sleep. I'll find you tomorrow and remind you." The captain headed toward the barracks door, leaving Burchard in the silent building. Taking a deep breath, he undressed, and then slid under the covers on his bed. He was asleep before his head touched the pillow.

A soft, warm piece of fabric was touching his cheek. Burchard's eyes fluttered open and he was peering straight into the golden eyes of Fang, her tongue lolling from her mouth. *Tongue, not fabric*, he corrected himself.

"Good morning," he murmured to the wolf, wondering how she managed to sneak into the barracks. Then, he realized he couldn't move. She was lying on top of him, and the bed was very narrow. He also was surprised at how much she weighed. Stretched out as she was, she happened to be almost as tall as he was. Sliding his arm out from under Fang and the covers, he ran his fingers through her coarse black fur.

Burchard heard a thud and some uneven steps at the end of the bunk, and then Ruschmann appeared in the pale light streaming through the shutters. He had a set of wooden crutches and was hopping around to avoid putting weight on the one foot. Ruschmann peered at Fang in concern.

"Scared?" Burchard teased.

"Aren't you a little bit? She could just end you right there in your bed, and you'd be helpless," Ruschmann countered.

Burchard attempted to shrug but wasn't sure if his friend could even see the movement with Fang on top of him. "Pretty sure if she wanted me dead, I'd be dead. How's your foot?"

"Better than it was when we got here last night. Captain Thomas wants the healer to see it today. He did what he could last night but felt it wasn't a broken bone, just bruised muscles, and that sleeping would not slow down the healing process," Ruschmann explained.

Burchard tried to sit up, but Fang was not moving. "Fang, I need you to move. I can't just stay in bed all day."

The wolf licked his face from chin to forehead before hopping off the bed. Then, he was able to sit up and slide his feet out from under the covers. His arm was stiff, but thankfully the pain had reduced to just a dull throb. He glanced at Ruschmann, noting he was dressed.

"Breakfast in the hall and then a meeting with the General?" Burchard guessed.

Ruschmann nodded in agreement. "Yep, that's what Sir Daniel told me. What are you going to do about Fang?"

Burchard paused pulling his shirt over his head. "If I don't keep her with me, then someone might try to kill her. You know how people usually are about wolves. I don't think she could pass for a dog."

"And the General?" Ruschmann prompted.

Burchard tugged his shirt the rest of the way over his head and tucked it into his fur-lined pants. "I will have to make him understand why I need her." Shirt tucked in, he sat in the chair and pulled on his boots, then his coat. "Ready. Let's go find our breakfast."

Together, the two squires and black wolf headed out of the barracks and into the great hall within the castle.

16

After breakfast, Burchard and Ruschmann went directly to General Wolfensberger's office. Precariously bracing his crutches under his arms, Ruschmann knocked on the partially open door before pushing it open the rest of the way and leading the way inside.

Burchard heard a familiar cough and found himself gazing at his father, whose piercing blue eyes were so like his own.

"Squires are not permitted to have pets," the General said harshly.

Burchard met his father's eyes. "This is Fang. She is not a pet. She is my companion." *I guess he cares more about the wolf than the men we lost.*

The General opened his mouth to speak, but Sir Peter stepped forward. "Fang is worth at least two knights in battle, sir."

Frowning at Sir Peter's interruption, General Wolfensberger rocked back on his heels and seemed to be inspecting the five of them from head to toe. The silence became almost unbearable to Burchard.

"I am willing to allow…Fang…" the General said, rolling the name out as though it was distasteful, "a chance to prove herself.

Be warned. If I hear of her attacking anyone or anything within Alderth Castle, then she will be treated as wild wolves are meant to be."

Burchard bowed, deciding that until any questions were directed at him, silence would be his best way to survive this meeting without his father deciding Fang should be killed. Reggie was standing next to their father and giving him a look he could not decipher.

The General spread his hands out on the papers on top of his desk, leaning over them. "I still feel as though the details of what occurred at Camp Tooth are too murky. You encountered a dark mage who killed everyone but you five?" The General paused. "From a commander's standpoint, I can understand letting one or two people go to report to their leaders, but five…that's difficult to believe. What is it that you're not telling me?"

Hands clasped loosely in front of him, Sir Peter spoke. "The dark mage had control over the knights who resided in Camp Tooth. We were forced to fight them, and in that process, everyone but us died. The dark mage unfortunately escaped. With the three squires wounded, Sir Tiniel and I felt it prudent to return here to Alderth Castle instead of pursuing the dark mage."

"You said all three squires were injured. I was not aware Reginald had any injuries." The General cast a sideways glance at his oldest son, who kept his face blank.

"Forgive me, sir, but Squire Reginald was knocked out by one of the knights, and we were concerned he could have injured his head," Sir Daniel chimed in.

To Burchard's surprise, his brother spoke. "When they woke me up, I was very dizzy. It took a while before I felt like I could sit on a horse without falling off."

Burchard bit the inside of his lip, drawing blood. *I can't believe my brother just lied to our father's face.*

"Very well then. Sir Windemere, you said that you also suspect this dark mage is working with the Stinyian rebels?" the General asked, giving Sir Peter a very intense look.

Sir Peter seemed unfazed by the General, as though they had done this dance many times before. "Yes. I believe the dark mage was working with Walter Pell and is the reason he was at Leosor Hollows with his own camp setup and so many men."

"I will take all of this into consideration and write to the king. As you know, any major changes to my plans must be approved by His Majesty," the General said in a tone of dismissal.

"Of course. We understand," responded Sir Peter in a monotone.

Burchard looked at his knight master uncertainly. He had never heard him use that tone before. The knight shook his head at Burchard, and Burchard kept his mouth shut.

Both knights and their squires bowed to the General and departed the office. Burchard avoided his brother's eyes as they left, still not sure what to make of Reggie lying to their father. Burchard expected Sir Peter to lead them to the healer or the barracks, but the knight seemed to have another destination in mind. They walked through darkened hallways in the castle, occasionally going up or down a short flight of steps. Finally, Sir Peter halted in front of a heavy wooden door with a brass knocker on it. He banged the knocker four times, and then the door opened silently.

The four of them plus Fang filed into the chamber, and the door shut with a thud behind them. Fang growled softly, then lamps were turned up and the room was bathed in dim golden light. Three knights were in the room. Burchard recognized the faces but couldn't remember their names.

The knight in the dark-green cloak stepped forward, his curly brown hair framing his face. In the lamplight, Burchard thought the man's beard was starting to turn silver, but he was not sure. "What did the General say?"

Sir Peter frowned. "I'd like to introduce you first before we get to business. Squire Burchard and Squire Ruschmann, I'd like you to meet Sir Marcus Waldorf." The green-cloaked knight inclined his head. "Sir Lucius Foxbright." The knight in the middle with short, clipped auburn hair and beard lifted his hand in greeting.

"Sir Andre Emberwood." A young knight with light-blond hair and the barest hint of a mustache gave Burchard a wink.

"What is this about?" Burchard asked, eyeing the knights uncertainly.

"I told you when you returned from your first visit to Camp Tooth that your father likely wouldn't believe anything we told him about the cannibal knights without proof. Unfortunately for us, what happened when we all went to Camp Tooth is not, in his mind, sufficient proof," Sir Peter explained.

"But…in the meeting he said he'd contact the king," Burchard protested.

Sir Peter tsked. "I forget you have not been around him when he is in a command position. What he said in our meeting is his classic response when the explanation provided is not enough to satisfy him. It is unclear how much we said that he believes, but one thing I do know for certain is he is not going to act on the information. He might interrogate some Stinyian rebels about Walter Pell, if he can catch any. I know that tidbit spiked his interest, but as far as a dark mage or whatever Ossa is? He doesn't care. I imagine if Ossa were to appear leading an army toward the gates of Alderth Castle, he would probably believe us then. But if that were to happen…it would be too late."

Burchard scraped his toe along the stone floor. "So, what exactly is it that you think we"—he waved his arm around the room—"can do without incurring the General's wrath?"

Instead of Sir Peter answering, Sir Waldorf did. "Straight and to the point, just as you said he was," the knight said with a chuckle. "Boy, we are here because like Sir Peter and Sir Daniel, we believe that the cannibal knights and Ossa are a threat."

Burchard bristled at being called a boy. Fang's low growl rumbled through the room.

"Hush, I am not insulting you," Sir Waldorf chided. "Lucius is the head of the Trinity Page and Squire School. He has the king's ear. Regardless of what General Wolfensberger does or doesn't tell the king about Ossa, Lucius will also send along his own report. While it may not change the king's mind on what course of action to take, at least the king will have all the pertinent information. Sir Andre and I have command over ten squads apiece. He also has ties to a group of mages at Onaxx Academy and has agreed to write to them requesting assistance here in the north."

Ruschmann coughed. Everyone's gaze shifted to him. "How will this help? A couple hundred knights against an old god? What about any orders the General gives you? All of us know he executes traitors on the spot."

Lamplight making his eyes spark, Sir Waldorf replied quietly, "Would you rather face the old god and his commanders by yourself?"

Burchard wondered if this was all some trick to get them in trouble with the General. He couldn't wrap his mind around why these five knights in this room were willing to go up against his father's orders.

"Show them," Sir Daniel said tersely.

Sir Foxbright thrust a scroll in Burchard's face. "Read that. Then we will answer your questions if you still have them."

Burchard untied the scroll and unrolled it, then proceeded to read it aloud so Ruschmann would know what it said.

"Ossa and Umbra will arise to prepare the way for their master. First, men will eat men. Then, when the fields are ripe for sowing, the dead will rise. Legions of dead, infinite in number, will herald his arrival. Mors, god of death and chaos, all will bow before him."

The writing on the scroll stopped about midway down. To Burchard, it felt as though there should be more. *This is what these grown men are willing to be called traitors for? Maybe my father is right and it is all nonsense.*

He shared a glance with Ruschmann, who looked just as incredulous as he felt.

"This sounds like nonsense to me," Burchard said, handing the scroll back to Sir Foxbright.

Sir Peter sighed. "Burchard, you told me that Eos helped you escape from Camp Tooth. Then, she sent Fang to you, and you learned she is the wolf goddess. Why do you think the wolf goddess would involve herself with you if there wasn't something going on, something bigger than the Stinyian rebels?"

Burchard slowly let out his breath. "I don't know why a goddess would care about me. Who am I—or we, for that matter—to understand why the gods do anything?"

Sir Emberwood chuckled. "You do have a point, squire. However, haven't you ever been told that if any of the gods decide to make themselves known, you should pay attention?"

Burchard shook his head. "No, my father does not find value in spending time studying or worrying about the gods. They were rarely spoken about in our household."

"I suppose I shouldn't be surprised. Then let me give you some more understanding. When the gods make appearances, in Etria and throughout the world, important history-altering events tend to take place," Sir Emberwood explained.

Burchard's mind raced at the idea that the gods *did* appear to mortals—that his encounters with Eos had not been strange dreams as he had assumed but actual visions of a real in-the-flesh goddess.

"Sir Peter told us that you've informed him the wolf goddess has spoken to you several times. What did she tell you when you were sleeping outside of Camp Tooth?" Sir Emberwood prompted.

Burchard brushed stray strands of hair out of his face. "She told me to leave."

"And when you didn't leave, what happened?" Sir Emberwood pressed.

"My dream continued, and I saw a dark knight who we now know is Ossa. Then, we were attacked and…" He paused. "You know the rest of what happened already."

"See, the wolf goddess gave you a warning, which you ignored, and then you were almost killed by Ossa," Sir Emberwood said, looking Burchard directly in the eye.

Burchard rubbed the back of his neck, still not completely convinced. "You said that when gods appear, history-altering events happen. I doubt if I had died at Camp Tooth yesterday that would have been considered history-altering."

Sir Waldorf scowled. "Andre didn't mean that all encounters with a god or goddess result in history-altering events; just that when they appear, those type of things have a tendency to not be far behind." He ran his hands through his hair before peering at each occupant in the room. "Why are we getting hung up on the small details? We need to move past this and figure out what our plan is before someone comes looking for us. Lucius, you're not even supposed to be in the north."

Sir Foxbright gave the squires a forced smile before focusing on Sir Peter. "Marcus is right. What is our plan?"

Sir Peter folded his arms across his chest. "Get as many of your men close to Alderth Castle as possible. I believe Eos coming to see Burchard now that he is here in the north and Ossa's appearance at Camp Tooth cannot be a coincidence. Whether or not Ossa is going to attack the castle directly remains to be seen."

"The king has been talking about sending the pages up here to learn about the strategy that General Wolfensberger is using to launch his campaign against the Stinyian rebels. Even though I am not supposed to be here right now, I do have a legitimate reason to come back," Sir Foxbright said.

Sir Waldorf tugged on the corner of his shirt before speaking. "Andre and I have been ordered to bring our men into the castle's vicinity to prepare for the first assault against the Stinyian rebels. We should be reachable by pigeon."

"Very good. Then if Eos gives Burchard any more details, I will be sure to send word as soon as we know," Sir Peter announced.

Burchard's chest was tingling. These knights seemed convinced that they would make a difference if Ossa were to appear again. But he was not so sure. How could a couple hundred troops defeat an ancient commander of a death god? What if Mors himself showed up? Burchard still didn't understand why two gods had decided he of all people was important. *I'm just a lowly first-year squire.*

Ruschmann nudged Burchard with the end of his crutch, drawing him out of his thoughts, which grew darker with each passing moment. "We're supposed to leave first."

Burchard nodded, chewing on the inside of his cheek. He followed Ruschmann out and down the hallway. His friend took a while to figure out where they were. Soon enough, they were approaching the door to the healer's suite.

"Ah, good, I was hoping you would come, Ruschmann," said the healer with a smile. "Come sit, and we can get your ankle taken care of."

Ruschmann propped his crutches by the door and hopped over to the chair. Burchard debated if he should stay or go. Fang brushed against his leg, and he realized she was probably hungry.

"I'm going to find Fang some food."

Ruschmann gave him a wan smile as the healer had already begun poking and prodding his ankle.

17

Burchard was lost in thought, staring at the trees in the forest surrounding Alderth Castle. He was bored, and he still had one more day of taking it easy before he could go back to using his sword or bow, or practicing hand-to-hand combat. That left him with few options to entertain himself: running, riding—which he was doing now—trying to find Lady Gladys, or asking one of the servants for a task he could do. He hadn't yet offered to help in the castle, afraid they would want him to mop or sweep the floor. When he tried looking for Lady Gladys yesterday evening, she had locked herself in her room. He had heard sounds that could almost have been the clack of wooden practice swords, but he realized he must have been mistaken, because why would Lady Gladys be using a sword?

Fang had been exploring around him, checking back in every once in a while if he hadn't moved from his last position. He wasn't sure why the wolf was content to stay with him when there was a wide-open forest just outside the gate waiting for her. Just then, Fang burst through the trees, glided to a halt a few paces from Burchard on Chip, and then faced where she had just come from, almost as though she was waiting for something.

Moments later, a young woman, no more than sixteen, with loose, long brown hair came through the trees, pausing a few horse-lengths from Burchard. It took him a moment to recognize the bow strapped to her back and then the owl that was perched on a low branch close to her head.

Eyes widening in recognition, Burchard spoke. "Jade?"

Jade grinned at him. "Hello, Burchard." He watched as her eyes went from him down to Fang and back. He could see her lips form the word wolf, but the word never reached his ears. He could feel the medallion the druids had given him, a solid weight on a chain around his neck, and the horsehair bracelet around his wrist. Jade continued inspecting him, and he could feel her eyes lingering on his neck, even though the medallion wasn't visible. He wondered if that was some sort of magic the druids possessed, that they could track the medallions given as a gift.

"What are you doing here?" Burchard asked, breaking the silence and hoping it wasn't too awkward already.

"I was in the area and was hoping to see you again. You look well," Jade replied.

Burchard couldn't help himself. He laughed. "I am not permitted to swing a sword until tomorrow; I'd hardly call that in good health. Ruschmann is in even worse shape."

Irritated, Jade squared her shoulders. "I see you don't know how to take a compliment."

Burchard took a deep breath. If Jade thought well enough of him to check in, then he should not ruin their budding friendship by being mean. Those actions were what Reggie would do, and he tried with every fiber of his being to not be like his brother or father.

"Sorry, I've just been cooped up. Most of the people at the castle, including my father, don't believe our story, even though we lost a full squad of knights and were accompanied by our knight masters."

Jade's eyes sharpened. "Lost a squad to the rebels?"

Burchard shook his head. "No, they would believe me if that were the case." He pressed his lips together, unsure about telling her the rest of the tale.

Jade swung the pack from her shoulder and held it up. "I have a blanket and some snacks. Why don't you tell me what happened?"

Burchard nodded, relief flooding through him. *Jade is a druid. She knows about magic. Maybe she can help.* He dismounted and led Chip a little bit farther away. When he came back to Jade, she had a blanket spread out, and she was sitting on it. The food she had brought was on a wooden plate. "You keep a plate in your pack?"

"Don't you?" she fired back.

Burchard smiled and sat down facing her. "No. I never thought about it."

He patted the edge of the blanket, hoping Fang would join them. Fang decided to oblige his request and lay down next to him, but she kept her face trained to the trees, watching.

"How did you end up with a wolf?" Jade prompted.

"Her name is Fang. I think the wisest thing would be if I start from what happened after we left you at Leosor Hollows," Burchard said, then launched into the tale of both encounters at Camp Tooth.

When he was done, the owl who had been perched on the tree was now directly in front of him on the blanket, wings flared. He looked at Jade, not sure what the owl was doing, but Jade's focus was on it.

"What?" he asked uncertainly.

"There's a legend," Jade began.

Burchard groaned. *Not another legend!*

"Do you have a problem with legends?"

"Only that they all seem far-fetched," Burchard muttered.

Jade clucked her tongue before continuing. "As I was saying… there is a legend about a man with a wolf companion who faced Ossa and Umbra and prevailed, preventing Mors from being able to rise again."

Burchard growled. "A legend is a story of past deeds, right? Not a prediction of future events like a prophecy."

Jade nodded. "Yes, that is true. But if you'll let me finish, I will get to that part. There is a *prophecy* in the druid lore that the man with the wolf companion will return when things are dire and Ossa and Umbra once again walk the world. Damos can recite it for you if you need to hear the full thing."

Burchard chafed. "I am a fourteen-year-old squire. I am not a man, certainly no mage. There's no way that I can be the person in the legend or prophecy."

"Of course," Jade murmured soothingly. "As you said, it's just a story." She scooted closer to Burchard so their shoulders were touching. The owl returned to her perch in the tree. "When you mentioned your brother, you sounded worried that he had joined Ossa. Is that something you would suspect him of doing?"

Burchard raised his eyebrow. "Reggie and I don't have the best relationship, but I feel confident he would not betray Etria." He was about to add how terrible his brother behaved toward him but decided to omit that information.

"Do you have any sisters?" Jade inquired.

Burchard chuckled. "I thought you knew everything about me. Shouldn't you know I have an older sister?"

Jade shrugged. "I never said I knew everything. Females in Etria are not treated the same way as they are in Mootia and other countries. You don't have any stories of female warriors, do you?"

"No…" Burchard replied.

"See, you just proved my point," Jade said, nudging him with her shoulder.

"Or you just proved that I don't read stories about female warriors," Burchard muttered to himself. His fingers trailed through Fang's coarse fur.

Jade laid her hand on his knee and gave it a squeeze, drawing his attention back to her face, which was now very close to his. He could see the exact shade of green of her eyes. He felt a flush creep up his cheeks.

"I really like you, Burchard," she said softly.

Before he could ask her what she was doing, Jade leaned in, and her lips met his. His whole body tensed in surprise. He felt like his heart was going to leap out of his chest, it was pounding so hard. She was practically in his lap, and he wasn't sure what to do.

At that moment, Fang stood up and shoved herself between the two of them, seemingly oblivious to what she had just interrupted. Burchard was grateful to the wolf and buried his face into her fur.

Until Jade's words caused him to lift his head. "I've been wanting to see what it would be like to kiss you since I first laid eyes on you," Jade replied matter-of-factly.

Eyebrow arched, he said, "Really?" Burchard never let himself dwell much on girls or kissing. He had one goal: finish his four years as a squire and become a knight. Then, when he was his own man, he could worry about finding a girl.

If I even have a say in that matter. It'll most likely be an arranged marriage, he reminded himself. He knew other squires did things with girls—even Ru had hinted of the things he'd done with his girl back at Port Riverdale—but they also sometimes ended up with more drama on their hands than it was worth.

"Is it so hard to believe that a girl would want to kiss you?" Jade inquired. "You are an expert swordsman, have had many successes in battle, and are nice to look at."

Burchard shrugged, his face heating up even more. *She thinks I'm nice to look at? What does that even mean?* he wondered. Instead of meeting Jade's gaze, he picked a spot on the tree behind her. "Why are you *really* here?"

"I told you that already. I was in the area, and I wanted to see you. No other reason." She raised her hand. "I swear."

Burchard let the silence fall around them, not sure how to respond to Jade. He couldn't decide if he wanted to kiss her again or even how he had felt after her kiss. A light breeze ruffled the few leaves left in the trees. High above them, squirrels tittered, and even higher they could hear birds calling. *Everyone has begun winter preparations,* he thought.

An idea came to him. Maybe Jade had information she could share with his father about other matters. "Have you found any more rebel camps after the one run by Walter Pell?"

Jade shook her head. "No, but Damos took us farther into the mountains. He doesn't think we should go home yet, but he felt like being so close to the brewing conflict between Etria and the Stinyian rebels was not within our best interests."

"What do you do when you're not fighting rebels?" he asked, genuinely curious. *This is a safer topic,* he mused.

Jade shrugged. "The usual. Train in weapons and magic, and then we hunt for our food."

"Have you traveled to many places?" Burchard asked. He dreamed of traveling. He knew the odds of it ever coming to fruition were slim. As a knight, he would be sent wherever the conflict was.

A smile formed on Jade's lips. "A little bit. We live in the country of Mootia. In the far west. I have been everywhere it is possible to go in Mootia and in most of Etria. I also was in Sneg once, but that was a long time ago and I don't remember much."

Burchard closed his eyes, trying to recall what he knew about those places. Slowly the information came back to him. "Mootia is a land of green grass and cows. In some places, the grazing areas seem to stretch forever. Sneg has mountains with tall peaks and snow deeper than a full-size man in winter. Moose are also said to only be found in Sneg." He opened his eyes, feeling certain he had forgotten some other tidbits from his reading.

Jade was staring at him. "You actually know about Mootia?"

Burchard shrugged. "I make it a habit to learn about places and people that I could one day interact with."

Jade blinked a few times. "Very unusual. But I appreciate your effort. It is far more than most people would ever attempt."

"You're not the first to tell me that," Burchard murmured, blushing again. He hesitated, debating if he should ask the question that had been nagging at him since they'd met at Leosor Hollows. "Can you tell me more about the druids?"

"Of course," Jade said, smiling again. The owl fluttered down to the blanket again. Burchard wasn't sure why. "Liala wants to make sure I don't forget the important parts."

Eyebrow raised, Burchard looked uncertainly at Jade. "Who is Liala?"

"The owl. I told you that the last time we met," Jade replied. "She is a druid. Some of us can shapeshift. But…let's not get sidetracked." She paused, moistening her lips with her tongue. "Druids. In general, we are a peaceful people and spend much of our time as caretakers of the land. Our magic is nature based. Many are drawn to plants and trees, with fewer to animals. Just like in Etria, weather magic is rare, but not unheard of, since weather is a natural force. Some druids are human, and others, like Damos, are different. Centaurs as you know are half horse, half human; however, it is not necessary to be part human to be a druid. In fact, many are wholly in animal forms."

"You mean there are horses that are druids?" Burchard asked.

Jade shook her head. "No, if you see a horse that is a druid, it is a shapeshifted one. I meant animal forms such as a unicorn, griffin, dragon, and more. Individuals who are often far more intelligent than any human."

"You say that as though you know some personally." Burchard struggled to believe what Jade was saying. *Dragons are real?* He ran his hand along Fang's back. *I suppose if I believe that the wolf goddess exists and gave me Fang, then accepting that a dragon is real would not be as big of a stretch as I would have thought a few weeks ago.*

Jade gave him a toothy smile. "Yes, back home in Mootia, there is a herd of unicorns and a mated pair of griffins that we share our land with. I haven't seen a dragon, but I know there is one somewhere in Sneg."

"How do you know they're all druids? Do they have a sign hanging around their necks that says 'I'm a druid!'?" Burchard asked, his face serious.

Jade giggled, then it turned into a full-throated belly laugh.

Burchard once again turned beet red in embarrassment. "You… you…"

Jade could barely stop laughing to speak. "You think they wear… signs?" She grabbed her stomach, holding it as she rolled over on the blanket laughing. Burchard couldn't help himself; he started laughing too, and soon they were both rolling around on the blanket, grabbing their sides.

Jade sat up, still grinning, but finally done laughing. "To answer your question, our magic allows us to identify each other. Usually, a druid who does not have a mouth capable of forming words in one of the human languages is able to speak mind to mind. Or if that's not the case, they will seek out a druid, like me, who can interpret for them." Jade picked up a piece of jerky and chewed on it slowly, as though she had tired of talking.

Burchard waited a few minutes, but she did not continue speaking. "Is that why Liala is with you…because you can help her communicate when she is in her owl form?"

Jade nodded. "Partly, yes. She also got stuck as an owl and is unable to shift."

To Burchard's surprise, Liala suddenly clamped her beak on Jade's index finger, drawing blood. Jade glared at the owl. "She didn't want me to tell you she is stuck in her shape."

"I can't help her, so I don't know why it matters if I know or don't know," Burchard said softly.

Jade bit her lip. "To us druids, if you are stuck in a shape, then it is a major vulnerability. It is not something that is shared lightly. I trust you, but Liala thinks that because you are not willing to believe the prophecy, you should not be trusted."

Burchard studied the owl and directed his next question to her. "Do you find that when someone tells you something that goes against everything you've ever believed, you immediately take their word for it?"

Liala flared her wings briefly, then became too busy preening to look at him directly. Jade to her credit didn't say anything, letting Liala's behavior speak for her.

Burchard snagged a branch that was digging at him under the blanket and then pulled out his pocketknife. He whittled the stick, only half paying attention to what he was doing—just enough to be sure he wouldn't accidentally slice open his fingers. "If druids are primarily concerned with being caretakers of the land, then why are you, Liala, and the centaurs here in Etria? I know we don't have any sort of alliance with the druids. I am not even sure King Roland is aware you exist."

Jade twirled a strand of her hair in her fingers. "It has to do the with the prophecy, the one I tried to tell you about earlier that you said was nonsense. Bits and pieces of other prophecies link to that one and talk about where certain things will take place and that we need to be there, otherwise Mors will certainly rise again."

"You just blindly believe the prophecy is true?" Burchard asked.

"We're not following it blindly. This is what we as a people believe in, that prophecies do exist, and they can come true. As long as your actions don't directly conflict with my…the druids' ability to follow the prophecy, then whether or not you believe is irrelevant," Jade said quietly.

Burchard peered up at the sky and realized that the sun was beginning to set. He hadn't thought they'd been there that long, but he knew time passed quicker when you were busy than when you were bored with nothing to do. "I need to get back before they shut the gate for the night." He was tempted to ask if she would be around the next day but couldn't decide if he wanted to see her again. She had definitely given him a lot to think about.

"I should head back too," Jade said, standing up. Liala flew back into the tree. Burchard swiftly folded the blanket and handed it to Jade before snagging Chip's reins. The mare had been dozing off and on during their conversation. She nibbled at his shirt, presumably eager to get back for her dinner too.

Burchard swung his leg over the saddle. "Thanks for the conversation." Then he steered Chip away and back to the castle. *Why couldn't I come up with anything better to say? I surely sounded like an idiot.*

He clucked urging Chip into a trot, hoping a hot meal would help clear his head.

Burchard settled Chip into the stable with a hot bran mash before finding his way into the dining hall. To his pleasure, Ruschmann was just ahead of him. He studied his friend's back and realized something was missing. "Where are your crutches?"

Ruschmann chuckled and peered over his shoulder at Burchard as they both got in line for food. "When you left me earlier, I was with the healer. Well, he used his magic and was able to repair most of the damage to my foot. He told me since he could use his magic it would be better; otherwise, the amount of time I wouldn't be able to put weight on my foot would set my training very far back."

"How long do you have to wait then?" Burchard asked.

"Tomorrow. We will be able to start practicing together," Ruschmann said, then began to fill his plate.

Burchard followed his friend down the table laden with food. When they reached the end, he had a few slices of wild boar, fresh bread, and an assortment of cooked vegetables. Inhaling deeply, he could feel his mouth watering in anticipation of the meal. They chose seats toward the end of a long table that was currently vacant.

When they were done eating, they sat at the table in companionable silence, sipping water from their mugs.

"What did you do today while I was with the healer?" Ruschmann inquired.

Burchard blushed, earning a smirk from Ruschmann.

"Did you kiss Lady Gladys?"

Burchard growled and smacked his friend's arm. "No! I told you before, Lady Gladys and I are just friends."

"Hmmm," Ruschmann said, tapping his fingers on his mug. "Then the only other girl we've seen recently would be Jade."

Ruschmann must have caught Burchard's lip twitch because he grinned broadly. "You kissed Jade?"

"Yes," Burchard said softly, sure his face was bright red. He could feel even his ears heating up and was grateful his hair was long enough to hide them.

"Are you going to kiss her again?" Ruschmann teased.

Burchard stuck his tongue out at his friend. "I don't know. She said I'd see her again. I haven't decided if I want to kiss her again."

"Hopefully you decide before you see her again," Ruschmann replied.

Burchard growled. He wasn't sure he wanted to keep discussing kissing Jade, not when he hadn't had a chance to think about his own feelings on the matter. He pushed his chair back from the table and took his plates over to the dirty dish bin.

Ruschmann followed him in silence. By the time they made it back to the barracks, he could tell his friend was having trouble staying silent. "What?" he asked grumpily.

"Well, I was just thinking, you saw Jade, and Sir Peter had some questions for the druids. Did you ask her anything?" Ruschmann asked.

Burchard sighed, "I really don't feel like talking about it now. It has been a long day. I'd like to get some sleep."

Ruschmann bowed his head and went to his bunk in silence. Burchard knew he had been short with his friend, but he just needed time to himself. He let out a sharp laugh, realizing that earlier, before he'd run into Jade, he had been bored and hoping for something to do.

I'm hopeless, he thought to himself.

Fang must have slipped inside the barracks because she brushed up against him, then jumped on his bed and fell asleep. *Fang has the right idea.* He undressed and then slid under his blankets, relishing Fang's warmth against his usually chilly sheets. He fell asleep almost instantly.

18

It was the third day after the meeting in General Wolfensberger's office, and clearly the General was not going to do anything about Camp Tooth. Burchard was running around the perimeter of Alderth Castle with Fang, her tongue lolling out of the side of her mouth and keeping pace easily beside him. Part of him hoped he'd run into Jade again; the other part hoped she would stay away. Their conversation had taken time to sink in and for him to realize that she was right. It didn't matter if he accepted that the prophecy existed or might even refer to him. What he was certain of was that the druids had a vested interest in finding and defeating Ossa. He had allies who were not subject to his father's authority or that of the king.

Burchard also had not figured out whether or not he wanted to kiss Jade again. He had admitted the kiss felt nice, but now was not the time or place to explore if it would turn into anything more.

The stiffness that had settled into his arm was finally gone, and Burchard was planning to do some light sword exercises after his run. The General was preparing to depart tomorrow with the majority of the men to engage the Stinyian rebels near Dry Bridge. After sneaking a peek at the map, Burchard had to admit his father's choice of battleground was a smart one. The Etrians would have the advantage of the high ground on the south side of the bridge. As long as the rebels didn't provoke the General to follow them into Dry Valley, the Etrians would likely keep the upper hand.

The decision also meant that there would be very few people left at Alderth Castle. Sir Waldorf and Sir Emberwood had been ordered to meet the General with all the men they had at Dry Bridge. They had tried to wheedle out of the order, but the General had given them an ultimatum: either they showed up or they would be executed as traitors when the battle was over.

Even with that unfortunate turn of events, Burchard had also learned that King Roland had indeed granted Sir Foxbright permission to bring the pages up to Alderth Castle, and they were expected to arrive late tomorrow evening.

I am not even sure how they are supposed to learn anything from the General if he's not here. I suppose I should be grateful Sir Foxbright's part of the plan is working in our favor.

Just at the end of the fourth lap, Burchard led Fang back inside. His whole body was pleasantly warm from the run. The castle yard was a flurry of activity, and he found himself having to weave and duck between people who were so focused on their tasks they weren't looking where they were going. When he made it to the edge of the yard closest to the training area, he pivoted and watched as two of the castle staff walked straight into each other. The basket of bread the woman was carrying spilled, sending small loaves and rolls everywhere. The bundle of medical supplies landed with a splat in a puddle and sprayed both in icy brown mud.

It took a split second for him to realize he should go help. He took off toward them at a jog and helped pick up the bread, using his shirt as a basket. When he reached them, he realized it was Lady Gladys and Captain Thomas.

"Are you two OK?" he asked with concern.

Lady Gladys sighed. "Yes, we're fine. The bread is ruined, but Captain Thomas thinks the medical supplies stayed dry since they're wrapped in leather."

"What do you want me to do with the bread?" Burchard asked, raising his makeshift shirt basket slightly.

"My basket is no good," Lady Gladys held up the basket, which was split in half. "If you don't mind carrying the rolls, we can go give them to the chickens. At least they won't mind the mud."

"Sure thing," Burchard said, nodding.

Lady Gladys led the way to the pen with the chickens. They were kept separate from the ducks because otherwise the ducks would break the chicken eggs, which had thinner shells. She waved a hand at the wooden trough where some old corn cobs had been deposited last night.

Burchard carefully emptied the rolls out of his shirt. The chickens began squawking as soon as the first one noticed the food. Burchard had to step away, the noise got so loud.

Lady Gladys giggled. "Too loud for you?"

Burchard nodded. "Yes! How do you stand it?"

Lady Gladys shrugged. "The same way you don't mind the smell of horses. Over time, you just get used to it."

In the distance, a bell rang. Burchard groaned. "I really need to go. Sir Peter is waiting. I'll see you 'round!"

Without waiting for her response, he took off at a jog back toward the training yard.

Sir Peter was waiting for him. "Let's see how your arm feels. I want to at least make sure that you can use your sword before we leave."

Burchard gave his knight master a sharp glance. "Leave?"

Sir Peter let out a heavy sigh, face expressionless. "I got orders that we are riding out, along with Sir Daniel, when the General departs."

"Then we're all going, right?" Burchard asked.

Sir Peter nodded. "Yes, you and Ruschmann get to come too. Now let's see how your sword arm feels after having a few days off. Ruschmann will be joining us to test out his ankle as well."

Burchard smiled. *We're finally going to get to do something useful while the General is present, so he will actually believe it happened.* "I will meet you there. I want to run a quick lap to finish my warm up."

Sir Peter nodded in approval, and Burchard took off at a run out the main gate. The first third of his lap was at fifty percent of his speed, the second at seventy five percent, and the final third at full speed. He found if he was using the running as a warm-up that ramping up how fast he was going instead of hitting full speed immediately seemed to have a better effect.

When Burchard made it back to the training yard, Ruschmann and Sir Peter were waiting. Sir Daniel was in a discussion with some other knights at the edge of the ring.

Burchard took a sip of water from his canteen and then set it down and stepped into the middle of the marked circle. Together the squires went through the basic drills, warming up with high, low, and middle blocks and strikes.

"Ready?" Ruschmann asked as he reset his feet and shook out his arms.

"Yep," replied Burchard. "One, two, three!"

Ruschmann started with a quick high and low strike combination, forcing Burchard on the defensive. Burchard let his friend lead for a few moments before giving his wrist a twist and sliding his sword up Ruschmann's. The metal screeched. He then rocked back on his right heel before shifting his weight onto his left foot and striking low, then doing a backhand sweep toward Ruschmann's middle. His friend hastily brought his sword up to block.

Burchard stepped to the right and executed another high-low combination, forcing Ruschmann to give up his space, before he recovered. Strike and parry, back and forth the squires went, neither gaining the advantage again. Burchard could feel sweat trickling down his back as they moved around the ring. He knew today was not intended for either one to push their limits. They just wanted to get a good practice in.

"And time!" announced Sir Daniel, walking toward the two squires.

Burchard and Ruschmann stepped backward in unison, swords lowered. Sir Daniel inspected each squire. "How did that feel?"

"Good," both replied.

"Excellent! You can have a few minutes' break, and then I want to see you over by the archery targets," Sir Daniel commanded.

Burchard sheathed his sword and snagged his canteen from the ground. He greedily guzzled about half of its contents before stopping. "Archery, eh?" he murmured.

Ruschmann shrugged. They headed over to the archery targets. Neither squire had brought their bows, and Burchard belatedly wondered if they should have gone back to the barracks to retrieve them. He started to change directions when he heard Sir Daniel's voice.

"You don't need your bows. We're doing something else."

Interest piqued, Burchard turned back toward Sir Daniel. As he approached the knight, his gaze went to the table next to Sir Daniel. It was covered in small, identical knives with hilts wrapped in strips of leather.

"You're going to teach us how to throw?" Ruschmann said incredulously.

"Absolutely. There is no rule that says squires aren't permitted to learn how to use throwing knives," Sir Daniel explained patiently.

Burchard picked up one of the small knives and ran his finger over the blade, testing it. It was not as sharp as he had expected. Sir Daniel must have noticed what he was doing because he chuckled.

"You didn't think I was going to let you try throwing them for the first time with sharp battle-ready blades, did you?"

Burchard looked away in embarrassment.

Sir Daniel said, "I am going to show you in steps. How you hold the knife and the motion of throwing it."

The knight selected a knife from the table and used a hammer grip on the handle with the blade pointing away from him. Burchard made note of the position of Sir Daniel's thumb—over the top, with the other four fingers wrapped around the handle. The knight set the knife down and picked it up several times, making sure the squires saw how he was gripping it. He set it down one more time and stepped away from them so he would have space.

"Now for the throw, we will try close range first," Sir Daniel explained. He then bent his wrist slowly back toward his forearm. He repeated that motion several times before adjusting his stance, putting his weight on his right leg since it was his dominant one, and raising his right arm perpendicular to the ground and bent at the elbow. The knight then shifted his weight from his right to left legs, creating the forward momentum needed so that when combined with swinging the forearm forward, the knife could be released in a straight line.

"Let me show you with a couple of knives, and then you can try first without a knife a couple of times and then with a knife," Sir Daniel said. He threw three knives. Burchard assumed that the knight could throw them way faster than he was for the demonstration, but he appreciated the slow speed because it allowed him to study the motions of the throw.

"OK, let's give this a try," said Burchard eagerly.

Sir Daniel nodded in encouragement as both squires went through the motion of the throw several times, then demonstrated they understood how to hold the knife properly.

"I think you are ready to try it," Sir Daniel said.

Burchard picked up a knife and set his feet so his weight was back on his right dominant leg. He adjusted his grip slightly on the knife and then, focusing on his target, swung his right arm out in front of himself and released the knife. It traveled in a fairly straight line but fell short of the target. Ruschmann tried and had the same issue.

"Everything you did was correct. You just need a little bit more power behind the throw to get the extra distance you need," Sir Daniel explained.

Burchard nodded. It made sense since he had decided to not get too carried away with the amount of power he put into a throw until he was more familiar with this type of weapon. He reset himself, closed his eyes, and took a deep breath. When he opened them, he tuned everything out except the center of the target. He swung his arm down, and everything was perfectly straight. He watched the knife sail through the air far faster than it had last time. It went over the top of the target and kept going. Eyes wide in horror, Burchard watched his knife glance off a knight in plate armor, a knight who happened to be walking somewhere no one was supposed to be—behind the targets. He began growling, at himself more than anyone else, at his stupidity.

"Who threw the knife?" roared General Wolfensberger.

Burchard felt the blood draining from his face. *I threw a knife at my father.* Beside him, he could hear Ruschmann muttering curses. Burchard kept his eyes trained on the ground, dread growing at what would happen when the General reached them.

"You!" snarled the General.

Burchard looked up, meeting his father's gaze. "Sorry, sir. My intent was not to hit anyone."

"Your intent?" sputtered General Wolfensberger. "Why would you be throwing knives at all? That is not a skill that is necessary for squires *or* knights to have."

Sir Daniel opened his mouth to say something, but the General waved him away. "Because of your utter disregard for the people around you, neither one of you will be permitted to join us when we depart to fight the rebels."

Ruschmann wisely stayed silent. Burchard waited for his father to say something else, to dole out a punishment even harsher than being left behind. But it never came. Instead his father turned his attention to Sir Daniel. Burchard stood there staring at the ground and listening to their discussion.

"I don't know what possessed you to teach these two squires to throw knives, but it is not a skill they need. Because of your thoughtlessness, they will now stay here with the pages instead of getting experience in a battle campaign. You and Sir Windemere, however, will still be required to come with the rest of us. Do not disappoint me again, or there will be much more severe consequences," the General said coldly.

Burchard kept his eyes on the ground until he heard his father move away.

"I'm sorry," said Sir Daniel. "I didn't expect the General to be nearby when we started. If I had known, then I could have waited to teach you this."

Burchard met the knight's gaze. He could see how upset the knight was at having put the squires in this position. "He didn't whip us."

"Yes, I suppose that is consolation. I know he enjoys punishing you in that manner. Anyhow, I will put the throwing knives away, and the two of you can go do something else for a while. I'd recommend staying clear of the General though, lest he changes his mind about your punishment," Sir Daniel said calmly.

"See you later, sir," Burchard said with a bow and departed.

The next morning was surprisingly warm. Burchard was heading to the training yard to begin his morning sword work when he crossed paths with Sir Peter.

"I'm sorry that you have been ordered to stay here and help with the pages when they arrive," Sir Peter said in a soft voice.

Shoulders slumped forward, Burchard felt as though all the energy had been sucked out of him. *His father didn't believe he deserved a place on the battlefield, again, but Reggie would be there at the General's side, no doubt.* "We get to babysit," he uttered.

Sir Peter reached a hand out and squeezed Burchard's shoulder. "I know you're unhappy, but it is out of my control. I tried, trust me—I tried to get him to change his mind. Nothing I said would sway him."

Mutely, Burchard took his sword and walked to the training yard, wanting to lose himself in his sword work and not waste another thought on his father.

Sweat trickled down his back and arms. Burchard could feel the familiar burn as he went through exercise after exercise, his muscles protesting at how long he had been working. Finally, Burchard lowered his sword. His canteen was on a strap hanging on the fence post. As he reached for it, he heard a delicate cough behind him.

Turning slowly, he met Lady Gladys's gaze and offered her a tentative smile. "Hi."

"This is for you," she said and shoved the tray she was holding into his arms.

He studied its contents, but when he looked back up to thank her, she was gone. Burchard glanced at Fang. *What was that about?* he wondered, then shrugged. *I'll have to see if I can play cards with her soon to make up for whatever upset her.*

Burchard found a bench and sat down, placing the tray carefully beside him. There was a roll studded with raisins and dusted in cinnamon, some sort of jam tart, and a small strip of raw meat.

"I think this is yours," he said, setting the plate of raw meat on the ground. Fang gobbled it up and then proceeded to wash the plate. They had been regularly hunting outside of the castle, so he knew she wasn't truly hungry, but he was touched that Lady Gladys had been kind enough to bring something for the wolf. Most of the people in the castle ran in the other direction when Burchard and Fang approached, their fear of wolves too long ingrained to be casually forgotten.

Instead of worrying about why Lady Gladys vanished so quickly, Burchard picked up the roll and took a bite. It was still warm. He savored the taste of the cinnamon and raisins and some other flavors he couldn't identify. He shut his eyes as he chewed. He felt Fang place her muzzle on his knee. He cracked his eye open.

"Do you want some?" he asked, offering her a piece of the bread. Fang sneezed and backed up a few steps. Burchard laughed. "That's what I thought."

He made quick work of the roll and the jam tart. When he was done, Burchard was ready to continue his sword practice. The healer wanted him to focus on stretching and strength exercises. Burchard was lost in his thoughts about different sword combinations when he heard a cough. He whirled, hand instinctively going to his sword.

"Are you going to stab me?" taunted Reggie.

Burchard bit the inside of his cheek to keep the retort that came so easily from passing his lips. He hadn't spoken to his brother since their strange encounter at Camp Tooth, and he was hesitant to believe that Ossa doing some sort of mind control was enough of a jolt to cure Reggie of his hatred for him.

"What do you want?" Burchard replied, keeping his voice even.

"I heard that you can use a sword today. I thought I would come spar with you before I have to go," Reggie said in a tone Burchard hadn't heard in a long time. It was almost as if he cared that they likely wouldn't see each other for a few weeks. *How odd.*

"Yes, I can use a sword today." Unwilling to openly invite his brother to spar, Burchard skipped that step and asked the next pertinent question. "Have you warmed up already?"

Reggie nodded. "Yes, I was just practicing with my bow before I came over here. I'm all warmed up."

"All right then." Burchard swung his sword a few times before stepping into position in the middle of the ring.

When Reggie was ready, they crossed swords. "One. Two. Three."

On three, Reggie sidestepped to the left before using a sweeping uppercut. The first thing Burchard noticed was the speed of the strike. Typically, Reggie came at him hard and fast. This strike, at least, was not that way. It was at a moderate speed, as one would expect at the beginning of a sparring match. Burchard smoothly brought his sword up, blocking, and then with a twist of his arm, disengaged their swords and parried, striking at his brother's middle. And so the match went, neither brother gaining nor losing much ground.

Burchard couldn't believe that his brother was behaving like a proper squire and was not out for his blood. Since it was only his second day back, Burchard had been hoping to not have to push himself to his limits. Sweat trickled down his back and neck. He gazed at Reggie, assessing what his next move was and taking note of any weaknesses. The sweat was rolling down his brother's face. Burchard grinned wolfishly at his brother before beginning his combination. Low right, feint high left backhand, swap to left hand, and finish with a sweeping undercut from the left. For this move, he added slightly more speed than they'd been practicing with. His brother was blinking rapidly, trying to clear the sweat out of his eyes, and didn't realize Burchard had feinted. Instead, he fell right into the trap, and the end of Burchard's sword caressed his brother's exposed throat.

"I yield," Reggie said softly, amusement dancing in his eyes. "Thank you. This was fun."

Eyebrows raised, Burchard, hesitated a second before replying. "It was."

"I'm…I'm sorry for before. It's just…Father pushes us both so hard. Sometimes it's hard to let go of old feelings," Reggie explained, catching Burchard off guard again.

He had not expected his brother to be civil or to ever offer him an explanation about his past behavior. Burchard couldn't wrap his mind around it. He sheathed his sword, then glanced at his brother. "Good luck. Against the rebels, I mean."

Reggie gave him a slight smile and a two-fingered salute. "Thanks, brother."

Burchard watched as Reggie walked toward the barracks. Then, Sir Peter walked over. "That went well."

Burchard glanced at his knight master. "Not what I expected."

"Maybe the encounter with Ossa made him realize the error of his ways," Sir Peter pointed out.

"Perhaps. But after six years of being treated like I'm worthless to him, I struggle to believe that one moment in his life has made such an impact," Burchard responded.

"How do you feel?" Sir Peter asked, his eyes roving over the squire as though looking for any outward sign that the sparring had pushed him too hard, too soon.

Burchard shrugged. "Like I had the perfect amount of exercise and that if I continued it would not go well."

Sir Peter smiled. "Good, I'm glad you are in tune enough with your body and the training to be able to judge what is enough or too much. Walk with me." Sir Peter started walking away before Burchard realized his knight master had asked him to come along. "When the pages come, I hope you will practice with them and help them if they are making mistakes. It is a good opportunity for you to work with others close to your age. One day, when you're knights, it's likely you'll be fighting side by side."

Burchard gave Sir Peter a confused look. "You don't want me to befriend all of them, do you?"

Sir Peter chuckled. "No that is not what I am saying. I just wanted to encourage you to work with them. Be friendly. People *remember* how you treat them, Burchard."

Burchard snorted. "I'm not going to bite them."

"Make sure they know that," Sir Peter said gently.

19

Burchard walked into the dining hall, which, like the rest of Alderth Castle, was strangely silent. The pages were supposed to arrive soon, which would help fill the void some. He'd never been at the castle when it was empty and never realized how much he enjoyed the buzz of knights and infantry going about their tasks. Shaking his head, he made a beeline for the table in the back that had a small assortment of food laid out: a basket of rolls, a platter with slices of cold meat, and a pot of stew. There was also a stack of plates and cups full of utensils. With the General and the officers gone, he knew that the meals would be far more relaxed. Or at least he hoped they would be. He didn't know Sir Foxbright or if he would demand the castle staff revert to formal meals upon his arrival.

Burchard was just finishing his last bite of stew when there was a commotion at the doors to the dining hall. They finally pushed open and a group of pages stumbled in and then landed in a heap. An amused smile tugged at his lips. *Eager bunch*. Burchard picked up his plate and set it on the second table along the wall for dirty dishes. Then, he made his way down toward the pages. By the time he got there, they were bunched together in a group. Some gazed at him with awe, others with indifference.

"There's food waiting on the table in the back," Burchard said, motioning behind him.

The pages surged forward around him, some almost running in their eagerness to reach the food. The last page in the group paused before him.

"Burchard," he said with a slight smile.

Burchard gazed at the page in surprise. *I forgot about my brother.* Frustration bubbled up in him. He bit his lip in an effort to keep it from his voice, since it was not directed at his brother, but at himself. "Theodore."

"You forgot," Theodore Wolfensberger said, green eyes locked with blue.

Burchard blew out his breath slowly. "I'm sorry, I did forget."

Theodore shrugged. "It's not a big deal. You have important duties as a squire that I'm sure keep you busy."

Burchard grimaced at the reminder. "It's not an excuse. I'll make it up to you, I promise. For now, let's get you some hot food."

He slung his arm over Theodore's shoulder, and together they walked in companionable silence to the table with food. Burchard had never been very close with his younger brother. Theodore was only training to become a knight because their father had insisted. He would have preferred to help manage the family castle than learn about weapons. Still, he had spent two years with him at the Trinity Page School. He shouldn't have forgotten.

More pages found their way into the dining hall until at last Sir Foxbright came in. Burchard hid his surprise, raising his hand as though to cover a sneeze, when the knight shut the door behind him. Burchard had been expecting more instructors to come since *all* the pages were here. He knew it wasn't his place to question, so he would not voice his concern aloud, but one knight to manage forty pages for who knew how long seemed unfair.

Father can command thousands of knights without needing officers. How hard can it be to manage forty pages? he reminded himself. *I guess I should see what techniques Sir Foxbright uses to keep the pages in line.*

Although he wasn't hungry, Burchard's curiosity about Sir Foxbright got the better of him. He went to the back of the line of pages and selected a roll, then found himself a seat.

A small boy—*page,* he corrected himself—sat in the seat to his left. The boy had deep red hair that stuck out every which way. Given his size, Burchard assumed the page was a first-year. To his right was another small page with curly black hair, although he wasn't quite as tiny as the redhead. Across the table from him were some clearly older pages who looked about twelve, Theodore's age. Burchard nibbled on his roll and tried to look relaxed. He wasn't sure how many of the pages remembered him since he'd only been a squire for about four months. Burchard had only been close to Ruschmann when he was a page. None of the others bothered to get to know him.

Not that I did anything to encourage them to get to know me, he thought.

A tug on his left shirt sleeve had him gazing into the light-brown eyes of the redheaded page. "Hello," he said.

"Hi!" said the page excitedly. "You're Burchard Wolfensberger, right?"

Burchard felt his lips starting to curve upward in a smile. "Yes, I am. Who are you?"

The page stuck his hand out, banging his shoulder into Burchard's. "I'm Armand. Pleased to meet you."

Burchard took the offered hand. "Burchard. Nice to meet you too. How do you know who I am?"

Armand gave him a broad smile. "Oh, everyone knows who you are. Especially after your last year as a page when you bested Sir Luther Fernwood during your final fourth-year sword test."

Burchard grimaced. He'd been trying to forget that test.

Sir Fernwood had entered the sparring circle confident and cocky. Burchard was the second-to-last fourth-year, and Sir Fernwood had already had gone against two other pages who quickly crumbled under his aggressive sword work. But Burchard had been watching Sir Fernwood, and he had been ready. The knight had some tells. He'd rock back on his right foot just before he would do an upper strike, and he would roll his left shoulder before pivoting. Burchard knew that he had to prove to his instructors he deserved to be promoted to a squire, so he couldn't just quickly defeat Sir Fernwood. He had to ensure they had time to evaluate his skill set.

Which meant that for his test he played a game of cat and mouse with Sir Fernwood. Letting the knight get in a strike here or there, making it seem as though Sir Fernwood was better at sword work and that Burchard's moves were more out of luck than skill. He could feel sweat trickling down his back and threatening to loosen his grip on his sword. When Burchard had felt certain that the demonstration had gone on long enough, he struck hard and fast. Sir Fernwood was caught off guard and barely had time to block Burchard's rapid set of high and low strikes. He then swapped his sword to his left hand and performed a sweeping uppercut, switched back to his right, feinted to the left, and pivoted. Sir Fernwood, sword waving wildly through the air but not accomplishing anything, failed at blocking Burchard's sword as it swept up and caressed his neck.

Burchard felt light tug on his sleeve. "Are you OK?" Armand asked with concern.

Burchard squeezed his eyes shut then opened them. "Yes, I'm fine. I was just…remembering." A shudder went through him as he recalled the rage in his father's eyes when he had looked up at him after Sir Foxbright had declared he had passed his test. He had known the General would react this way if Burchard used the sword skills he had and defeated Sir Fernwood. The General considered defeating an individual who is a higher training level or rank than one's own as being disrespectful, regardless of how difficult such a feat would be. Just as he had reacted when he had seen Burchard defeat Reggie the day he was leaving to become a page.

"Are you sure? You keep getting the strangest look on your face," Armand queried.

Burchard frowned. "Yes, I'm sure. Just a bad memory is all."

"How would passing your fourth-year test be a bad memory?" Armand asked.

Burchard gaped at him, wondering how the page had known what he was thinking about. "If you knew about my relationship with my father you would understand," he muttered, then clamped his lips shut before he said anything else—anything that would earn him a whipping if his father heard about it.

"If he wasn't proud of you for that test, then he must not know how amazing you are," Armand declared.

"You were there?" Burchard asked suspiciously.

Armand laughed. "Of course I was there, silly! My father is Sir Foxbright. He wanted me to see how the year-end tests went so that I would know what to expect for the next four years. Seriously though, the way you executed your test was absolutely brilliant. How did you know what to expect?"

Burchard shrugged. "I have learned to observe my opponents if possible. If you study someone long enough you can discover any tells or weaknesses and then use them to your advantage."

"Can you teach me?" Armand asked eagerly.

Burchard looked away. *This page doesn't even know me, and he wants me to teach him. I should say no, but...I can't forget what Sir Peter said.* "If we have time, yes, I can teach you. Since all the knights are gone, other than Sir Foxbright, it will be more difficult for you to learn. But I am sure I can teach you something. Maybe we can talk Sir Foxbright into sparring with Ruschmann."

Armand was practically bouncing in his seat. "I am sure Father will agree. Let me go ask him."

Before Burchard could open his mouth to protest, Armand had leapt out of his seat, practically toppling it over in his haste, and raced down to where Sir Foxbright was eating at the head of the table. He watched as the knight gave his son his full attention and was even smiling as Armand explained what he wanted. The last thing they did was hug before Armand came bouncing back toward his chair. Burchard realized then that some fathers did actually love their children. He just wasn't one of the lucky ones.

Beaming, Armand slid into his seat. "He said yes. But he wants to give everyone a few days to settle in and get into our new routine before adding a new skill to learn." The page then turned his attention to his bowl of stew and dug in. Burchard let out his breath in relief and took a large bite of his roll.

Focusing on the roll, Burchard jumped when there was a familiar tug on his sleeve. He glanced at Armand's bowl and saw it was completely spotless.

"Hungry?" Burchard teased.

Armand smiled. "I think I'm always hungry."

"There's still some stew if you want more," Burchard replied

Armand shrugged. "I'm fine for now. I might grab a roll to take with me, just in case. Have you met everyone?"

Burchard raised an eyebrow. "I know the castle staff."

Armand tilted his head to the side. "I meant the pages. Have you met the pages yet?"

"No, you lot just arrived. When was I supposed to meet them?" Burchard responded, trying to keep his voice light.

"Right, sorry." Armand said, smile falling.

From Burchard's right side came a whiny voice. "You haven't stopped talking long enough for Burchard to talk to anyone."

Burchard peered at the page with curly brown hair for a moment, then back at Armand. "He does have a valid point."

Armand shrugged. "Everyone says I talk too much. But if you stay silent all the time, then you don't learn anything new. You never know when valuable information will come along. It certainly won't if you just stand in the corner brooding."

The curly-haired page huffed out his breath. "I do not stand in the corner and brood."

Burchard covered his mouth with his hand to hide his chuckle. "What's your name?"

The curly-haired page looked up at him, hazel eyes bright. "Frederick, but everyone calls me Freddy."

"Nice to meet you, Freddy," Burchard stated. He heard the scraping of chairs along the table as pages started to stand up to clear their plates. "I think that's my cue to leave so you two can follow whatever orders Sir Foxbright needs to give you."

Armand gave him a frown.

"I'm not leaving the castle." *Not that I have anywhere to go.* "I'll see you tomorrow for training." With that, Burchard shoved the rest of his roll in his mouth, dusted off the crumbs from his pants, and departed.

20

Burchard lay in his bed, wide awake. His hand trailed idly over Fang's back, mulling over his conversation with Armand and the other page, Freddy. At some point, he must have fallen asleep.

Burchard found himself in the foggy white space. He waited, deciding if Eos was going to come to him, it would be better to stay in one place than to wander around and risk Ossa finding him. He wasn't sure how much time passed, though it felt like hours. Then, Eos appeared in front of him, as though she'd been there all along. She sat down. Her eyes seemed to glow in the odd light of this place.

We are running out of time, she said, speaking into his mind.

Time for what? he replied. He'd almost spoken aloud before remembering that would be detrimental to both of them.

*Things were set in motion when you found the druids at Leosor Hollows. If certain tasks don't happen within the predetermined amount of time, then…*She shuddered.

Then what? he prompted.

She shook her white head. *I am not permitted to tell you directly. It is for you to discover.*

If I fail at discovering the tasks? Worry coursed through him.

We don't want to find out, Eos said, peering over her shoulder. Her eyes lingered on the mist behind her, then returned to his. *I need to go. But…trust yourself. Trust your friends.*

I only have one friend, Burchard said softly.

That is not true. You just have to look inside yourself, Eos said, then vanished.

Burchard woke with a start. His hand was clenching Fang's fur tightly. He was surprised that the wolf hadn't bitten him or moved in protest for how hard he was gripping her. She gave a low woof and licked his hand. He loosened his grip on her fur, allowing his fingers to just lie on her back instead.

"Eos said I have more than one friend. Who are my friends?" he asked. "Do you count as a friend?" Fang let out a high-pitched yip. "I'll take that as a yes." Fang licked his hand again. "That makes two, but she seemed to imply that I have many friends. Hopefully, she didn't mean that us defeating Ossa is hinging on my ability to properly count my friends."

Fang didn't do anything to indicate she understood the question.

Burchard sighed and decided he should just get up and start his stretches. He threw the blankets back, covering Fang in the process. The wolf didn't seem to mind, though, and snuggled into them. Burchard stood up, shivering as the cool air hit his bare chest. Once he was away from the top bunk and certain he wouldn't hit his head, he bent over, touching his toes. He repeated it a few times, holding the position until he could really feel the pull on his muscles. He then worked his way through the other stretches for both his legs and arms.

His bed squeaked behind him. Burchard spun, fists raised, and saw Ruschmann sitting on the edge of the bed, eyeing Fang. The wolf's mouth was open, teeth visible, almost as though she were smiling.

Burchard chuckled. "She likes you."

Ruschmann wouldn't take his eyes off the wolf. "If you say so. Did you see the pages last night?"

Burchard nodded, then proceeded to get dressed. "Did you want to go for a run with me before breakfast?"

"Not really. It's cold," Ruschmann replied from the bed.

Burchard clicked his tongue. "You're being lazy."

"It's only one morning," Ruschmann replied.

"One morning turns into two, and soon it's a whole week," Burchard chided, turning to face his friend as he tucked in his long-sleeve shirt.

"Fine. I will join you. But then we must eat before the pages steal all the food," Ruschmann declared.

Burchard rolled his eyes. "I doubt they will steal everything. However, we will of course eat after the run. I just…I had a weird dream last night, and I think the run will help settle me before we do training, since it'll be with the pages."

"Will you tell me about the dream?" Ruschmann inquired.

Burchard sat down in the chair and tugged his boots on, then stood up, pulling on his coat. "Eos, the wolf goddess, was talking to me, saying she couldn't tell me what I needed to know. I had to find it out myself. And…that we're running out of time."

"Very cryptic," Ruschmann muttered, standing up, careful not to jostle Fang.

"That's what I thought. But she would not elaborate," Burchard said. He strapped his scabbard around his waist, then slid some soft gloves over his hands. "Let's go."

Fang jumped off the bed and brushed against Ruschmann. Her tail held high, she led the way to the door. Ruschmann opened it, and Fang shot outside.

Burchard grinned. "I guess she needed out."

Fang rejoined them when they reached the gate. Once through the gate, the three of them increased their pace till they were running. Burchard wasn't sure how to classify what Fang was doing. She would keep pace with them and then dart away and disappear into the trees before reappearing. He assumed she was just hunting and wasn't being successful. Or was not putting in a strong enough effort to be successful. He was not too concerned with it though. If she was hungry, she would catch prey.

Ruschmann finally broke their silence. "Did Eos say something else? You seemed to be holding back earlier when you told me what she said."

Burchard huffed, his breath visible before him in a wispy cloud. "She told me I need to trust my friends and that I have more than one friend."

Ruschmann's steps faltered and he fell back before speeding up and keeping pace again. "She's right. You do have more than one friend."

"Who else do you consider to be my friends?" Burchard replied testily.

"Captain Thomas, for one. Lady Gladys, Sir Peter." Ruschmann paused, breathing heavily.

They were on their fifth lap of what was supposed to be short run. "I don't consider Sir Peter a friend," Burchard admitted.

Ruschmann stopped moving. Burchard kept going before he stopped and turned around, wondering where he'd gone. "How can you think Sir Peter isn't your friend? He has defended you to the General several times. He has tried to ensure that we can stay together as much as possible."

Burchard growled. "You think those things make him my friend? Isn't that what normal knight masters do?"

"Have you seen Reggie's knight master do any of those things?" Ruschmann demanded. Burchard kept quiet, knowing Ruschmann was probably right.

"I guess I just assumed that he was behaving in a way that was typical for a knight master with his squire. I didn't realize it was because we were friends or know that it was even possible for adults to be friends with fourteen-year-olds," Burchard said defensively.

Ruschmann gave him another look. "What happened when you were growing up that you don't know these kinds of things?" he said softly.

Burchard frowned. "You have seen my interactions with my father. The way he behaves here is not much different than when we were growing up. He has always been a knight first, then a lord, then a husband."

Ruschmann stepped toward Burchard until he was close enough to reach out and grab his hand, giving it a reassuring squeeze. "There is nothing that says friends or family have to be related by blood. You are a squire now. You can choose for yourself who will play those roles in your life."

"Really?" Burchard said, voice barely a whisper.

"Really," Ruschmann said firmly. "Come on, let's go get breakfast. When you suggested joining you, I thought you meant for one lap, not five! I'm starving."

Burchard gave his friend a half-hearted smile before turning toward the castle gate and taking off at a fast run.

21

Higigh, middle, low." Sir Foxbright's voice carried over the training yard as three rows of pages and the two squires went through a hand-to-hand combat drill. The explanation at the beginning of the training session was to help them warm up. The group began with Sir Foxbright standing in front, but as they eased into a rhythm, the knight walked the lines, pausing by each page and correcting them individually.

Burchard let his hands drop to his sides as he observed. What was most fascinating to him was how quickly a page would improve. Once the knight moved on, Burchard found himself continuing to watch the previous page and could see that they remembered how they were corrected. Sir Peter taught him that way, but it was usually one on one. Most of the instructors preferred to stand in front and shout instructions. If one was doing it improperly, the instructor would repeat the demonstration, but never took the time to walk through and give individual instruction.

Burchard heard a rasp at his side and turned slightly to see Sir Foxbright studying him. A blush crept up his cheeks. He had been observing instead of warming up. "Sorry, sir."

To Burchard's surprise, the knight shrugged. "I know you ran five laps around the castle before breakfast with Ruschmann. I'm not worried about if you're warmed up. Do you have any thoughts on my methods?"

Burchard blushed even deeper. "They work," he said.

Sir Foxbright chuckled. "Yes, they do. It's amazing how much more willing a page is when you take the time to explain what they're doing wrong and how to fix it, instead of just telling them they're wrong." He paused. "Sometimes it is a challenge even for me to figure out what a page is doing incorrectly. When you see a move that is almost right, but just a little off."

"Being even a little off can be the difference between surviving or dying," Burchard said softly.

"Yes, I know. Which is precisely why I teach them this way. To ensure they learn now, before it is harder to undo improper footwork or a stance," Sir Foxbright agreed.

"Why weren't they teaching like this when I was a page?" Burchard asked, hoping the knight wouldn't mind the question.

"It wasn't until I saw your fourth-year tests that I realized how much you already know, and how far behind everyone else is," Sir Foxbright revealed.

Burchard nibbled on his lip. "I don't understand."

"General Wolfensberger ensured you never learned the improper way of using your body when you were just a small boy. You live and breathe it, so it did not impact your training much over those four years. But most pages don't have the luxury of learning under the eyes of General Wolfensberger."

"They're better off," muttered Burchard.

Sir Foxbright ignored his comment. "My point is that I have been requiring the combat instructors to start walking the lines, helping the pages individually, so they correct their mistakes sooner than later."

"Is there anything you want me to do, sir?" Burchard asked.

Sir Foxbright shrugged. "If you want to walk the lines too, you are more than welcome to do so. Just keep in mind not all of the pages will appreciate being told what to do by a squire."

Burchard nodded and waited as Sir Foxbright moved on to Ruschmann, who had continued to do the drill. Then, he went to the end of the row he was on and started walking down it. He decided instead of finding things for the pages to fix to just observe each page more closely to get a feel for what they were doing. He slowly made his way down all three lines.

Just before he reached the last page, Sir Foxbright called everyone to attention. "Now that we are warmed up, I want everyone to grab the wooden practice swords and pair up." Burchard caught Ruschmann's eye, and the other squire shrugged and walked over to the massive pile of wooden practice swords.

Burchard picked one up and found a spot clear of the pages and gave his sword a few practice swings. For starters, it was unbalanced, and it was very lightweight. He was tempted to just use his regular sword but wasn't sure what Sir Foxbright was planning on doing with them.

Ruschmann walked over to him, smacking his hand with his wooden sword. "This is going to be fun."

"Do you miss having your fingers whacked?" Burchard asked with a smirk, then jabbed at his friend with his sword, poking him in the side.

Ruschmann twirled his practice sword in his hand, then smacked Burchard's shoulder with it. "Do you?"

"Pair up! Get in a line!" ordered Sir Foxbright.

Burchard winked at Ruschmann as they fell into the double line formation. Thankfully, they were at one end. They scooted farther away from the pages closest to them, wanting room to maneuver, and also to stay clear of any stray strikes.

"Ready begin! High, low, middle. Left side strikes, right side blocks," Sir Foxbright ordered.

Burchard nodded to Ruschmann, who started with a high strike. Burchard met it with a high block. Down the line there seemed to be some confusion as whines and yelps echoed.

"I guess they don't know what left or right is," muttered Burchard.

"Hopefully they figure that out before they're on a battlefield," Ruschmann replied darkly.

Just as with the hand-to-hand warm-up, Sir Foxbright walked the double line, helping each pair of pages. When he got to the two squires, he just watched them without comment for a few moments before returning to the beginning of the line again. The knight walked the line three more times before Ruschmann got bored and stopped doing the prescribed exercise of high, middle, and low blocks.

"What are you doing?" hissed Burchard, blocking his friend's strike.

"Practicing," retorted Ruschmann, feinting to the right and jabbing his sword at Burchard's unprotected side.

Burchard rolled his eyes. He had to admit that the drill was incredibly boring, but training was still training. Mastery of those three blocks and strikes had been useful more than once when he was in the field. He stepped sideways and chopped down at Ruschmann's sword. They slid farther and farther out of the line, but as he felt himself relax more, he admitted how right Ruschmann had been; the basic drills were boring. They did serve as a good warm-up, but beyond that, for two squires with combat experience, they were not terribly helpful.

The wooden practice swords crossed, and Burchard adjusted his grip. Sir Foxbright had not interrupted their practice, but Burchard was sorely tempted to ditch the wooden swords altogether.

At the front of the group, an ahem, and then Sir Foxbright's voice reached them. "Pages, go take a water break. Squires, please come here."

Burchard groaned. "See what you did. Now we're going to get in trouble."

Ruschmann ignored him completely as they stopped in front of the knight, both squires offering him a formal bow.

"Would you mind doing a demonstration?" Sir Foxbright asked.

Ruschmann smirked at Burchard before answering. "What kind of demonstration?"

"Sword work with your real swords. It doesn't have to be long. I just want them to see how steel is different than wood. I'm also having the castle staff set up a table with a variety of swords and other weapons, wooden and real, for them to examine after your demonstration," Sir Foxbright explained.

"Sure, we would be happy to do the demonstration," Ruschmann said brightly. Sir Foxbright turned and walked over to the pages, presumably to explain about the demonstration. Once the knight's back was turned, Ruschmann elbowed Burchard in the middle.

A growl escaped Burchard's lips. "What was that for?"

"You're just standing here like a statue," Ruschmann retorted.

Lip curling, Burchard glowered at him. "I wasn't aware that we both had to respond. You do know I would have said I disagreed if that were the case." He stepped away from Ruschmann, nostrils flaring, and took a deep breath. *I need to chill out. He's just teasing me.* He glanced over to where the pages were. Sir Foxbright had found some old benches that looked like they had seen better days, but all forty pages were seated. Some were observing the two squires, others chatted quietly among themselves.

Burchard continued to take deep breaths, willing himself to calm so that he could focus on the demonstration. He slowly made his way to the center of the training ring and unsheathed his sword, holding it in his right hand. He did a few experimental swings to readjust to the comfortable weight of his weapon.

"Ready when you are," he said softly to Ruschmann.

Ruschmann nodded and they crossed swords. "One. Two. Three."

Burchard darted to the side, trying to come up behind Ruschmann, but Ruschmann was anticipating the move and pivoted, parrying the strike. Each strike and parry was executed quickly. Burchard wondered if the pages could follow what they were doing or not. He hesitated, and Ruschmann took the opening, running his sword tip along Burchard's ribs.

"What?" Ruschmann asked, taking a step back.

"Are we going too fast? Can they see what we're doing?" Burchard queried, before slicing the air with a high strike.

"I think Sir Foxbright would tell us if it was too fast. But I can slow down a hair if you want," Ruschmann replied, then stepped to the left as he swung in a low strike.

Burchard swept his sword down to block, then he swapped his sword to his left hand. When he used his left, he didn't have the same amount of speed as with the right, but he was just as accurate. He watched as Ruschmann adjusted his position before stepping forward and slashing for Burchard's middle. Burchard blocked the middle strike, twisted his hand, and the swords slid against each other. He braced, adding more pressure. Ruschmann stepped to the right, disengaged his sword, and swung low at Burchard's legs. Burchard jumped over the sword and, grinning, swapped hands again. Ruschmann's momentum with the low strike carried him forward past Burchard, and Burchard brought the flat of his sword down, slapping Ruschmann's back. Ruschmann let go of his sword and fell flat on the ground.

Burchard chuckled, removing his sword from his friend's back. "Wasn't that a little overkill?" he said, offering Ruschmann a hand to get up.

Ruschmann shrugged. "Eh, they're just pages. They don't need to know how to get out of that particular attack yet."

Together they walked over to the benches. Sir Foxbright smiled with approval.

"Thank you. The two of you are welcome to join us or do your own thing for the rest of the day. After the weapon review, the pages will have lunch, and then we will review battle strategies from the Forest War of 557."

"I need to think about it," Burchard replied.

"I'm in," Ruschmann said. "Thanks for the invite."

Burchard was about to respond again when his stomach gurgled loud enough that even some of the pages pointed at him and snickered. "I'll see you in the dining hall."

In one quick motion, he sheathed his sword and headed at a brisk walk in the direction of the dining hall, not bothering to see if Ruschmann was following or not.

22

Burchard was in the stable, tacking up Chip. The lessons in battle strategy with Sir Foxbright had been fascinating, but after two days of being cooped up in the castle, he was restless. Today, instead of accepting the invitation to join the battle strategy lesson, he was going for a ride. A small part of him was hoping he'd run into Jade again and that she'd kiss him. He had finally decided that he was interested in being more than friends with her, if that was what she wanted. The other part was really hoping she wouldn't be there and he could enjoy the solitude he was craving, just him, Chip, and Fang in the forest. For that reason, he had packed his bow. He wasn't sure if he'd get even remotely close enough to a deer to shoot it with Fang accompanying him, but he knew the cook would appreciate the fresh meat. Alderth Castle was well stocked in pro-visions that would easily last them for months, but the meat stores were mostly salted. Which was better than nothing, he supposed.

With one last tug on the strap holding the saddle onto Chip, Burchard gathered his reins and led the mare out of the barn. He swung into the saddle, checked his bags one last time, then clucked to her. They went through the gate at an ambling walk, and once they were clear of the castle, she sped up into a smooth canter down the road. Fang shot out of the forest and met them on the road, tongue lolling out of her mouth.

"Good afternoon, Fang," Burchard said to the wolf. She gave a little yip and matched Chip's pace. Burchard felt the tension melting away as they cantered down the road. When they were about two miles away from the castle, he slowed Chip down. He knew if he wanted to try to get a deer that he would have to have some distance from the castle and the road.

"Let's go hunting, Fang," he murmured. Fang woofed in acknowledgement. Quietly as possible, the three of them slipped into the forest. Fang kept her nose to the ground, ranging ahead and to the side of Burchard and Chip. Burchard kept his eyes peeled for any sign of a deer.

When Burchard saw indications that a deer could be nearby, he halted Chip and dismounted. He retrieved his bow and quiver, strung the bow, and then slung the quiver across his back. He snagged an arrow and set it before moving forward. Chip would stay where he left her. He couldn't see Fang, but he was fairly sure she was nearby, stalking the deer. Finally, he caught a glimpse of the deer. A large ten-point buck that had to weigh over three hundred pounds.

I have to not miss, he reminded himself. Not that he was in the habit of missing, but a moving target that was also a living, breathing, and thinking creature was different than shooting into a target back at the castle.

Burchard found a spot where he was mostly hidden by the tree and he could get a decent angle on the buck to shoot straight into the heart. Or that was the plan. He set the arrow and drew the bowstring back. Just as he loosed, the buck sprang forward, and the arrow thudded into the tree behind it. Burchard was fumbling to grab a second arrow when a streak of black shot out of the trees across from him and seemed to fly through the air. *Fang!* The wolf's wide-open mouth clamped down on the buck's throat. Burchard watched in horror, afraid that the struggling buck would surely injure Fang with one of its sharp hooves or antlers.

With a whistling breath, the buck fell to the ground with a thud. Fang kept her jaws locked around it until Burchard came over.

"It's dead," he announced to Fang, although he was fairly certain the wolf knew the deer was dead long before he had.

Burchard let out a sharp whistle to call Chip before he returned his attention to the buck. It was even bigger than he'd thought. *I suppose I will be walking back. I don't think Chip can carry me and a buck this big.* He set down his bow and pulled out his long knife. Fang was watching him, her mouth dripping blood. The buck's neck was in shreds from her teeth. He did a quick inspection of the rest of the buck and found it seemed to be in good shape. Then, he began the task of field dressing—removing the organs. By the time he finished, Chip had appeared. She seemed tense but willing to cooperate. Burchard cleaned off his knife and sheathed it, then opened one of his packs. He had brought a piece of canvas and some rope in case he did successfully catch a deer.

Swiftly, he wrapped the deer in canvas and tied the bundle shut. Then, he carefully kneeled down and picked it up. Slinging the carcass over his shoulder, he swayed precariously as he stood all the way up, taking a few unsteady steps toward Chip. The mare, as though she could read his mind—which he knew was impossible—sidestepped toward him, closing the gap.

"Thanks," he said breathlessly. Then, he awkwardly shoved and pulled the deer over the saddle. When he was sure it was balanced and wouldn't slide to the ground, he let go. Using what was left of the rope, he tied the deer to Chip to ensure it wouldn't budge, even if she had to trot. Next, he gathered up his bow and quiver and secured them to the saddlebags.

He glanced at Fang. "Are you ready?" Fang came over and licked his hands a few times, covering them in bloody saliva. "Eww, that is gross." He ran his hand through her black fur, returning the mess she had deposited on his hand. Fang wriggled away and paused in front of Chip. To his surprise, the wolf and horse touched noses before Fang stepped in front and started walking in the general direction of Alderth Castle.

Burchard went around to Chip's left side and snagged the reins, just in case she tried to bolt. He was confident Fang would pick a path appropriate for a fully laden horse. They settled into an easy walk. Judging by the light filtering through the mostly bare trees, it was midafternoon. He still had ample time to get back with the buck and for Cook to possibly use some of it for that night's dinner.

Lost in his thoughts, Burchard jumped at the sound of flapping wings as a huge great horned owl glided over his head to land on a large rock directly in front of them. The owl had something grasped in a talon. Burchard studied the owl, then it dawned on him why it looked familiar. "Liala?"

The owl clacked her beak in response. He hoped that meant yes. She raised up her right talon, which held a scroll. Burchard let go of Chip's reins and cautiously went up to the owl and took the scroll. He opened it, not sure what to expect.

Meet me at the edge of the forest when it gets dark. – Jade

Burchard reread the note a few times. Then, he turned to the owl. "Do you know what she wants to talk about?"

Liala tipped her head this way and that before hooting. Burchard had no idea how to interpret what she was saying, not without Jade there.

"I will be there," Burchard said solemnly with a bow. The owl, seemingly satisfied by his answer, flapped her wings twice before flying deeper into the forest.

One of the pages had to have seen him from the wall as he was approaching Alderth Castle. Cook met him at the gate herself, beaming. He halted so she could inspect the buck properly.

"Fantastic job, Burchard!" Cook exclaimed.

Burchard couldn't help the smile tugging at his lips. "Fang did most of the work," he replied.

Cook was practically glowing. "Let's bring Chip up to the door closest to the kitchen. Some of the castle staff are waiting to help unload the buck. I've got the table cleaned and ready."

Burchard followed as Cook led the way to the kitchen door. Sure enough, there were four men waiting for them and Lady Gladys.

"When I am done butchering the buck and have everything cleaned up, I will make sure you get the antlers. I will set aside some of the meat for Fang as well," Cook announced, daring any of the men to object.

Burchard untied the buck and held Chip's reins to allow the four men to slide the buck off the horse. "If you don't need me for anything else, I need to go get Chip cleaned up." The canvas wrapping had protected the mare from most of the mess, but she still had some dried blood on her sides. When Cook nodded and waved in dismissal, Burchard turned and led Chip toward the barn.

He could hear steps following in his wake. Burchard halted, wondering who was there.

Lady Gladys walked over to him. "That was nice of you to get such a large deer."

Burchard shrugged. "I just got lucky. Usually I don't have enough time to wait for the biggest one to come along. Without the host of knights here, if we want fresh meat, I know I'll have to go out and get it."

Lady Gladys raised her eyebrows. "There are other people here who are capable of hunting."

"Yes, but they also have other duties. Hunting permits me to practice with the bow. Trust me, I don't mind," Burchard said in what he hoped was a reassuring voice.

"Well, just don't forget if you run out of things to do, I am here and I miss our card games," Lady Gladys said, then glanced behind her. "I should get back into the kitchen to help with the meat. See you 'round."

Burchard smiled and watched as she left. A card game would be fun, if he could find time. "C'mon, Chip, let's get you untacked and cleaned up."

Chip nickered softly in agreement.

Burchard had Chip tied in the stable aisleway. He was just finishing wiping her down with some wet rags when Armand poked his head through the barn doors. "Hello!"

Burchard smiled. "Hey."

"Everyone is talking about the huge buck you brought back," Armand said with a glance at Fang, who was lying in the aisleway. Burchard had cleaned the worst of the blood from Fang too.

"Fang did most of the work," Burchard said softly with an affectionate look at the wolf. "Did you need something?"

Armand shook his head and sat down on a bale of hay. "Nothing in particular. The other pages think I'm annoying and told me to go away."

Burchard turned away so Armand couldn't see his amusement. "You're welcome to help me with Chip." The mare had taken a liking to the page since his arrival. She didn't like very many people, so Burchard took it as a good sign that she approved of Armand.

"Thanks, but no thanks. I was in the group of pages assigned to the barn today. I'd rather just sit here," Armand replied.

Burchard chuckled, then grabbed the stiff brush off the ground and worked his way down Chip's body, starting with her neck. The other horses in the stable were quietly eating their hay.

"Do you mind telling me about the druids?" Armand asked hesitantly.

Burchard put the brush down and unclipped Chip from the ties, then led her into her stall. When he was done putting her away, he took a seat next to Armand on the hay bale. "No, I don't mind. But how much does your father share with you?"

"He tells me everything," Armand said softly.

Burchard raised an eyebrow. "He's not worried about you telling someone you shouldn't?"

Armand frowned. "No. Why would I tell anyone?" The page gave Burchard a look, and then his expression softened. "I forget that your father is General Wolfensberger and that he doesn't tell you anything. Instead, he has taken Reginald under his wing." His voice dropped even lower. "The brother who is not worthy."

Burchard gave Armand a sharp look but wasn't sure he wanted to know who told the page that Reggie was not worthy of the General's attention. "Do you know what a gladius domini is?"

Armand sucked in a sharp breath, eyes widening. "It's a sword master, but where did you hear it called that?"

"One of the druids, Damos, used that term before I faced Lieutenant Commander Walter Pell. Damos said he wasn't worried about me against twenty rebels because I am a gladius domini," Burchard responded.

Armand's eyes got even wider. "He said that you *are* a gladius domini, or will become one?"

Burchard's lips twitched before he answered. "Damos said I am a gladius domini."

"You're only fourteen!" Armand almost shouted. "King Roland won't permit a squire to take the sword master test. You must pass your knight's test first."

"I am aware of that," Burchard said tartly. "I just am not sure I believe Damos that I am a gladius domini."

"Damos probably knows more about you than your father does. Druid magic is very different than what we are used to. Some of them can talk to the trees, and if a tree witnessed something, then they can access the tree's memory. As you know, there are plants and trees all over Etria. A druid with that type of magic would be able to learn many things without ever having to interact with a person," Armand explained.

"Ah," Burchard murmured. Now he understood how Jade had known so much about him when they met at Leosor Hollows.

A single bell rang out in the courtyard. Armand leapt to his feet. "Dinner!" the page exclaimed before racing out of the barn.

Burchard chuckled and finished cleaning up the aisleway before finding his way to the dining hall too.

23

Alderth Castle was quiet when Burchard slipped out. The sky was completely dark, dotted only by a few scattered stars not hidden by clouds. Given the hour, he decided that he would be better off walking. The edge of the forest wasn't far, and he didn't want to alarm anyone unnecessarily by taking Chip. After explaining what he was doing to Fang, the wolf had decided to follow him. He wasn't sure why but decided her presence wouldn't change anything.

Burchard had his hands stuffed in his coat pockets. Even with the fur-lined gloves, the wind that was picking up was cold. *A bad winter is coming,* he predicted. Fang, of course, seemed unruffled by the cold. In fact, she was bouncing around, as one would expect from a puppy, not an adult wolf. He picked up his pace, hoping the faster movements would warm him up. He didn't want to run, worried that Jade would get the wrong idea.

At the edge of the trees, he saw a flickering light. *She made a fire?* Just another hundred paces or so and he'd be there by the fire. A slight movement in the trees stopped him in his tracks. Fang had noticed too. She gave him a quick lick before disappearing into the trees. He didn't see the movement again. Shaking his head, he walked the rest of the way to the fire.

The fire circle was tiny, with only a handful of kindling and a short, thick branch surrounded by a ring of rocks. But the heat it generated was far greater than what it should have been. Jade caught his eye from the other side of the fire.

"I thought we should be warm instead of trying to not freeze while we met," Jade explained.

Burchard studied the fire ring again. "How is it giving off this much heat?"

"Magic," Jade said, wiggling her gloved fingers in the air.

"I didn't know you could do fire magic," he said.

Jade shrugged. "I don't think you ever asked what kind of magic I have."

Burchard held his hands out to the fire, relishing the warmth that trickled through his gloves. "What kind of magic do you have?" he asked, taking the bait.

"A little of this and a little of that," Jade said with a smile. "I told you before I can communicate with animals and druids who are shifted. I can also amplify heat or light that already exists. Like I'm doing with the fire."

"Convenient," murmured Burchard.

Fang had not returned yet. He wondered if he should worry or not. He turned his back to the fire and peered into the dark forest. Jade slipped close to him so they stood with their shoulders touching as they looked out into the forest. Tentatively, she slid her hand into his.

Burchard took a deep breath, trying to settle his nerves. "I thought you wanted to talk to me."

Keeping their fingers laced together, Jade turned to face him, her brown hair looking almost red in the firelight. "I do. Damos wanted me to share some information with you," she said softly. Burchard raised his eyebrows. "I told you last time we met that I really like you, Burchard. I was serious." She leaned forward and kissed him.

A shiver ran through him as cold air worked its way up a gap between his shirt and pants. He stepped forward without thinking, pressing his body to Jade's tightly. He had to brace his hands against her shoulders to keep from toppling them both into the fire. When they were balanced again, he pulled away slightly, uncertain what to do.

Maybe I should speak to Ruschmann again about how to talk to a girl, so I don't sound like a bumbling idiot! "Damos said…" he prompted.

Jade licked her lips in a way that made his blood thrum in his veins and had him hoping she'd kiss him again. "I can tell you later."

"But—" he protested, part of him wanting to stick to the task at hand, the information Damos had wanted passed on. *It could be critical for the safety of those within the castle*, he reminded himself.

His words were cut off as she captured his lips once again with hers. This time she was more demanding. Her hands traveled down his chest. Burchard closed his eyes. He didn't think he was ready for anything beyond kissing but had no idea how to tell her so without embarrassing himself. He kissed her and ran his hands along her back, then pulled away. Jade had said that Damos had something important for him to know and he wanted to know it—then they could kiss more.

Jade stuck her tongue out at him, "You're ruining the fun. Damos wanted you to know that there are no…"

A loud crunch in the forest just in front of him. Burchard's whole body tensed. To his horror, it wasn't Fang who materialized from the dark forest, but Ossa. His long gray hair fell around his face and down his back in greasy clumps.

"How sweet, the two of you together." Ossa's cold voice wrapped around them. Jade whirled, fists raised, earning a harsh laugh from Ossa. "You are going to make this even easier than I thought." Ossa grinned, flashing his razor-sharp teeth at them.

Burchard could not suppress the shudder that ran through him. "What do you want?" he demanded through gritted teeth.

"You, of course. I'm surprised you haven't figured it out yet," Ossa replied. "Eos should have chosen better. Too bad for her, there won't be a next time. Once Mors is free, she will be the first god to die."

Interesting that Ossa let it slip that Mors will be the one to kill Eos. I wonder if that is true of the other gods. If only a god can kill a god. He tucked that revelation away, hopeful there would be time later to examine it further.

"Are you waiting for something? You could just kill us now and be done with it," Burchard growled.

Ossa stared at Burchard until Burchard had to look away from his burning eyes. "You mortals have your prophecy and we have ours," Ossa finally responded.

Burchard glanced at Jade, wondering if the druids knew anything about the prophecy Ossa was using as guidance. Jade gave him a slight shake of her head. Burchard opened his mouth when Fang came flying through the air, jaws snapping. At the last moment, she had to twist to avoid colliding with Burchard because Ossa had disappeared. Fang stood up and shook herself, sending dirt and leaves into the air.

Jade met Burchard's gaze. "I need to warn Damos. If Ossa appeared this close to Alderth Castle, they must be planning an attack soon. You must warn whoever is still in the castle. Prepare as best you can. The timing is not ideal, not with the General and all the knights going after the rebels. Even if we got a message to them and he decided to send help, the odds are low they'd make it in time."

Burchard shrugged dismissively. "I doubt General Wolfensberger would believe any message we sent to him unless the message was accompanied by Ossa's head. Then he might believe us."

"You know that is not going to happen," Jade chided him.

"I know, I know. Let's go warn everyone, and hopefully we'll get lucky," Burchard responded.

Jade nodded, then gave him a quick kiss. "I will see you soon." With a wave of her hand, the fire went out.

Burchard whistled for Fang and then sprinted for the castle. *How long will it take for Ossa to attack? Or for Jade to bring help?* Burchard felt his speed waning and willed himself to press on. *I should tell Sir Peter first.* He stumbled and almost fell on his face as he realized that Sir Peter wasn't there, nor was Sir Daniel. Sir Foxbright was the only knight in the whole castle.

Fang nuzzled him, as though she could read his thoughts. "I will find Sir Foxbright," he said to her.

They were almost to the gate. He could see Ruschmann's silhouette in the darkness. His friend had agreed to make sure the gate would stay open till he returned from his meeting with Jade. The castle staff had a rotating schedule for who would open and shut the gate each morning and evening, but otherwise the gate and wall remained unmanned. General Wolfensberger had not considered it important enough to leave even a few sentries, declaring the squires or pages could take that task if needed. What had surprised Burchard the most was that no one had protested the decision to leave Alderth Castle utterly defenseless.

"What's wrong?" called Ruschmann as he stepped out to meet Burchard.

"Ossa," gasped Burchard. He bent over, placing his hands on his thighs, taking slow, deep breaths.

"What do you mean?" Ruschmann asked, voice an octave higher than usual.

"He appeared when Jade and I were talking," Burchard said. He could feel the blush creeping up his cheeks and was grateful Ruschmann wouldn't see it in the darkness.

"He said that I'm right where he wants me. I need to go tell Sir Foxbright," Burchard said and brushed past Ruschmann.

Ruschmann grabbed his sleeve, stopping him. "Help me get the gate shut first."

Burchard nodded, and they went into the guard house. Together they turned the wheel to lower the metal gate. It thudded into the stone, and he sighed. He knew the gate would not protect them for long, but at least it was something. Ossa wouldn't be able to just waltz right into Alderth Castle.

"Are we going to wake everyone up if we go talk to Sir Foxbright?" Ruschmann asked.

Burchard shook his head. "No, he's in the barracks where there's an officers' quarters at the back with its own entrance. As long as we aren't too noisy, we shouldn't disturb the pages."

Burchard's body was tiring rapidly. After a long day of drills, multiple runs, and then his sprint for the castle, he was ready to sleep. Instead, he had to warn Sir Foxbright, and then he wasn't sure what. They walked to the barracks, Ruschmann seemingly content to go at whatever speed Burchard chose.

They went around to the back side and up the three steps. There was no light spilling under the door. Burchard raised his fist and knocked twice, then waited. He was about to knock again when the door opened. Sir Foxbright peered at them for a moment. "Come in." The knight turned away from the door, then moved farther into the room and lit a lamp. Ruschmann shut the door behind them to keep as much of the cold air out as possible.

Burchard spoke. "I'm sorry to disturb you, sir. But I was talking to my friend Jade." Sir Foxbright gave him a confused look. "She's one of the druids," Burchard clarified. Sir Foxbright nodded and motioned for him to continue. "When I was talking to her, Ossa appeared and said that he was looking for me and I was right where he wanted me."

Sir Foxbright's eyebrows narrowed in concentration. "Did he say anything else?"

"He did say that they have their own prophecy, which is different from the druid prophecy," Burchard replied.

Sir Foxbright's jaw clenched. "You never mentioned anything about a druid prophecy."

Burchard shrugged. "I didn't think it mattered."

The knight stood up and paced. "After our meeting with Sir Waldorf and Sir Emberwood, you didn't think a prophecy would matter?"

Burchard shrugged again. "No, I think it's all nonsense. Which I told you and Jade." He watched as various emotions flickered across Sir Foxbright's face.

In a surprisingly calm voice, Sir Foxbright responded. "Do you recall any of the druid prophecy?"

Burchard licked his lips, trying to remember what Jade had said. "She said something about 'the man with the wolf will return, and Ossa and Umbra will walk the world.' Possibly also mentioned Mors returning, but I honestly don't remember." He covered his mouth to stifle a yawn.

"You are the only person I know of who has a wolf companion," Sir Foxbright said matter-of-factly.

Burchard rolled his eyes and another yawn escaped before he could stop it. "I'm not sure why everyone seems to think the prophecy is about me. I'm just a squire. I'm not important."

Sir Foxbright rubbed his temples. "You look like you're about to fall over from exhaustion. The two of you should go get some rest." He glanced down. "Fang too."

"Are you sure? What if the druids come?" Burchard asked.

Sir Foxbright clicked his tongue. "First off, you are no good to me if you are too tired to stand, let alone fight. Second, other people in this castle can help. I will talk to the head of the castle staff about starting a watch immediately. Third, I have been the head of the Trinity School for nine years and a knight for another ten even before that. I do know how to properly handle interactions with fighting forces from other lands. I will not do anything that would cause the druids to decide to not aid us if Ossa attacks. However, you're also assuming that Jade can gather the druids quickly. It could take days, not just a few hours."

Burchard bowed his head. Sir Foxbright was right on all accounts. "Promise you'll get us if Ossa shows up?"

Sir Foxbright gave him a sharp smile. "Absolutely. Until then, get some rest while you can."

Ruschmann opened the door and quietly went down the steps. Burchard was about to follow him when out of the corner of his eye he saw Fang shove her nose into Sir Foxbright's hand, as though they were acquainted.

"Come on, Fang. Let's go to bed," Burchard murmured softly. The wolf brushed by him, then leapt down the stairs and out of sight.

24

At breakfast the morning after Burchard's encounter with Jade and Ossa, the dining hall was oddly silent except for the clink of silverware on plates. When Burchard finished his food, Sir Foxbright motioned for him to come over.

Burchard shared an uncertain glance with Ruschmann before heading over to Sir Foxbright.

"You wanted to speak to us, sir?" Burchard asked, tucking his hands behind his back.

"Yes, I need you to lead the pages in their drills this morning while I coordinate preparations with Cook and the other castle staff. In the early preparation stage, I think you lot would just be underfoot. Instead of making the pages—especially the first-years—nervous, I think training will help keep everyone focused," Sir Foxbright explained.

"Are you sure? I'm just a first-year squire," Burchard said hesitantly.

Sir Foxbright chuckled. "I am confident in your ability to teach the pages. You have a natural ability to teach and lead, Burchard. It's time you try it out." He paused. "Besides it's not like if you make mistakes your first time that you will hurt them. They like you already."

Burchard bit his lip. "OK, but Ruschmann is helping too, right?"

Sir Foxbright nodded. "Yes, Ruschmann is welcome to help. Just head out to the training yard once you grab your gear, and I'll make sure the pages are there and ready."

Burchard bowed. "Very well, sir."

A little later, Burchard was in the training yard. He had brought a selection of his weapons. Fang decided to lie down next to his weapons and take a nap. Just as Sir Foxbright had said, the pages were there, ready for training. Burchard gave Ruschmann a nervous glance and tilted his head, indicating they should go to the front of the group.

When they stood before the pages, Burchard licked his lips nervously. The pages gazed back at him, waiting. "Good morning. Have you warmed up yet?"

Armand, who was in the front row, giggled. "We just finished eating. We haven't warmed up, and neither have you."

Burchard almost rolled his eyes at his friend but then caught himself. If he was going to lead the pages, it wouldn't do for him to be rolling his eyes at them. "OK then, since you haven't warmed up yet, we will jog three laps around the training yard."

His announcement was met with loud groaning. Ruschmann stepped forward. "If you think three laps around the training yard is a lot, then you should try three laps around the whole castle. That's what Burchard does every morning. Sometimes it's five laps."

Some of the pages' mouths fell open in surprise. The comment had the desired effect; the pages hastily formed a line and began jogging around the training yard. Burchard and Ruschmann picked up the rear.

When the three laps were completed, Burchard had the pages line up, making sure there was plenty of space between each of them.

Then Ruschmann led everyone through a sequence of stretches. Afterward, Burchard found himself front and center again. From his years of training, he had always found that the natural progression from stretching was working on simple hand-to-hand combat techniques. He started calling moves from the front and then began walking the lines, with Ruschmann taking his place at the head of the group, making the calls.

"No, no, you're doing it all wrong," Burchard said gently to his brother Theodore.

Theodore gave him a look. "Are you sure you're not just picking on me because I'm your brother?"

"Yes, I'm sure. Here, let me show you what you were just doing." Burchard gave his brother's arm a tug and pulled him out of the line. He demonstrated, showing his brother how his shoulders had been drooped and his feet turned in, making it difficult for him to keep his body straight for the punches. "Now if you stand like this instead…" Burchard squared his shoulders and straightened his feet, and then did a mid, high, low punch sequence. "See how my arms are straighter?"

Theodore nodded. "Yes, I can see that now. So I just have to roll my shoulders back and straighten my feet?"

Burchard smiled. "Yep. Try it."

Theodore tried, and Burchard could see the relief on his brother's face at how the posture changes had made a significant difference. "Thanks, brother," Theodore said with a smile, and then went back into line.

Burchard worked his way through the pages twice before returning to Ruschmann's side. "Now what?" he asked uncertainly.

"Well, I think they probably want a water break," Ruschmann pointed out.

Burchard grinned. "Yes, I suppose that would be a good idea." He turned his attention back to the pages. "Good job. You may take a water break."

The sigh of relief at the announcement was audible from the pages. *I guess when I was a page I tired easily too,* Burchard reminded himself.

When he deemed the water break long enough, he called the pages back into line, instructing them to get their wooden practice swords.

Burchard stepped to the front of the group. "Just like with the hand-to-hand practice, we will start with the basics: high, middle, and low strikes and blocks. Once I am sure you are doing those correctly solo, we will pair up." He unsheathed his sword and raised it. "Ready, begin. Strikes first. High." He swung his sword in a high strike. "Low." He demonstrated low and then middle. "Now for the blocks. High." He brought his sword up in a high block, followed by low and middle. He slid his sword back into its sheath and kept repeating high, low, middle. When the pages fell into the rhythm and did not appear to need him to continue saying the maneuvers, Burchard walked the lines.

He paused here and there, adjusting a stance or grip. Every adjustment he made, he had the page demonstrate for him they could do the strike or block with the change before he made his way to the next page. Satisfied that he had made any necessary adjustments, Burchard went back to the front of the group and watched for a few more minutes.

"OK, I think you are ready to pair up. To begin with, I'll allow you to select your own partners. Then, I need you in two lines, but make sure that you have plenty of space."

It took a while for the pages to get themselves organized, but they finally stood in two lines with plenty of space between each pair. "Good. Now we will start with the simple stuff. The page on the left will strike first and the page on the right will block. We will do each set twice and then you'll swap."

"Ready, begin. High…low…middle," Burchard called. He kept repeating the commands as he worked his way down the line. The first pass he was just observing, wanting to see if the pages had changed because they were paired up or if they remembered the corrections he told them. For the most part, it appeared as though they remembered. He was pleasantly surprised but also was beginning to feel the monotony of the basic drills getting to him.

He clapped his hands together. "OK, we are going to take another quick break, and then I want to change things up." He could hear the pages murmuring at his announcement. *Good, let them wonder.*

Ruschmann walked over to him. "What exactly are you planning to have them do?"

Burchard chuckled. "I was going to pair them up, but only have four pairs at a time and let them spar. Think about it—the drills are good, but when you are fighting an enemy, they don't always stick to the basics of the drill. The pages are decent enough in the drills to have a chance to spar. Besides, maybe some of them could benefit from learning more advanced moves. This way we can see who that is."

Ruschmann shrugged. "If you say so. Just tell me where you want me."

Burchard nodded, then found himself examining the pages. He didn't know everyone's names yet, but he was familiar enough with their techniques.

"We will start with four pairs. When I call your name or point to you, you will come here," Burchard announced. "We will swap in a bit so everyone gets a chance to try this."

"You and you." Burchard pointed to two fourth-year pages. The first one was the tallest of all the pages and was even taller than Burchard; the second fourth-year had pale, almost white hair and was average height. He chose two more pairs of third- and fourth-year pages before calling his last set. "Theodore and Armand." A gasp went through the pages. Burchard knew they were all wondering why a first-year had been called.

"Now, space yourselves out. You get the whole ring, so don't bunch together. I expect you to use more room than you're used to.

The task is to spar. Use what you know. If all you are comfortable with is sticking to the high, middle, and low strikes and blocks, then that is perfectly OK. However, do *not* turn it into a drill," Burchard explained. He took a spot on the edge of the practice ring. "You may begin."

The four pairs hesitated. He could see each pairing making light, almost comical strikes at each other, as though they were afraid. Rolling his eyes, he realized he had to speak again. "You need to strike like you mean it. If the page in front of you were a Stinyian rebel, what do you think would happen if you were striking without any power?"

Armand replied, "We would get skewered."

"Yes, or at least the likelihood of being injured would be much greater. For this part of training today, I need you to make sure you are practicing as though you are going against a rebel. Make sure your strikes and blocks are strong and full of intent," Burchard said. He waited for the eight pages to nod in understanding. "OK. Let's try this again. Begin!"

This time, he could hear the wooden practice swords connect. He wasn't sure if the pages had been afraid to hurt each other last time or if they hadn't really understood the purpose of this exercise. The pairs he had chosen to begin were what he considered the top quarter from the drill today and from the other times he'd spent observing them since their arrival. Which meant once it was clear they understood the assignment, he did not have to adjust their stances or hand holds; he was able to just watch.

Burchard was a little surprised that the only pair doing any additional maneuvers beyond high, middle, and low was Theodore and Armand. He moved closer to them. Armand lunged forward and brought his sword down in a sweeping middle strike. Theodore spun out of the way and then parried with a low backhanded strike aiming for Armand's legs. Armand blocked but put pressure on Theodore's sword, forcing him to back up several steps. Theodore gave up the steps begrudgingly and then twisted his wrist and popped Armand's sword out of his hand.

Burchard clapped. "Brilliant!"

Theodore turned to him. "You're just saying that because I'm your brother."

Burchard shook his head. "No, I'm not. You were able to come up with a solution to get out of a situation where Armand had the upper hand. I can tell you've been watching some of the knights practice. Because that is not a move that you would have been taught as a page."

Theodore eyed his older brother. "Actually, I learned that from watching you. I wasn't sure it would work, but you had said earlier that we could use any strikes or blocks that we wanted to. I figured I could at least give it a try."

Burchard nodded. "Well, it worked. And Armand, great job putting pressure on Theodore and forcing him to give ground. Often when you put pressure on an opponent, it forces them to make bad choices and gives you an advantage."

Just then the bell rang indicating lunchtime. *Already?* He hadn't realized so much time had passed. "OK, everyone. We will pick up after lunch with another set of groups. Since Sir Foxbright is busy, I think we will just continue weapons practice since I don't think I'd be very successful at teaching you battle strategy."

The pages stacked the practice swords in a pile and filed into the dining hall.

Burchard and Ruschmann hung back a little. "I think that went well," Ruschmann said.

"I guess so," Burchard replied uncertainly.

Ruschmann smiled. "You have a way about you. I know you were focused on instructing, but the pages just soak up everything you say. Even when the four pairs were sparring, the pages on the bench were watching. Even Sir Foxbright has trouble keeping their attention this long."

"If you say so," Burchard said with a shrug and then led the way into the dining hall.

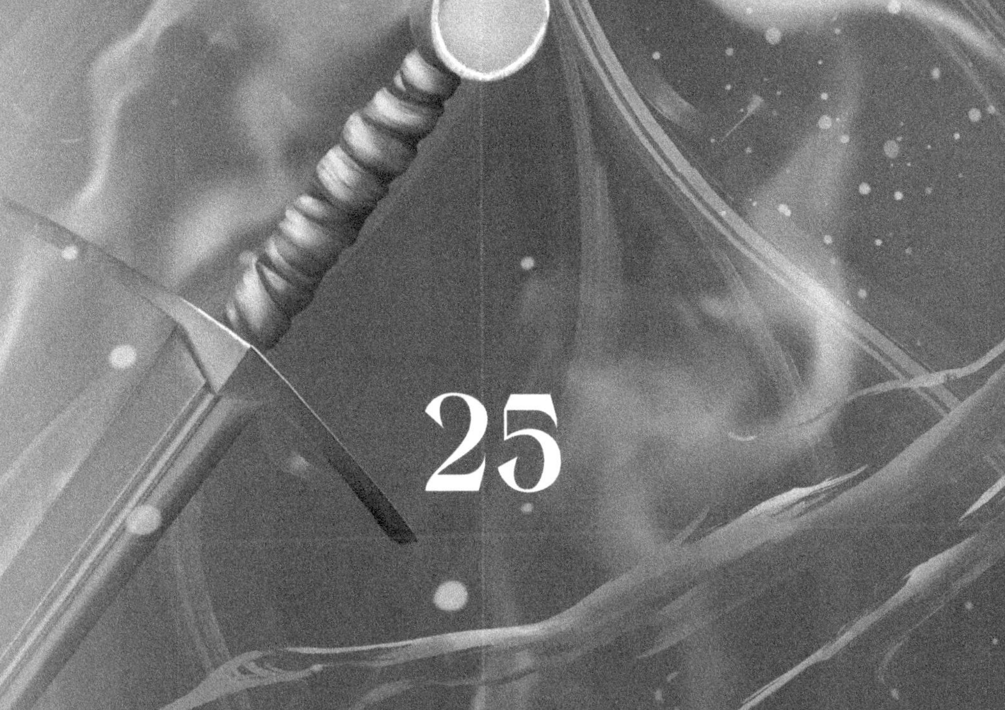

25

Burchard and Ruschmann stood on the wall and peered out into the gray mist surrounding Alderth Castle. This was the third morning since he'd met with Jade and had the encounter with Ossa. Neither Jade nor Ossa had shown up yet. Burchard wasn't sure whether to be worried or relieved.

Burchard blew out his breath and turned around to gaze upon the people in the castle yard. Forty pages, led by Sir Lucius Foxbright, were beginning their morning weapons training. Forcing himself to hide his feelings as the eager young Armand Foxbright caught sight of him and waved, Burchard raised his hand in acknowledgement before facing Ruschmann.

"I guess for now we might as well continue our morning routines like Sir Foxbright is doing. I know Sir Foxbright sent the General a message, which I'm sure he received and is ignoring. I don't know if Sir Foxbright would tell us if he had gotten a reply, though, unless it was specifically saying reinforcements were on the way," Burchard said before muttering under his breath, "If he'd even deem us worthy of rescue."

Fang whined, leaning into his leg. "You're right. Let's go find a morning snack, and then go practice some sword work."

Burchard, Ruschmann, and Fang headed toward the kitchen. With the number of residents in the castle now barely at one hundred, the decision had been made to only use the main kitchen and that everyone would eat meals together in the castle's dining hall.

Burchard pushed open the outer door slowly. He'd already found out the hard way that sometimes one of the kitchen staff was behind the door. It had taken over an hour to clean all of the stew that had splattered. Lesson learned.

Fortunately, no one was behind the door.

"Burchard!" called Lady Gladys from somewhere in the kitchen. Burchard found himself blushing.

Ruschmann elbowed him. "Are you *sure* you're just friends?"

"Yes!" growled Burchard.

Lady Gladys wiped flour from her hands as she strode toward them. "Let me guess," she said, peering from one to the other. "Morning snack?"

Cook laughed and thrust plates into their hands. "I told you, Gladys, they're boys. They are *always* hungry." Cook disappeared again and came back, eyebrow raised. "Are you just going to stand their gawking or are you going to sit and eat?"

"Excuse our manners, Cook. Thank you," Burchard said with a bow before sliding onto the bench of the nearest table. It happened to have an assortment of chopped vegetables on it with barely enough space for the two of them.

"Fang, I did not forget you," Cook said with a smile before placing a metal bowl full of raw fish in front of her. The black wolf gave Cook a quick lick of thanks. Burchard glanced between the two of them in surprise.

"You're friends?" he inquired.

"Of course we're friends," Cook said, running a familiar hand along Fang's back before heading back into the depths of the kitchen.

"Does my…" Burchard said quietly.

"No, your father doesn't know. But there are many things he is not aware of in the castle," Gladys said tartly.

"Oh, really?" Burchard said in surprise. He knew Gladys had become friends with Fang, but he hadn't realized the wolf was making friends with other people in the castle. His father had been very adamant that Fang did her own hunting outside of the castle. Every other day, Burchard, sometimes with Ruschmann, would take her outside and allow her to hunt. Maybe this was why she wouldn't always eat more than a squirrel—because she wasn't as hungry as he thought she was.

Gladys gave him a smile and went back to the counter where she was preparing rolls to go into the oven for lunch.

Burchard raised his arms over his head and stretched before sliding out from the bench. "That was delicious. Thanks!" he called into the kitchen. Gathering up their empty dishes, Burchard deposited them into the sink before heading back outside.

When they reached the sword training yard, they unbuckled their scabbards and went through a series of stretches.

"Are we running first?" Ruschmann asked.

"Yeah, how about just two laps. I'd like to help the pages some too," Burchard replied.

Ruschmann nodded and they took off at a run, keeping their pace steady. As they ran around the castle grounds, Burchard forced himself to let go of all his concerns over his father's actions.

Burchard and Ruschmann sheathed their swords and walked over to the rows of pages. Sir Foxbright was leading the third- and fourth-year pages through sword drills, while an injured Captain Edward Russell was carefully supervising the first- and second-year pages on the archery range from a chair.

Sir Foxbright motioned for them to come over. "Squire Burchard, would you please walk the line and make any necessary corrections?"

Burchard bowed before he made his way down the first line of pages. Here and there, he had to adjust a page's stance. A couple of them were so misaligned that he wasn't sure how they weren't just whacking their neighbors. Occasionally during the week the pages had been in residence, Sir Foxbright had asked either him or Ruschmann to walk the lines and help the pages. Much to his surprise, Burchard found he really enjoyed helping the pages and seeing their excitement when they finally understood what they were doing wrong and how to fix it.

Burchard was about to walk past Armand when Fang's warning howl pierced the air. Burchard leapt out of the line away from the pages, trying to pinpoint where Fang was. Glancing over his shoulder, he saw Ruschmann's gaze settle on the open gate. Yanking his sword out, Burchard sprinted out the gate and slid abruptly to a halt, almost falling on top of Fang, who was running toward him.

Burchard ran a hand along her back, trying to steady himself. He was shocked when he could feel Fang shaking. Tearing his eyes from the wolf, he looked where she had come from and began cursing. Swaying to regain his balance, he shouted, "Shut the gate! Shut the gate!"

Burchard ran as fast as he could, but it didn't feel fast enough as he watched the gate slowly close. He slid through and collapsed just as it slammed shut.

Fang licked his face, and he grabbed handfuls of her fur, pulling her close. They were both shaking.

"What's wrong?" Ruschmann asked, looking perplexed.

"It's coming!" Burchard shouted.

Sir Foxbright was staring at him. "I ordered the gate shut as you requested…but there's nothing out there."

"The blackness is approaching!" Burchard spat, his temper flaring.

Sir Foxbright gave him a sympathetic look. "I didn't say I don't believe you, but none of us can see whatever you and Fang saw."

Burchard took Ruschmann's offered hand and ran up the stairs onto the wall, taking two or three at a time. "There's nothing there," he said in surprise. The big black wall that had been approaching at sickening speed was nowhere to be seen.

"What on earth is going on?" Ruschmann asked.

"I swear to you I saw it!" Burchard growled.

Fang echoed his growl, but hers continued as she peered out over the wall.

Ruschmann ran a tentative hand along Fang's back. Burchard watched his friend uncertainly.

"Fang, can you still see the blackness?" Ruschmann asked.

Fang nodded.

Burchard stared as his friend. He had known Fang seemed smarter than most animals, but…she just answered a direct question. *Did I know she could do that?* he wondered.

"We know you don't have magic, Burchard. So, what if something in Alderth Castle is blocking it?" Ruschmann asked.

"Like magical protection?" Burchard asked skeptically.

"If we're lucky. I don't recall the General ever saying that the castle has any magical defenses," Sir Foxbright chimed in.

Burchard studied Sir Foxbright's face, debating his next words. Since Sir Foxbright was also a lord, he was the highest-ranking man residing in the castle, which meant he would be giving orders leading to fight against whatever awaited them beyond the castle walls. "What would you like us to do, Sir Foxbright?"

The knight opened his mouth to respond and then snapped it shut. "Gather your armor and inform the pages to collect whatever gear they have." Turning on his heel, Sir Foxbright walked over to the bell and rang it four times, warning any within the walls of Alderth Castle and those nearby that they were under attack and needed aid.

"Chain mail…what about shields?" Ruschmann asked as he and Burchard rushed into their barracks.

"It would probably be wise to bring the shields. Then we have them if we want them," Burchard replied as he quickly pulled on his heavy leather pants followed by a chain mail shirt. The links quietly clicked together as it settled on his shoulders. Burchard smiled grimly. *Whatever this enemy is, we will face it,* he thought.

On his small armor stand was a helmet and another sword in a scabbard. He snatched the helmet and put it on his head, before his gaze fell back on the sword. It was heavier than the sword he usually used. Shrugging, he picked it up and belted it so it sat on his right hip with his usual sword on his left hip. Shield slung over his shoulder, Burchard gave one last searching look to his space before meeting Ruschmann outside.

Ruschmann stared at the second sword. "What are you doing?"

Burchard shrugged. "I thought I might need a spare."

"What could you possibly be planning on doing that would require a spare?" Ruschmann paused and shook his head. "Never mind. Please don't tell me."

Burchard gave Ruschmann a smirk before they made their way back to the castle steps where Sir Foxbright wanted them to regroup. As they approached the steps, Fang reappeared at his side. Burchard looked down in surprise, realizing that the wolf had not been with him in the barracks.

When they could see the steps, Burchard stumbled to a halt, taking in the scene before him. The pages were organized in rows. They had an assortment of leather armor pieces, and a few of the larger kids found some chain mail that mostly fit. About half had long knives, and the other half had bows with full quivers.

Burchard stepped up to the side of Sir Foxbright. "Do we have any fire arrows?" he asked quietly.

"Yes, the pages that have the green quivers have only fire arrows. I also had some extra quivers placed along the upper wall so that if anyone runs out, they will have more," Sir Foxbright said without taking his eyes from the pages. "I'm going to have the archers primarily on the wall. I will command from up there. Those who are good with a sword…well, I couldn't find small enough swords, so the long knives will have to do."

"It's better than being unarmed," Ruschmann replied.

"Yes, it is better than being unarmed." Sir Foxbright said.

Just then, the castle doors opened, and the servants and castle staff filed out. They were a motley crew. Cook was holding her butcher knife and gave Burchard a small smile. Gladys had plate armor, a bow with a full quiver of arrows over her shoulder, and a long knife tucked into a belt.

Burchard gulped. *Plate armor on a girl? How did I not know she had armor? Or could shoot? I am a terrible friend if I don't even know those things.*

Gladys winked at him and stepped aside so more could come out of the castle.

"Thank you," Sir Foxbright said, meeting the eyes of each and every person there. Burchard watched as the knight's gaze paused for the barest moment on each person and that person grew taller, stopped shaking, and seemed less afraid. *He gives them confidence by acknowledging they are here.*

"We don't know yet what we face, but we will face it together. For only by working together can we be successful in battle. No matter what comes through those gates, *you are not alone,*" Sir Foxbright said in a firm but certain voice. Raising his sword in the air, he shouted, "For Alderth Castle!"

"For Alderth Castle!" the pages, servants, and squires shouted in response.

"For Etria!" Sir Foxbright shouted.

"For Etria!" everyone chorused. Even Fang joined in and gave one short howl.

The gate blasted open, and a huge creature with red eyes slowly materialized from within a billowing black cloud.

Burchard almost dropped his shield in shock. He had no idea what it was other than evil and definitely *not* Ossa. The creature had the head of a man with curly black hair, but at the base of its neck it changed and was no longer human. It looked like a beast. It had four legs with huge paws. Each step forward, he caught a glimpse of razor-sharp metallic claws. The tail started off with the tawny fur of its body before changing into hard black scales, ending in a wicked spike. Its tail curved up behind it and almost over the top of its back.

Burchard felt Ruschmann's hand brush his, a reminder that it didn't matter what they were facing because they had to come up with a plan to defeat it. Taking a deep breath, Burchard settled his shield on his left arm and drew his sword with his right. He could hear Sir Foxbright softly giving orders to the pages behind him.

"Charge it on three," whispered Ruschmann. Burchard nodded in confirmation.

"One…two…three!" Together both squires sprinted toward the creature.

"Stop!" came a familiar voice of a boy behind them.

Burchard wouldn't stop. He kept running.

"It's a manticore!" the voice shouted, filled with terror.

Manticore? wondered Burchard. *I have no idea what that is.* One more stride, and they would be within striking distance of the manticore. Tightening his core muscles in preparation, Burchard was not expecting the manticore to leap over them and into the group of pages.

Panting, Burchard glanced at Ruschmann, wondering if they should turn around or not. "Is it only one?" he asked uncertainly.

Ruschmann gazed around the area in front of them. The darkness seemed to be lifting some, and there was no evidence that the manticore had companions. "We should go a little farther out to check."

"What about the pages?" Burchard said quietly.

"Sir Foxbright can handle them. The last thing we need is more of the…manticores…to come charging at us unexpectedly," Ruschmann replied.

Burchard nodded in agreement. Cautiously, the two squires crossed the final section of the bridge. No people, animals, or creatures came leaping out at them. As they stepped off the bridge, they were engulfed in darkness. Fang snarled, but it sounded muffled. The two squires and wolf continued their slow, cautious advance even though they couldn't see anything.

Just because I can't see doesn't mean my other senses are useless, he chided himself. When he took his next step, he put his foot down slowly. It felt like the road, just as he remembered it with hard-packed dirt. He inhaled deeply and then started choking.

Ruschmann pounded him on the back. "You OK?"

Careful to not repeat the same mistake, Burchard inhaled in small breaths. When he felt like he could breathe normally, he responded, "Yes, thanks."

Suddenly, the black began to shift, lightening. Burchard thought he saw shapes but couldn't be sure as it seemed like unnatural mist or fog around them.

A sharp barking laugh came toward them. Burchard adjusted his grip on his sword and raised it. Suddenly, the mist disappeared completely, and the midmorning sunlight washed over them. Burchard gasped in shock, his sword dipping, as he gazed upon what the sunlight revealed. Row after row of people. They were moving slowly, with strange, jerky motions. He was trying to figure out why they were moving so strangely when two of the people noticed them. They emitted groans and grunts but no words before running straight at them, arms clawing at the air as though they would rip the two squires apart.

"What are those?" hissed Ruschmann.

"No clue," replied Burchard, equally puzzled. Then they had no more time to talk because the two people reached them. Each squire attacked one of the people with short, precise strikes to the unprotected bodies. An arm launched through the air and landed somewhere behind them. Something about them was off. They had no weapons and were just trying to attack with their arms and fingernails, which were sharpened as though they were claws.

When the first two collapsed, more filled the gap they left. Burchard found himself easily working his way through the people as they kept coming.

"They're not bleeding!" Burchard exclaimed, a shiver of fear running through him. *What does that mean? Doesn't everyone bleed?*

"I don't think they're alive," Ruschmann said, voice shaking.

Burchard paused his attack, and the person he was attacking succeeded in clawing at his hand, leaving bloody scratches. Growling low in his throat, Burchard swept his sword across the person's neck. The head went sailing through the air, and the body collapsed in a twitching heap. He gave it a kick with his foot, and it turned into a pile of dust. "I think you're right. They're not alive."

Burchard could hear Fang's growls and snarls as she took out her share of these strange dead people. He knew the three of them would not be enough. The surging mass of dead stretched far down the road. Some were even starting to come out of the forest too.

"We need to get back into the castle."

Without needing further urging, Ruschmann turned and bolted for the castle gate. Burchard quickly followed, whistling for Fang. Fang reached them just as they were squeezing their way through the small opening in the fortified gate, which some of the pages helped cover once they were inside.

Burchard ran right into Sir Foxbright, who put a hand out to steady him. "Easy, squire."

Burchard peered at Sir Foxbright, then at the pages behind him. "What happened to the manticore?" He had been expecting them to be decimated by the creature, but instead the pages all seemed to be accounted for.

Armand shoved his way forward. "It was an illusion. It disappeared as soon as it landed in the group of pages, which I believe is when you went into the darkness outside."

Sir Foxbright examined the two squires. "What were you fighting out there? We could see you fighting, but it was difficult to make out what your enemy was."

"Dead people," Ruschmann said flatly.

Sir Foxbright raised his eyebrow. "Dead people?" He opened his mouth to say something else, then snapped it shut. "Do you mean…risen dead?"

Burchard nodded. "Yes. They didn't bleed, they carried no weapons, and they made strange, jerky movements."

Sir Foxbright shut his eyes. "'His coming will be heralded by an army of the dead…'" His voice trailed off.

"*That* is what an army of the dead is like?" Ruschmann said in disbelief.

"What did you think it would look like?" Armand asked.

"Enough," Sir Foxbright said, raising a hand to stop Burchard from replying to the page. "We need to prepare. We do not have much time before they come to the gates. The castle staff has been working on heating any tar or oil they could find. There are large pots of it around the wall. One of the pages can do a little bit of magic and is able to keep them hot. He is working his way around the wall and will continue to do so. He can also deliver messages if needed. I think we have about six pots total. The pages who can shoot a bow and hit a target consistently have also been put on the wall. There are about ten of them. The rest are currently here," he said gesturing to the pages behind him. "I was hoping you could lead them, Burchard. Ruschmann will be with the castle staff, and I'll be stationed on top of the wall."

"Me, lead?" Burchard sputtered, balking at the suggestion of formally leading anyone.

Sir Foxbright chuckled. "What do you think you've been doing the past few days practicing with the pages?"

Burchard's mouth gaped open. "Practice."

Sir Foxbright shook his head. "Not entirely. I have known since you first set foot at Trinity that you could be a leader."

"Like my father?" Burchard asked hesitantly, not sure he wanted to lead if it meant being like his father.

"Yes and no. I am sure if you want it, you could be a general too. But I meant that you could be a truly great leader. A man that people wouldn't hesitate to follow, no matter the circumstances. Anyone can earn the title of general, but it takes a true leader to earn the respect of your fellow knights—respect not based on fear," Sir Foxbright said with such certainty that Burchard wondered what the knight saw when he looked at him.

Ruschmann couldn't seem to decide who to look at. Burchard watched as his friend's eyes darted between him and the knight. "What about the previous plan?"

Sir Foxbright shook his head. "I was not anticipating this many enemies. The new plan is better."

The gate began rattling as the dead reached it and pounded on it.

"How smart did you say the army of the dead is?" Burchard asked as he fell back toward the group of pages.

"It depends on how much control Ossa is using on them," Sir Foxbright replied. "Good luck, and I would recommend praying." The knight turned on his heel and ran up the stairs to the wall, readying the long bow that had been strapped to his back as he went.

Burchard looked a Ruschmann. "See you later." The squires hugged, then Ruschmann took off at a jog for where the castle staff was waiting. Burchard gazed at the thirty pages now under his command, including Armand.

He took a deep breath, trying to keep his voice from shaking. "If we can keep the dead from spilling all the way through the gate, then we might have a chance." *A tiny chance,* he added in his mind, but he wouldn't tell the pages that. Not as they gave him hopeful looks as though he, a first-year squire, would be the solution to defeating the army of the dead.

"For Etria!" he shouted, raising his sword high in the air.

"For Etria!" the pages and everyone else in the castle echoed.

Boom! Boom! The fortified gate fell away, the pieces of wood used to brace it blasted across the courtyard by something

Burchard couldn't see. He glanced down at Fang. "Do what you need to do, Fang." She nuzzled his hand, then leapt away into the shadows.

Four abreast, the dead came through the missing gate. Arrows were sticking out of several. To his chagrin, Burchard realized the arrows were not doing much damage. *That is not my concern.*

"Charge!" he shouted and ran forward, the pages hesitating behind him, then rushing ahead. He didn't mind their hesitation. It gave him time to slam into the dead and hopefully give the pages a chance to pick off the ones he missed.

Slashing his sword right and left, Burchard was able to hamper the progress of the army of the dead entering through the gate. But he was not pushing them back beyond the gate, merely preventing them from overwhelming the pages. He could hear screaming on the wall above them and concern flashed through him as he realized that perhaps Ossa was taking more control, as Sir Foxbright had indicated could happen. If they were somehow able to climb the wall, then the meager numbers up there would be overcome quickly.

Not my problem, he thought, trying to convince himself to stick to the plan. *If I help Sir Foxbright, then I will have to abandon the gate.*

As though Fang could read his thoughts, he heard a loud howl from atop the wall. Body parts began raining down on the pages behind him, followed by yelps and mutters of "Eww, gross!" Burchard couldn't help but grin.

Encouraged by Fang's commitment to helping the pages, Burchard sped up his strikes and parries. Instead of striving for good technique, he wanted to annihilate as many as possible. Out of the corner of his eye, he could see Armand just a hair behind him to the right. Not wanting to be distracted by the page, he kept his focus. He barely nicked one of the dead that twisted and skipped to the right, just in the perfect spot for Armand's sword to skewer it. Burchard flashed a grin to his friend before taking a large step forward. Armand mimicked him, taking advantage of the gap that was in front of them to drive the dead back to the gate.

A couple more dead tried to come through the broken gate, but Burchard and Armand quickly finished them off. It was hard to discern what was beyond the gate. A lot of the bridge was obscured by fog again. The pages behind him cheered, but Burchard glanced over his shoulder to look at them. Some had smudges of dirt or the dead dust, but otherwise they seemed remarkably in one piece.

One of the pages let out a scream of terror. Burchard whirled, sword up, but was too late. Ossa, who had appeared behind Burchard, had sliced Armand's right arm. Blood splattered on the page and on Burchard. Cursing at himself and Ossa, Burchard glared at him. Not wanting to know what awful words Ossa would spew this time, Burchard flung himself at Ossa, sweeping his sword to the left. Ossa blocked easily and then parried with a strike of his own.

Burchard grimaced at the force behind that strike. Dead emerged through the gate again. With Burchard focused solely on Ossa, it would be up to the pages to handle them. High strike, followed by a middle strike, then Burchard pivoted and did a backhand aiming for Ossa's armpit, since that move had worked well at Camp Tooth.

Ossa laughed. "You remember the weakness of my minions, I see. Too bad for you it is not my weakness. I don't have a weakness."

Burchard growled. "Everyone has a weakness."

Ossa's dark pits of eyes flashed bright red, and a blast of power shot out of his sword. Burchard rolled and barely missed getting struck by the magic. He jumped to his feet and whirled, starting a combination move, when Ossa sent another blast of power at him. This time it knocked him backward.

Burchard slid several feet on his butt. Snarling, he once again got up. "You're cheating."

Ossa shrugged and leapt with his sword raised. Burchard brought his sword up to block it. The strike was so hard that he could feel his teeth rattling. *I cannot give up.* Pushing back against Ossa's sword, he was able to disengage the blades and skip to the left. He ducked under a careless swing Ossa made and came up behind him. The strike hit its mark, and the clang rang throughout the yard. Unfortunately, Ossa's dark armor did its job, and other than making noise, the strike didn't injure Ossa in any way.

Strike, parry, block, repeat. Back and forth they went. It didn't matter what maneuvers Burchard tried, Ossa was always there and ready. Burchard could feel his body tiring and knew Ossa was watching for the moment when he could deliver the killing blow.

Suddenly, the ground shuddered, and a blast of white light from somewhere out in the field was visible through the gate.

Ossa hesitated, turning toward the gate. "Umbra," Ossa murmured.

Burchard wasn't sure what was happening in the field, but Ossa gave him the opening he needed. He swung his sword two-handed for extra power and was a hairsbreadth away from slicing through Ossa's head when the knight disappeared.

"No!" howled Burchard in frustration. He spun around, sword ready. The pages were no longer in a good formation. A couple of them were sitting or slumped on the ground. Most had cuts on their faces or arms.

"Armand!" he gasped, looking around for his friend. "Do you know where Armand is?" he asked the pages. He went to each one to check them over and ask them the same question. But no one knew where he was.

Burchard checked the spot where they'd been fighting before Ossa appeared. There was a concerning pool of blood there, but no sign of his friend anywhere.

A dark voice filled his mind. *If you want your little friend back, come over the bridge alone.*

Sir Foxbright came down the stairs. "Where's Armand?" he said. Burchard realized the knight had heard him calling.

"I don't know, but I will find him," Burchard promised.

"You don't need to risk yourself for my son. We know that Ossa wants to kill you. It would be stupid to hand yourself over like this," the knight said sadly.

Burchard shook his head. "He is my friend. I cannot abandon him."

Sir Foxbright didn't reply. Instead, he bowed his head, perhaps realizing that unless he restrained Burchard, the squire was going to go find Armand.

Wiping his hands on his pants to try to dry the sweat from them, Burchard took a firm grip on his sword and strode briskly out the gate, hoping no one would be stupid enough to follow him. He knew it had to be a trap, but he didn't care. There was no other reason Ossa would have taken Armand, especially not after Ossa had told him that *he* was the target.

Burchard crossed the bridge and halted a few feet away from it. No one was out there, which he thought was weird. *Did the army of the dead just vanish? Or is it hiding somewhere?* He shook his head. *Armand is my concern now.* The minutes ticked by, and he thought Ossa was not going to show after all.

The air in front of him rippled with darkness. Then Ossa appeared, his hand gripping Armand's shoulder. From the page's expression, Burchard knew the hold had to be excruciating, yet the page didn't make a sound.

"I thought you weren't going to show," Burchard said gruffly, trying to mask his feelings.

Ossa just stared at him, eyes of endless black somehow glowing. Burchard was about to say something again when Ossa finally spoke. "If you come with me, then Armand can walk back into the castle now."

"That's all this is? A trade?" Burchard demanded.

"Yes, a trade. You for your little friend," Ossa said, digging his fingers deeper into Armand's shoulder. The page yelped.

"Don't do it, Burchard!" Armand pleaded.

"I don't have a choice." Burchard met Armand's eyes with his own. He hoped the page would understand that he would not willingly sacrifice one of his friends if he could turn himself over instead.

"There's always a choice," Armand said in barely a whisper.

"Ossa, I will accept your trade. Now let Armand go," Burchard said firmly.

Ossa grinned with all his sharp teeth visible. "I was hoping you'd agree."

Burchard stepped forward and Ossa released his grip on Armand's shoulder. Armand passed Burchard, and Burchard whispered, "Run as fast as you can."

Armand didn't hesitate and took off at a run. Burchard watched for a moment before turning to face Ossa. "You have what you want."

Ossa laughed. "Not quite, but close. Now come here." Ossa beckoned Burchard to walk toward him. Burchard felt a tug on his bellybutton, almost the same as when he'd been at Camp Tooth and his brother had been calling to him. He tried to fight it, but he could not keep his feet from moving forward.

"What did you do?" he hissed.

"An insurance policy. So that you can't run. You didn't think I'd let the page return unless I was certain you couldn't just run after him? I have been around for thousands of years, boy. I know all the tricks," Ossa said in a cold voice.

Burchard was almost within Ossa's range. A tremor of terror went through him. He wasn't sure if he could get free once he got to Ossa. Trying to mask his terror, he replied, "You can't know them all, or you'd have killed me at Camp Tooth."

To Burchard's satisfaction, Ossa replied, "I told you three days ago, there is a prophecy. I cannot just kill you outright—or, I should say, I couldn't. Now, though…I believe it is safe for me to kill you."

Ossa closed his fist and Burchard found himself being yanked into him. Ossa pinned Burchard's arms to his side and stepped behind the squire, running his nose over Burchard's throat. Burchard could feel the sharp teeth graze his neck, and then his sword belt slid off. He heard a soft thud as he assumed Ossa tossed it out of his reach.

There was a loud screech followed by the sound of huge flapping wings. Burchard found himself wanting to duck for cover, but his body would not respond. He could hear the wings again, and then the creature came into view as the fog momentarily parted. A huge great horned owl, razor-sharp talons outstretched, flew by.

Ossa let out a shriek of rage, and black blood sprayed off the top of his head. Droplets landed on Burchard's face and arms. He dug his heels in and tried to take a step backward. It didn't work. The giant owl banked and came back. This time, Ossa pushed Burchard out of his way and prepared to attack. Sword raised, he slashed upward as the owl passed over the top of him. White feathers scattered across the ground.

The ground vibrated with a familiar thrumming sound. Almost like hoofbeats. An arrow sailed through the air and narrowly missed the top of Ossa's head. It landed with a thud at Burchard's feet. At that moment, he realized that he no longer felt the tug on his bellybutton; the spell that had prevented him from moving must have broken. Keeping his attention on Ossa, Burchard slowly kneeled and broke the arrowhead off the shaft. Using his hand to hide his new weapon, he straightened, waiting.

The fog vanished, and Burchard's eyes went wide as he saw what had to be at least fifty centaurs charging straight at them, followed by what seemed to be a squad of Etrian knights and a handful of riders in colorful robes. *Who on earth is that?* At the head of the group was Damos, the air around him crackling with threads of his green-and-gold magic. The centaurs were armed with an assortment of weapons, including swords, axes, and spears.

Ossa raised his hand and a dark, billowing cloud shot toward the centaurs. Burchard was sure Damos was going to die. He was pleasantly surprised when a green-and-gold oval, almost like a shield, erupted from Damos. The light and dark magic collided and sent a shockwave blasting throughout Alderth Castle, the road, and the forest. Burchard's feet were knocked out from under him, and he almost lost his grip on the arrowhead.

He could feel the ground trembling as the centaurs and the knights behind them launched their attack on Ossa and the army of the dead. *I guess they were not affected by the shockwave.* Burchard slid his knee under his chest and pushed himself up off the ground. Now that help had arrived, the army of the dead had also returned with seemingly renewed energy. Damos and Ossa were fighting off to the side, while the rest tried to push Ossa's army away from the castle. He could see flashes of magic coming from the robed people when it dawned on him who it was. *Sir Waldorf and Sir Emberwood said they had men who could help and access to Onaxx Mages.*

Burchard was debating if he should slip back into the castle when another clash of dark and light power created a second shockwave. He heard a crack and twisted to look at the castle. Some of the stones were falling off the wall.

I must end this, or the castle is going to crumble. There are innocent people in there. His mind set, Burchard crawled on his hands and knees, creeping closer to Ossa and Damos. He knew it would be slow this way, but if he stood, he risked Ossa seeing him or being knocked down again if there was a third shockwave. Gritting his teeth, Burchard pressed onward, pausing as needed to ensure he wouldn't be seen. During one of his stops, he inspected the arrowhead and was surprised to see it appeared to have been dipped in something. He raised it to his nose and sniffed, then began gagging. Desperate to keep his presence hidden, he curled into a ball, waiting for the feeling to pass. *It must be some sort of poison—a guarantee that Ossa will die. Just the weapon I need.* He ripped a piece of his shirt off and carefully wrapped the arrowhead in it to protect himself from the poison, hoping that would be enough.

He finally could see Ossa and Damos. The centaur had several nasty-looking slices across his chest and flanks. He was limping slightly too. Ossa's head was slick with black blood, and pieces of his armor were missing completely, revealing that his arms underneath also sported the skull tattoos.

There was a rock outcropping not too far off, and Burchard angled himself toward it. When he reached the rocks, he stood up. Ossa's back was to him, and he hoped that Damos would spot him and understand what he intended. Burchard fingered the broken shaft connected to the arrowhead. He knew his plan would likely result in his death, and he was OK with that. If he could get close enough, he was certain it would kill Ossa.

Burchard hunkered back down so he was hidden by the rocks but could still see. He winced in sympathy as Ossa's blade sliced deeply into Damos's front left leg. The centaur stumbled but used his momentum to drive Ossa back toward the rocks. Ossa took the opportunity to slice at Damos's other leg, bringing the centaur crashing to his knees as his front legs gave out completely. Damos caught Burchard's eye and gave the slightest nod.

Burchard lunged forward and wrapped his arms around Ossa. Ossa struggled and Burchard almost dropped the arrowhead. Damos let out a small blast of power, momentarily stunning Ossa. That was all Burchard needed. He drove the arrowhead deep into Ossa's exposed left arm and then let go, throwing himself backward.

Ossa spun and looked at him in disbelief before he burst into a poof of black dust. Burchard threw out his arms just in time to keep himself from slamming into the rocks. Panting heavily, he stared at the spot Ossa had been moments before. He hadn't expected the poison to work that fast. His gaze then slid to Damos. The centaur had slumped to his side; his eyes were closed, and Burchard could see blood still leaking out of his wounds.

Cautiously, Burchard stepped forward. "Damos?" he said softly.

The centaur's eyes opened a slit. "I'm not dead."

"You could have fooled me," Burchard muttered, earning a chuckle followed by a groan of pain from Damos.

"I will heal," Damos said.

Burchard kneeled beside the centaur and watched as the bleeding seemed to slow a bit. "Do you need my help?"

"Only if something else comes our way. I don't think I can even use my magic right now," Damos confessed.

"Are you worried that more will come after us?" Burchard said, peering out beyond where they were. He couldn't see much. Clumps of fog blocked most of his view. He also couldn't hear the sounds of battle.

"Umbra will come," Damos said confidently.

"Today?" Burchard asked.

Damos coughed, then shrugged. "I don't know."

"I saw Liala. I didn't realize she could get huge," Burchard said, awe lacing his voice.

Damos's eyes slid shut, and Burchard wondered if the centaur was going to go to sleep. "Some druids who shapeshift can also change the size of their animal form."

When it was clear that Damos was done speaking for now, Burchard looked down at himself. His body felt battered, and he could sense the exhaustion creeping up on him. A clip- clop of hooves had him standing defensively in front of Damos, sword raised.

A pair of centaurs appeared. A male with short-cropped bright blue hair and olive skin had horse fur that was a mix of blues and browns. The female had black hair that was in tiny braids— some were vibrant purple instead of black—and dark-brown skin. Burchard's eyes traveled down her face to her torso and he found himself blushing. Across her chest was the strap of the baldric holding a pair of axes across her back. Other than the baldric her chest was bare, leaving her breasts quite visible. Burchard gulped audibly and forced his eyes to go back to her face. A twitch of her lips was all the indicator he had that she had noticed.

"We need to get Damos into the castle," announced the female centaur.

"Who are you?" Burchard said. He knew that they had to be part of Damos's group, but he didn't want to just turn Damos over to anyone.

"I'm Thaleis, Damos's second-in-command, and this is Charos," the female centaur said.

Burchard was surprised that Damos's second-in-command was female. He knew that not all cultures shared Etria's aversion to women leading, but this was the first time he'd met a female leader in the flesh rather than just reading about one in a book.

"How do you plan to move him? I don't think he can walk."

Thaleis chuckled. "You didn't think that Damos is the only one in our group who has magic, did you?"

Burchard shrugged. He honestly hadn't spent much time considering what skills the centaurs might have, only that they had joined the fight. As he stood there, both Thaleis and Charos made small motions with their hands. Ropes of whiteish light—*magic*, his mind supplied—swirled around their hands, then wrapped around Damos. When Damos was covered in the white magic ropes, he rose into the air till he was about knee-height off the ground.

High enough to not hit anything lying on the ground, Burchard mused.

"Get on," Thaleis said in a tone that was almost an order. Burchard just gave her a blank look. "Climb on my back." She shifted closer to him.

Burchard took a hesitant step forward. "You want me to ride you?"

Thaleis nodded. "Yes, we can move much faster than if you walk. I don't want to give Umbra a chance to get her hands on Damos… or you."

Burchard wrapped his arm around her torso and swung himself awkwardly onto her back. It felt like being on a horse, but not quite. Then, Thaleis began moving, and he almost fell off. A tendril of white magic wrapped around him. Burchard blushed in embarrassment that the centaur felt she needed to use magic to keep him on. Then they leapt into a gallop, and he was grateful for the magic. Thaleis and Charos galloped side by side with Damos hovering in the air between them. They galloped right through the opening where the gate had been cleared and into the courtyard before coming to an abrupt halt.

Ruschmann, leading the castle staff—or what was left of them—ran forward, weapons raised. He must have recognized Damos or seen Burchard because he halted and shouted orders for weapons to be lowered. "You're alive!"

Burchard hopped off Thaleis's back, and Ruschmann pulled him into a hug.

"I am not sure how, but yes, I am alive. Did Armand make it back?" Burchard said into Ruschmann's ear. He didn't want to let go of his friend, worried if he did so that he'd wake up and be back with Ossa again.

Ruschmann took a step back, letting his arms drop. "Yes, Armand made it back, and we got him patched up."

"Who else was wounded?" Burchard asked.

Ruschmann shook his head. "Let me show you." Ruschmann turned to lead the way to wherever the wounded were being kept when a battle horn sounded.

Burchard pivoted so he was facing the gate. "He decided to show up now that all the work is done."

Sir Foxbright also facing the gate, replied, "But he did come."

Burchard refused to comment, not sure what he wanted to feel about his father coming, just not in time.

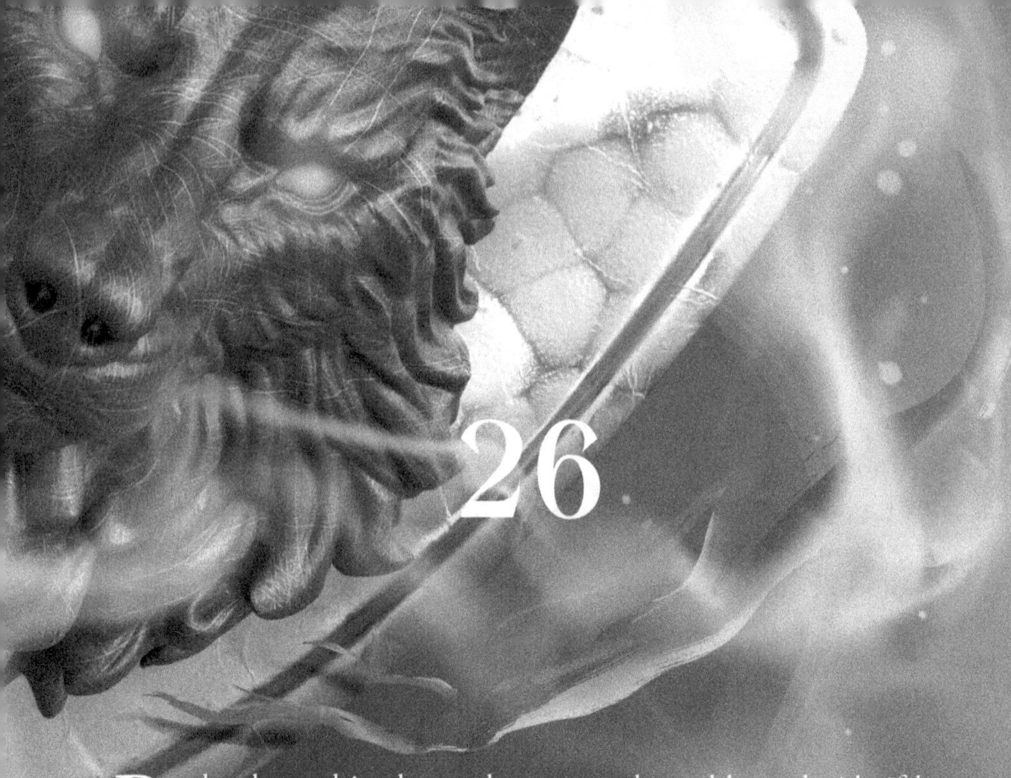

26

Burchard stood in the castle courtyard, unable to decide if he should follow Ruschmann to see the wounded or give his father a piece of his mind. He watched as General Wolfensberger rode into Alderth Castle as though he had been the one who just fought the battle. Anger filled Burchard. *How dare he.* A nudge to his armored leg had him looking down into Fang's golden eyes. The black wolf no longer looked black. Her coarse fur was plastered to her with a mixture of black and red blood and grayish dust. On her left hip, a patch of fur was missing, and she had a fresh scar.

"I guess you can heal yourself too," he said, trying to let go of his anger.

Burchard stepped backward as Sir Foxbright, his plate armor covered in ashes and blood, strode forward to greet the General. Burchard hoped he could just find someplace to disappear and not have to listen to whatever nonsense his father was going to say. *I know what happened, whether or not that is the tale the General deems worthy of retelling.* His back collided with a stone wall. He glanced to the right and then left and realized he had actually made it to the building. Ruschmann caught his eye from where he was waiting at the top of the stairs.

Not wanting to waste time, Burchard ran up the steps and slipped inside the castle. "Are they in the healer suite?"

"No, there were too many wounded, so we had to use the dining hall," Ruschmann replied solemnly.

Burchard bit his lip. There had been barely one hundred people in Alderth Castle. *How many were injured?* Keeping his thoughts to himself, he dutifully followed his friend, Fang periodically brushing against his leg as though to comfort him. When they entered the dining hall, he gasped. Everyone except for Sir Foxbright seemed to be in there. Some were walking around sporting bandages and helping with what they could. Others were sitting in chairs as though they were too injured to walk but could at least be upright. Then there were five laid out across the top of the long table.

Burchard's face blanched as he gazed upon the still forms. *The reality of battle*, he reminded himself. Step by step, he slowly walked forward, clenching his fists, willing them to stop shaking. Pages and castle staff offered subdued greetings when they saw him. He took his time to acknowledge each individual who addressed him before he finally made it to the table. As much as he wanted to rush to see who was on the table, it dawned on him how much the pages and castle staff needed those few words he said to them.

The first person laid out on the table was one of the groundskeepers. His body was covered in a white sheet and only his face was uncovered. Given the grayish tinge to his skin, Burchard knew without asking that the man was dead.

Pinching his lips together, he moved down the table to the next person. This one was a page. The white linen bandage wrapped around the boy's head was already soaking through with blood. His left hand was partially bandaged too where his ring and pinky fingers were missing. Burchard spent some time peering at the page, when he realized why under the dirt and grim the face was familiar.

"Theodore?" the words came out barely more than a whisper. The page didn't move.

Ruschmann bumped Burchard's shoulder, causing him to jump; he had forgotten his friend was with him. Burchard tilted his head so he could see Ruschmann frowning.

"Yes, that is Theodore. I forgot he's your brother, otherwise I'd have directed you to him first." Ruschmann paused. "I think with a healer he will be fine. I doubt his missing fingers can be grown back, but at least it's on his left hand."

Burchard nodded solemnly and gave his brother's uninjured right arm a squeeze. He wasn't sure if Theodore could hear them or feel the squeeze, but if he could, he wanted his brother to know he was there.

The next two badly injured were pages that Burchard didn't know, but based on his quick assessment of the severity of their injuries— one had a bandage around his abdomen that was already soaked through with blood, the other was missing a leg and was leaking blood and something else from his head—Burchard doubted they would survive, even with a healer's assistance.

As they approached the last figure on the table, Burchard immediately recognized Armand's red hair and rushed forward. "He ran back into the castle after I got him free of Ossa. What happened?" he growled.

Ruschmann clicked his tongue. "The shockwaves. You were closer to them, I think. Didn't they do damage on the battlefield?"

"Yes, but—" Burchard began.

Ruschmann raised a hand to cut him off. "He fell off the wall, Burchard. He was on his way to give Sir Foxbright a report when the second one hit. He lost his balance and…" Ruschmann closed his eyes as though he was reliving what had happened.

"My father has a healer with him. Surely that will help him and my brother," Burchard pleaded, unwilling to accept that this young, eager page who had so quickly worked his way into Burchard's heart could die.

Ruschmann shook his head. "I don't know. None of us can really tell how badly Armand was injured from the fall. He hasn't woken up since it happened. Your brother had a piece of the wall hit him on the head, but he didn't fall twenty feet. You should know that between the two of us, your skills with the medical supplies far outshine mine. We will just have to see what the healer can do."

Tears slid down Burchard's face. He felt so helpless. He lost track of time and was only brought back to awareness by a commotion at the doors to the dining hall. Several voices were shouting, followed by loud growls and snarls. Burchard's eyes snapped open; he was surprised to find himself sitting in a chair. *When did I sit down?* he wondered.

Directing his attention to the doorway of the dining hall, he saw the General's head healer, wearing a white robe that even from where Burchard stood looked as though it didn't have a speck of dirt on it. Fang was nipping at the healer's heels, driving him forward, while several knights were trying to block their progress. Burchard was frozen in the chair. He knew he should help. He just couldn't find it in him to correct Fang. *So what if she bites him?*

Burchard watched them. Fang was relentless. Every time the healer tried to stop, she'd snap at him. He could see a few times when her teeth grazed the healer, and small drops of blood were beginning to fleck his pristine robe. Finally, the head healer's eyes met Burchard's. Something Burchard was doing must have been enough for the healer to run over.

"Where are you hurt?" the healer said, taking Burchard's hand in his.

Burchard snatched his hand back. "It's not me you need to attend to. It's the pages, Armand Foxbright and Theodore Wolfensberger." He pointed to where Armand's small body lay on the table. The healer nodded and turned toward Armand, letting his hands hover over the page.

"Wolf," a voice said, causing Burchard to jump in his chair. He realized he must have dozed off again.

"Wolf," the voice repeated. Burchard looked around for the voice, then heard a giggle coming from the table. Sure enough, Armand was sitting on the table with his legs dangling off of it, and Fang was sitting in front of Armand, tongue lolling to the side. She was back to being clean and pure black.

Someone must have given her a bath, Burchard thought.

"Wolf," Armand repeated.

Burchard was confused. "Why are you saying wolf? She has a name, you know. Fang."

Armand giggled again. "I am aware of Fang's name, silly. I'm calling you Wolf."

Burchard scratched at his cheek. "I don't understand."

Armand rolled his eyes. "I'm giving you a new name. From now on, I am going to call you Wolf." The page paused. "When Damos woke up from his healing sleep, that is what he called you. Lýkos. I figured that most Etrians would probably freak out if your nickname was in a different language, so it's just Wolf."

Burchard was dumbfounded. *The centaurs gave me a nickname?*

Armand slid off the table and gave Burchard a big hug. "You don't need to understand, just be aware everyone is going to call you Wolf from now on. Besides…Burchard is such a mouthful."

Just then an all too familiar voice shouted across the noise in the dining hall. "Squire Burchard Wolfensberger, your presence is required."

Burchard sighed and gave Armand a rough hug, relief flooding him as he realized that Armand was truly healed. "How are you feeling?" he asked gruffly, emotions filling him.

Armand shrugged, "Like I slept for way too long, and now I need something to do."

Burchard laughed, then gently pushed the page out of the way and stood up. His whole body was stiff and had him wondering how long he slept in that chair for. "Let me answer the summons. Don't go too far. I will be right back!" He walked slowly to where the voice had come from, trying to shake the stiffness out of his arms and legs.

Just before he reached the General's makeshift desk, Lady Gladys intercepted him. "Hi," she said softly.

"Hi," he replied, his eyes running over every inch of her, wanting reassurance that his friend was OK. He took note of the dark blue dress and the long knife in her belt.

"I should have told you before that I can use a bow and knife. It's just…my father was worried about protocol and such," Lady Gladys explained quietly.

Burchard opened his mouth to reply when a shout came toward them. "Squire Burchard!"

He gave her an apologetic smile. "Hopefully after whatever I'm being summoned for, we can talk."

"I'd like that. Thank you for risking yourself for the safety of everyone in the castle," she replied and stepped forward, giving him a kiss on the cheek before disappearing among the milling people in the dining hall. Burchard bit his lip, not sure what to make of the kiss, and then finished making his way to the voice who summoned him.

It appeared as though his father had set up his office temporarily in a corner of the dining hall. The General was sitting in a large chair, almost throne-like, behind a large table that was covered by a map. Damos stood at the edge of the table as far as he could be from the General and still see the map. Sir Foxbright was on the other side. Reggie stood next to their father's chair.

"General," Burchard said with a bow before he approached the table.

"Damos has asked me to launch a search party for one of his druids, who seems to be missing," the General said in a cold voice.

Burchard bit his lip. He could guess the next words out of his father's mouth.

"I cannot spare any knights or infantry to help. I must regroup and make sure everyone has recovered from the devastating battle," the General said, confirming what Burchard had thought.

"Did you fight the rebels?" Burchard asked.

The General glared coldly at his son. "No, the rebels were not there. I was talking about the losses that happened here at Alderth Castle."

Burchard tilted his head so he could see Damos better. "Who is missing?"

"Jade," Damos said sadly.

Eyes widening, Burchard glanced at his father, then at Damos. "What happened?"

Damos sighed. "I believe Umbra has her."

"Umbra is a myth. Like I said, I do not have anyone to spare, druid." The General said the word *druid* as though it put a bad taste in his mouth.

"Let me have the two squires then, if they are willing," requested Damos.

General Wolfensberger laughed. He grabbed his sides, he was laughing so hard. When he finally got control of himself, he said, still gasping, "You want Squire Burchard Wolfensberger and Squire Ruschmann Blackwell to help you find your druid? Fine. Take them. I don't care. Just get out of my castle by dawn." The General stood up and walked away, not giving anyone a chance to say anything.

Burchard looked at Damos. "I guess I should go pack and tell Ruschmann."

Damos let out a breath. "You do not have to come if you don't want to." The centaur paused, before bringing his hand to cover his heart. "But it would be an honor, Lýkos, to have you at my side."

Burchard nodded, feeling overwhelmed by the emotions washing through him. He bowed to Sir Foxbright and Damos and then left to find Ruschmann.

Later that evening, Burchard found himself going for a walk around the outside of the castle. He had told Ruschmann and Sir Peter it was to clear his mind, but the reality was he needed to escape.

Everyone who had been in the fight at the castle kept thanking him as though he had been their savior.

We all worked together, he thought. *Why won't they accept that it was a joint effort and leave me alone?* He let out a raspy breath. *Maybe it's good I'm leaving; then my father won't punish me for getting too much attention from everyone.*

Fang walked somberly at his side. Together, they inspected the damage to the outside of the castle, skirting or climbing over piles of rubble depending on how unstable they looked. Just as he was about to head back in, he heard a soft clip-clop.

"Who's there?" he called, hand going to his sword hilt.

"It's Damos," the centaur replied and stepped forward. He raised a hand and a small ball of light formed and floated into the air above them, providing a soft glowing light so they could see each other better.

"Lýkos," Damos began. "When we first met back at Leosor Hollows, I had promised I would explain things to you, and then things with the rebel camp escalated and I did not have the chance before you departed. I thought before you embark on a journey with me that I, at the very least, owed you more information."

Burchard tugged on his lip before replying, "OK." He stuffed his hands in his pockets and waited patiently.

Damos took a deep breath, making Burchard wonder what exactly the centaur had omitted during their first meeting. "The wolf goddess Eos came to me months ago when I was in Mootia and told me that I needed to be at a precise location with Jade and Liala to find you. She said no matter what happened between the time she spoke to me and the day our meeting was ordained, the three of us must be there or necessary events would not happen."

Burchard opened his mouth to speak, but Damos held up his hand, and Burchard snapped his mouth shut. *This all sounds absurd. He was told to find me at Leosor Hollows months ago?*

"Unlike Etrians, druid culture believes strongly in the gods, specifically the animal gods. We also rely on prophecies to lead us to the history-making moments. When Eos came to me, I knew that it would be critical to the druids, not just my own clan of centaurs, for me to follow her instructions." Damos sighed and swished his tail. "It was a challenge to follow her directions to let my five clanmates get captured and do nothing about it, to wait until you came along. Especially when I knew my chances were high to free them before they reached the rebel camp. However, the events that have happened since make me realize that Eos was right in giving me those instructions and I was right to follow them, no matter how much it pained me to do so." A heavy pause. "I know now who you are, Lýkos, and it is an honor to have you at my side to recover Jade."

Burchard's jaw dropped. He wasn't sure what he had been expecting Damos to say, but it definitely was not that the wolf goddess's instructions had led to their initial meeting. Confusion filled him. Damos was right. There was a significant difference between the druid culture and the way he had been brought up.

"I guess I don't really understand what you're trying to tell me. Eos, the wolf goddess, told you to meet me at Leosor Hollows. So what?" He tried to soften his tone a little, but given Damos's expression, he wasn't sure it worked.

Damos huffed and then explained, "As I said, you don't seem to care much about prophecies. I discovered after she appeared to me that there was indeed a prophecy that roughly says in your language, 'When the wolf goddess appears, follow the directions explicitly, and the tools needed to defeat Mors will make themselves known.'"

Burchard shifted his weight back and forth between his feet. The cold was creeping up his toes due to his lack of movement, and he regretted not putting on heavier socks. "Does that mean I am your tool to defeat Mors?" Damos must have noticed Burchard's discomfort because he was suddenly enveloped in warmth. He blushed and mumbled, "Thanks."

Damos shrugged. "Yes, you, Ruschmann, and likely Fang, although she did not join you until your initial encounter with

Ossa, are all the tools that Eos was referring to. As Jade had also mentioned, there is another prophecy about the man with the wolf companion. My clan believes it is all tied together. Regardless of the prophecy, several things were made clear on the battlefield. You have an unprecedented amount of skill for one so young, and you have come up against Ossa not once but three times and are still alive. Those things alone should be enough proof that you would be welcome to fight at my side. I am sure many of your friends within the castle would not hesitate to say the same thing. Especially the young Armand."

Burchard was studying Damos's face when he mentioned Armand, and then the centaur's eyes turned completely white. Burchard gasped in shock.

The voice that came from Damos was deep and gravelly, as though the stones themselves were speaking. "The lýkos and flóga agóri are the key to the final battle with Mors. You must first recover Nefrítis." The centaur's eyes returned to their normal color and he stumbled backward a few steps.

"Are you OK?" asked Burchard, laying a hand on Damos's arm.

Damos shook himself, setting the beads in his hair rattling and dislodging Burchard's hand. "What did I say?"

Burchard gave him a curious look. "You don't remember?"

Damos fingered his axe before replying. "No, but from your expression and actions, I can assume that my eyes changed color and I said something."

"Has it happened before?" Burchard inquired.

Damos stomped his hoof. "Maybe…now if you would be so kind as to tell me what I said?"

Burchard muttered a few incoherent things under his breath before clearing his throat. "You said…the lýkos and flyga agari are the key to the final battle with Mors. You must first recover Nefrati." He scratched his head. "Or that's what it sounded like to me. Some of the words were in a different language."

Damos gave him a slight smile. "Was it flóga agóri and Nefrítis?"

Burchard snapped his fingers. "Yes! Those were the words."

Damos tapped his lips with his finger for a moment. "I believe what I said was…the wolf and flame boy are the key to the final battle with Mors. You must first recover Jade."

"Who is the flame boy?" Burchard asked. He didn't know of anyone who was called that or who even had the job of lighting the torches around the castle.

Damos shrugged. "I think that is for us to discover. However, now we know that Jade must be recovered before the final battle with Mors can happen. Or at least for us to have a shot at defeating Mors."

Burchard peered around him. The sky was completely dark. There were torches at the top of the castle wall, but they only cast enough light to walk safely at the top of the wall. "It sounds like we must focus our efforts on rescuing Jade then. I do have one more question for you. How did you get the Etrians to help?"

Damos tapped his arm with his fingers. "I know Jade failed to pass on my information to you about the rebels not being at Dry Bridge. When I discovered that, I went searching for Sir Waldorf and Sir Emberwood. Eos had told me they would be open to aiding the centaurs if the circumstances were dire. Which, as you know, they did."

Burchard felt his eyelids drooping and forced them open to look at Damos. "If you don't mind…" he said, yawning, "I'd like to go to bed."

Damos nodded. "Yes, I sometimes forget that humans have different sleep requirements. I apologize for keeping you from sleep. Let me walk you back to the barracks."

Burchard nodded and turned, heading toward the gate. To his surprise and pleasure the bubble of warmth stayed around him, as did the light. When they reached the barracks, Burchard gave the centaur a slight bow before retiring inside.

The silver light of dawn, with small tendrils of pale pink, greeted Burchard and Ruschmann as they stepped out of the barracks.

Their knight masters and Sir Foxbright had discussed this development for hours. The squires had gone to bed, wanting to get as much sleep as possible before facing whatever lay on their road to find Jade.

Burchard hefted his saddlebags over his shoulder, grunting with the weight. Their knight masters had insisted they pack what Burchard deemed too much gear. Damos was waiting by the gate with Armand Foxbright.

Captain Thomas emerged from the barn with Chip and Cricket. The two squires quickly tied their saddlebags to the saddles. Ruschmann mounted while Burchard walked over to Damos and Armand.

Locking gazes with Armand, Burchard spoke firmly. "You were not given permission to come with us."

Armand sighed deeply. "I know. I just wanted to tell you before you leave that I believe in you, Lýkos. In you and Fang. We will see each other again." A tear trickled down Armand's face. Burchard wrapped the page in a hug.

"Yes, we will see each other again," Burchard murmured. He glanced at Damos. "Are you ready?"

"Yes," Damos said.

Burchard mounted Chip and they walked through the gate. When the two squires, centaur, and black wolf reached the other side of the bridge. Burchard had a tickling feeling on the back of his neck. Chip turned to face the castle of her own accord. To Burchard's surprise, his father was up on the wall along with Sir Peter, Sir Daniel, Sir Foxbright, and most of the pages.

There on the bridge, he presumed visible to all based on the gasps and shrieks coming from within the castle and wall, was a huge white wolf. Larger than a horse.

"Safe travels, Lýkos," came the musical voice of Eos.

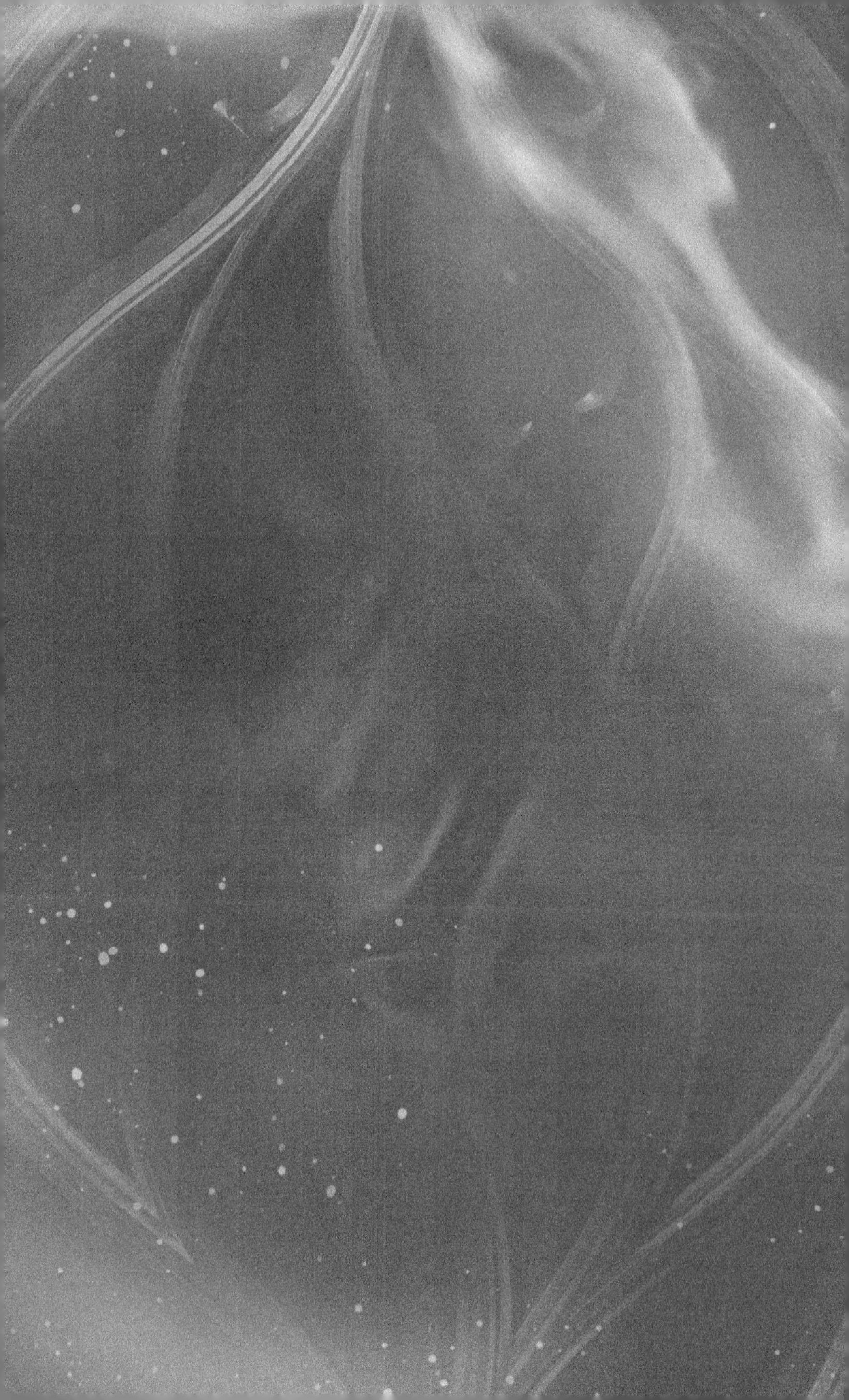

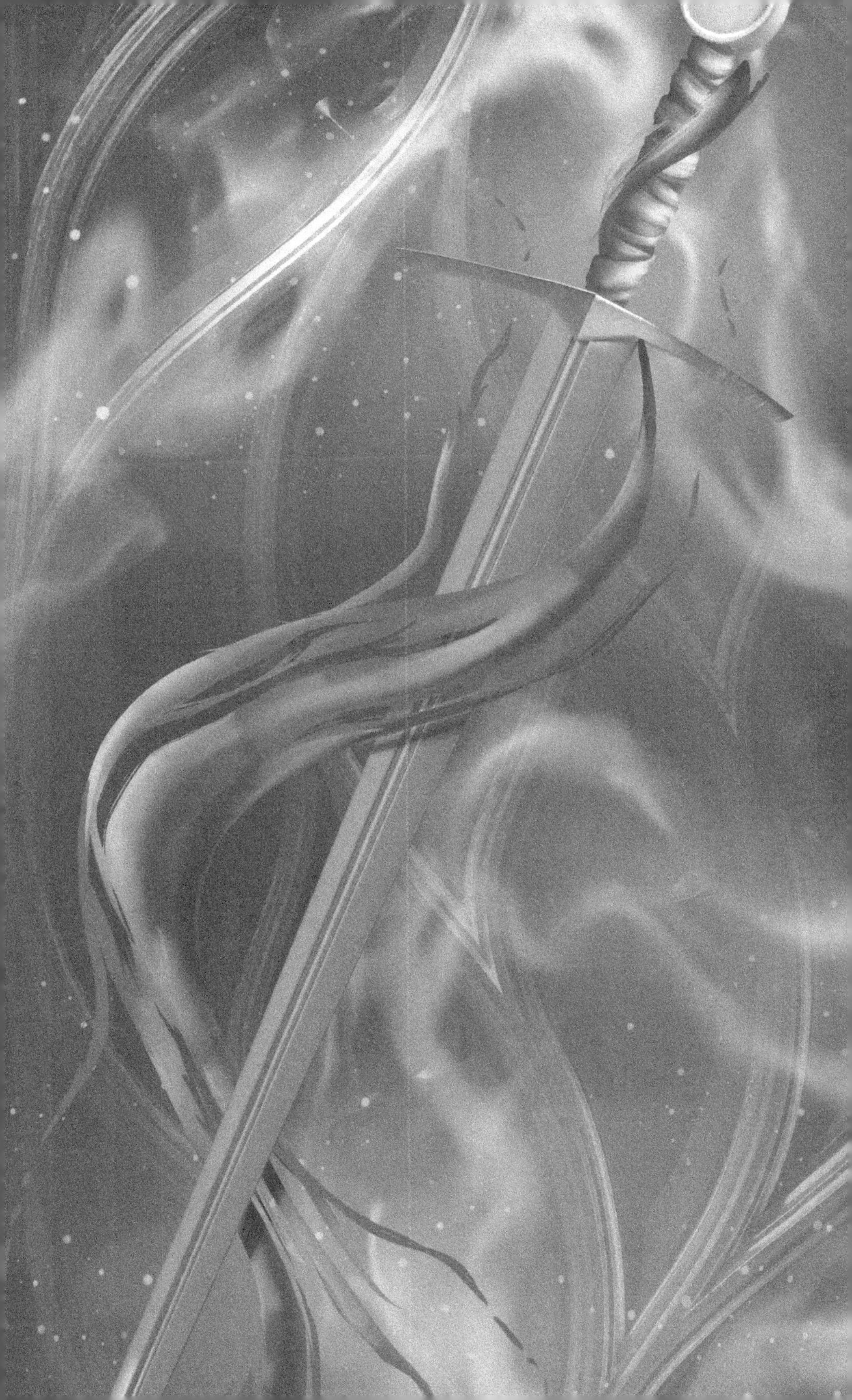

ACKNOWLEDGEMENTS

Thank you so much to everyone who has contributed to the creation of this book. It would not have turned out this well without you. Thank you to my readers whose continued support encourages me to keep writing the stories that are in my head.

ABOUT THE AUTHOR

Elizabeth R. Jensen is an award-winning author and Arabian horse and German Riding pony breeder in Atlanta, GA. This is her fifth book. All four of her previous books have won awards in numerous categories including Best Series, Cover Illustration, and Audiobook Production.

Elizabeth has a bachelor's degree in animal science, a master's of business administration and a master's of organizational leadership. In elementary school, Elizabeth was introduced to creative writing in an after-school poetry class for gifted students. Since then, she has continued to write poetry.